ETERNAL NIGHT

A Novel by: Sarah E Betts

Dedication:

I would like to dedicate this book first and foremost to those who have passed on. Mom, Pappaw and Grandma Watts. Though you aren't here to see this day, I know you're still proud, and that is enough. I would second like to thank my family, and friends who pushed me every day, and helped me through the entire process of this project! I couldn't have pushed forward to this day without any of you. Thank you do my Dad, Brother Zack, Grandma, Aunts, Uncles, Casie, Amanda, Chi, Patti, and LeAnna.

A special thank you to Tim, and his family.

Last but not least, the readers. Without any of you, this would not be possible.

Thank you all so much!

Prologue

An empty ballroom where the sweet sounds of a string quartet echoed. An exquisite chandelier was dimmed just enough to create the perfect ambiance for a romantic evening of dancing and cordiality. A handsome man with his black hair slicked back, dressed in an all black suit escorted a stunning woman with cascading red hair, adorned in the same color, down the stairs and to the ballroom floor.

The man bowed deeply to his partner, she gave him a curtsy. They joined together and began to waltz to the music echoing in the almost empty hall. The two danced, spinning round and round the floor, laughing. The song came to an end, and the man gently kissed his partner's hand.

"It was certainly a pleasure to escort such a stunning woman to this birthday party. I must say thank you Lilith, for your wondrous dancing." Adoration sparkled in the man's haunting silver eyes. His features were perfectly chiseled, his body tall, and lean. An ageless elegance bled from his being.

"My dancing would be nothing without your lead, my dear Samael." Lilith said, the same adoration shone on her face. She shared the same mysterious silver eyes as Samael. Her face was soft, angelic almost, with a frame of fiery red curls.

Samael took Lilith's hand and led her to a table at the end of the hall, and handed her a wine glass, with a gorgeous red liquid inside. He took one for himself. "To our dearest daughter! May she live a long and prosperous life. Reika dear, may this be the happiest birthday of your young life thus far. Happy 18th Birthday!"

Lilith smiled up at Samael. She raised her glass, and tapped it against his. "Happy birthday, my little demon! How excited we are for you to return home!"

"Yes indeed." Samael chimed. "How terribly ecstatic we are for your homecoming!" The couple grinned at each other, and took a drink from their glasses. Samael set his glass down, and made his way to the window. He looked out upon the small Ohio town and chuckled. "I hope you enjoy your new life, my dear child. This town, this world isn't your domain. What I will give you as your birthday gift will be unlike anything your friends have received. My dear, your gift will be much more glamorous."

Lilith joined him, looking out over their school campus. "You are correct. Locke Academy is just a training ground for what is to come in your blossoming life."

Samael wrapped an arm around Lilith and pulled her close. "Precisely, my love. It is the beginning of your new existence. We will teach you everything you need to know, you reign as the princess of death."

"Beautifully stated my love." Lilith said, looking up to him. "Shall we continue the festivities?"

Samael peered down. "Of course." He brought his lips down, and laid them upon hers. "Let us return home for the evening."

Chapter One

Sun poured through the cracks of the heavy black and red curtains. Reika rolled over in her bed, trying to avoid eye contact with the warm rays. She heard her phone buzz, and she sleepily searched for it, one eye opened but just barely. She tapped the screen, bringing the message up, *'We're on our way!'* greeted her squinting eyes. She sat her phone down, groaned and rolled out of bed. On the wall behind her was a poster of a foreboding castle-like prison.

Reika's feet hit the wooden floor of her bedroom. It was scattered with dirty laundry, books and hair ties. She shuffled her feet, making her way to her mirror while rubbing her eyes. Around the edges of the over-sized mirror, she had placed photos of her with loved ones, and ticket stubs from concerts and movies she attended.

At the top was a photo of her at age ten, hugging a middle aged man around the waist. She was dressed in a purple tee shirt, and plain jean shorts. The man wore a plaid shirt, tucked into a pair of khaki pants. The two were standing in front of a sign at the old Ohio State Reformatory. The two looked ecstatic to be standing before the haunting, ominous building. Reika remembered the trip as if it were yesterday.

"Daddy, are we there yet?" Reika asked. She sat in the front seat, kicking her legs out in front of her. She was antsy after being in the car for what seemed like hours.

The man with black hair, a gentle smile and soft brown eyes turned to face her. "We're almost there, I promise."

Reika watched out the window, getting a better view of the skyline of Mansfield. Off in the distance, she could see the old prison standing out among the grimy industrial buildings. The sinister old building caught her eyes, and she couldn't look away. "Oh my God, no way!" She shouted out. "We're going to the prison?!"

"Yes we are, Lily."

Reika smiled. She had read books about haunted buildings in Ohio, and was absolutely enamored with the Reformatory. She had gotten a poster for Christmas the year before, and she hung in above her bed.

William exited the highway, and took them towards the prison. They pulled down the long drive through the wrought iron gates and parked. He exited the car, and went to Reika's side, and opened the door for her. She took his hand and hopped out. She looked up at the Prison in awe.

"Whoa!" She exclaimed. The prison loomed above her. The presence surrounding it was grim. It was filled with death and suffering. It fascinated Reika deeply.

"Happy Birthday, Lily." William said. "We're going on a tour today!"

"We are?!" Reika jumped up and down. "Thank you Daddy!"

"Let's go have one of those people take our picture up front here. Would you like that?"

"Of course!" She shouted out. She ran off with her father's camera and asked if they would take a picture for them. She came back with a red headed woman holding the camera for her.

"Alright, let's get in front of the sign here!" She said cheerfully. "Ready, on the count of three? One, two, three!" The woman snapped the picture and handed the camera back to Reika.

"Have a happy birthday, little one!" She waved at Reika and her father and made her way back to the group she was standing with.

"I can't wait! I want to put this picture up in my room!"

"I'll make sure I make an extra copy, just for you!"

A tear trickled it's way down Reika's cheek. She shook her head, and looked at the mirror again. Pictures of her and her sister, Yuri, on the first day of the past few school years were there. Each year, their style had progressively gotten darker. First, they were dressed in band tee shirts, ripped up jeans and had dark eyeliner on. Reika wore a Pantera shirt, and Yuri had a Breaking Benjamin shirt on.

The photo next to it, showed Reika in a black and red corset style top, a long black skirt and her hair was long and straight. Yuri was wearing a pleated pink and black skirt, and a white button down shirt, the collar and cuffs were black, her hair was dyed blonde, and she had a black bow in it. Both were still wearing intensely dark make up.

Each year, the style changed, but the dark make up stayed the same. Throughout the years, Reika and Yuri had pestered

Meredith, their mother, to take them to concerts. They had gone to see many bands over the years. Her ticket stubs decorated the edge as well, anything from Avenged Sevenfold to Slipknot. She smiled, all the memories from going to the concerts with Yuri were wonderful. They had brought the two close through the years.

The girls were actually close for sisters. Reika always stood up for Yuri when they would go out together. The two lived in the small, picturesque town of Callisto, Ohio. The population of the town was very narrow minded. Reika and her sister were the subject of constant ridicule in the town. Many times, Reika found herself in a fist fight, because someone would call her and Yuri names, or stare at them. Though she had experienced minor issues before, her anger issues came to full bloom not too long after the passing of their father. Reika was thirteen when William passed away. She tried to forget the day as much as possible, but special days, like today, the memory sneaked into her mind once again.

It was February nineteenth, Reika was in English class, and was called into the office. Her and Yuri came in at the same time. Their Mom, and a police officer were waiting in the office. They were brought back to a vacant office, and were told the news.

William was hit by a semi truck, on a business trip to Columbus, Ohio. He worked in Callisto's hospital, in the I.T department. William was heading for a conference, when the truck lost control and struck his car. Upon hearing the news, Reika bolted from the room, ran out of the building at to the park her and her father frequented. She sat alone on a dock overlooking the frozen pond, sobbing. Her body was numb to the cold.

"What the fuck are you doing here, freak?!" An older boy taunted Reika.

"Look at her! She's bawling like a baby!" His companion said.

"What, did someone hurt your feelings by calling you a goth bitch again?!"

"No." Reika said softly.

"I guess you need reminded, then!" The first boy said. "You're such a fucking freak! You're going to end up alone. No one can love someone as weird as you."

"Yeah!" The second boy laughed. "God, I'm surprised your parents even love someone as weird as you! I bet you've got daddy *issues too. Is that why you're always wearing make up. Trying to*

cover up bruises, or something?"

"What did you say?" Reika growled out. She sprung to her

feet. "What the fuck did you just say?!"

"You heard me! I bet you've got major daddy issues!" The

second boy laughed.

Reika grabbed his coat collar and punched him in the nose.

"The only issue I have is with you two!" She screamed through her

sobs. She hit the boy once more, let go of his coat and he fell to the

ground. She turned to the other boy, and he had already run away.

Reika's eyes were overflowing with hatred for the two before her.

She looked down at the boy's bloodied face. He started crawling

backwards, scrambled to his feet and ran off after his friend.

Reika fell to her knees and cried once more. "Why?! Daddy!

Why did you have to leave me?!"

Once again, Reika found herself looking at her reflection, her

eyes brimming with tears. She quickly wiped her eyes and went to

her closet. She pulled out a pair of her favorite ripped up black jeans.

She exchanged her pajama shorts for them, and searched for a shirt.

She ran her hands over the many hangers full of black tops she owned. Her hand stopped over top a deep red shirt. She pulled it out, and looked at it fondly.

The collar of the shirt cascaded in an old fashion. She removed it from the hanger, then her own shirt and unbuttoned the one in hand, and slipped it on. Sebastian had given it to her. He hadn't named any other reason, aside from "I thought you would look pretty in it." She smoothed the front of the top down gently, looked at her reflection and laughed. Her hair was still a mess, which she quickly remedied.

After running a brush through her layered black hair, she teased and styled it to look a mess once more. She then applied her standard eyeliner and mascara. She shook her head, sprayed hairspray on it, and jumped, dropping the hairspray can when she heard a knock at the door.

"Reika, Sebastian and Lynde are here!" Her Mother's voice called from the other side of the door. She added the final touches of her outfit by placing her black ribbon choker on, and adjusted the red rose to sit in the center of her throat. She grabbed a pair of socks, quickly put them on and ran from her bedroom down the stairs.

"I'm ready guys!" She grinned, entering the living room. "Is Yuri even ready yet?"

"I've been ready for an hour!" Yuri groaned. "I swear, you can't ever get to bed on time, let alone wake up on time!"

"Sorry Yuri! Usually we're waiting on you! I did some extra training yesterday, and slept through my alarm." She chuckled. "Again. Mom said Bas and Lynde were here. Where are they?"

"I'm right here, Dear." Sebastian came around the corner from the kitchen to the living room. Reika smiled at the tall man. He wore a black and green plaid button down shirt, black pants, and a pair of black boots. His black hair was styled in a perfect mess similar to Reika's. His green eyes sparkled as he smiled back at her.

"Good, you're here!" She smirked. "Class yesterday didn't kill you?" Reika and Sebastian studied at a local martial arts studio, learning Aikido together. Reika had been a member of the studio for two years, but Sebastian joined only three months ago.

He laughed, "It didn't. Though, I gotta say I'm really sore still."

She shook her head. "I am too. Though, I put in twice the amount of training as you did." She smirked. "You'll get used to it someday."

Sebastian shook his head. "I hope so, it's been three months already!" Reika smiled up at him, wrapping her arms around his waist. Sebastian smiled too, pulling her in for a hug.

Meredith returned to the living room with a basket full of plastic forks, paper plates and a knife. "Are we ready now?" A boy with short brown hair and blue eyes, standing almost the same height as Sebastian followed her out with a cake box. His clothing was rather plain compared to the other three. "Thanks, Lynde for helping!"

Reika laughed softly. "Yeah, it looks like we're ready."

They headed out to the car, driving off to the park near their house. Reika looked out the window and watched the people as they passed them on the sidewalks. She noticed a couple walking towards the park entrance A tall man in all black, and a woman with bright red hair, dressed in black and burgundy. She had seen them before, but couldn't place them in any specific moment.

Meredith pulled into the gravel entrance. The small park was for fishing, and picnics. Near the entrance, there were trees scattered in clusters, paired with tables. Across from the parking lot was a wooded area, with trails for hiking. Farther into the park was a reservoir protected by another wooded area. Meredith pulled the car into the picnic parking lot near the park bench lined sidewalk.

The group got out of the car, each taking something with them. They picked the farthest picnic table from the car. After setting up the table quickly, they went off in pairs towards the treeline. Meredith sighed, sitting down at the table, and immersed herself in a novel she pulled from her bag.

"I'm really glad you were able to make it today, Bas." Reika said, as they walked over to one of the trees nearby and sat underneath it. "It kinda sucks we're celebrating a day early." She sighed. Reika's birthday was August twenty-seventh, the same day they all moved into their dorms for her and Sebastian's last year of high school at Locke Academy. "Are you ready to go back?"

"Yeah, I'm glad we're going back. I actually like school." Sebastian smiled. "Mostly because I get a break from my parents.

Don't get me wrong, I love them, but I love the freedom school gives me."

"What's it like living in the dorms?" Reika asked him. For Reika, it was her first and last year at Locke Academy. She was well known in their small town Callisto, Ohio for her violent outbursts. She attended a different school in the area each year of school due to fights. This would be her first year in a boarding school. She only hoped she would be able to make it through the year without any incident.

"It's not too bad. You'll have a roommate. Usually they put siblings together, you'll probably end up with Yuri. Lynde and I lucked out, since we've been best friends since elementary school. The food isn't bad, the classes aren't either." He shrugged. "I think you'll like it."

She smiled. "I hope so. Are the people cool?" She brought her knees to her chest and wrapped her arms around them. "I really have to try and not fight. Mom worked hard with the school board to get me in for my last year. I can't screw up." She sighed. "Either way, I feel uneasy about this year. I feel like something bad is going to happen."

Sebastian wrapped an arm around her shoulder. "Don't worry so much, Rei. I'm sure everything is going to be fine."

"No, I don't think it's going to, Sebastian. I've had this feeling for a while now and it's usually right." Reika leaned against him. "I think something weird or bad is going to happen but I don't know what. I know I can handle whatever it is, I just wish I knew what's coming."

He held her close. "You're right. Whatever is coming, you'll be able to handle it. I've never met a stronger person than you, Rei. I might not be of much assistance, but I'll always try to help, even if it's just listening." He gently kissed the top of her head. "You know how good I am at listening." He smirked.

"I do know, and I'm not sure how much help you'll be!" She winked at him.

He shook his head, laughing. "You got me! Honestly, though, if something does happen, please don't be afraid to talk to me. I'll do anything I can to help you."

"Thanks, Bas. I'm glad I can count on you." She looked out at the park, looking at all the people enjoying the day. She looked over at a couple sitting on a park bench close to where they had set up their party. It was the same couple she had spotted walking towards the park on their drive. They were staring right at her and Sebastian. She felt a shiver go down her spine. She shook her head and turned her attention back to Sebastian.

"Hey, are you alright?" He said, rubbing her arms gently. "You have goosebumps all of a sudden." He frowned.

"Yeah." She nodded. "I'm alright."

Sebastian continued to rub her arm. "Just making sure."

Reika smiled. Sebastian made her feel safe, the only other person who made her feel safe was her father. She had first seen Sebastian in the local record store.

Reika had gone to pick up a CD she ordered, when he walked in. Reika could feel his stare on her. She turned and looked at him, he had the dumbest look on his face. All Reika remembered was telling him to take a picture if he wanted to stare, and flipping him off on her way out the door. She saw him a few weeks later, again he stared at her. Reika was shocked when he took a picture this time.

She grabbed his phone and tried to delete the photo, but he had already sent it to someone. She remembered the caption clearly. The message said "I found the most beautiful girl in the world." Since that day, Reika and Sebastian became inseparable. She even convinced him to join Aikido classes. They worked well together in class, even her instructor was surprised to see how much of a change there was in Reika's attitude since Sebastian became part of her life.

"Hey, do you want to work on some weapons training?" Reika asked him with a grin.

He nodded, "Yeah, lets do it." He smiled as she hopped up and turned to him.

"I'll be right back!" She grinned, running off to the car to grab her weapons. She always had a set in her Mom's car. She opened the car door and looked around. The weapons were gone, but were replaced with five brightly colored pool noodles. She laughed and took them from the car. When Reika turned from the car, she dropped them to the ground.

Reika's eyes widened as she saw the couple walk past her. The red haired woman turned her head and looked into Reika's eyes. The woman gave Reika the most dazzling smile, and flipped her hair. She froze in place, watching them walk past. Once the woman broke eye contact, Reika shook her head. *'Her eyes were silver.'* She thought to herself. *'No, you're imagining things. Chill out, Lily, you're fine.'* She grabbed the pool noodles up from the ground with a sigh.

She turned and walked back to the table, her pool noodles in hand. She grinned as Sebastian looked up. "I found something better!"

He laughed some. "What are we going to do with these?"

She grinned. "We're gonna have a noodle war!" She gave him the blue noodle, and took a purple one. "Yuri, Lynde, come get one!" Reika yelled out. Meredith looked up from the table.

"I see you found my surprise." Meredith grinned. "I knew you would want to practice with the weapons, I figured I'd replace it with something a little less scary to the public."

"Mom!" She groaned some. "Us wailing on each other with pool noodles is less scary? I don't see how! We don't even hit each other with the real weapons!"

"The fact you can move so fast with the weapons is what's scary." Meredith gave her a chiding stare. "The last time you two practiced in the park together, you were brought home in a squad car."

"They just gave us a ride home!" Reika grumbled. "We didn't get arrested, they even admitted it was a misunderstanding! The bitch who called the cops on us should have minded her own damn business!"

"Reika Lilin!" Meredith growled. "Watch the language."

Sebastian laughed. "Yeah, My Dad wasn't too happy about that one either."

"The Officer even explained to him it was a misunderstanding. Why was he still mad?" Reika asked.

"He hates cops."

Reika shook her head. "He hates everyone. Am I ever going to meet your parents?"

Sebastian sighed. "I don't know if you will or not. They're insanely reclusive."

She shrugged. "It's their loss."

Yuri and Lynde finally joined them. They each took a pool noodle, and looked at Meredith.

"Is this some joke?" Yuri looked confused.

"No, I want to see you beat each other up with brightly colored foam tubes." Meredith grinned.

"Why is there an extra noodle?" Lynde asked.

"If the fight ends up too one sided, I'll help you." Meredith smiled, and put her hands up. "Ready yourselves! I want to see a battle extraordinaire!" Reika and Sebastian looked at each other and grinned. Yuri and Lynde exchanged worried expressions. "Begin!"

Reika and Sebastian stood side by side, waiting for the other two to attack. Regardless of the nature of the game, battles weren't taken lightly. The first to attack was Lynde. He ran forward and tried to hit Reika in the head. She laughed, and turned, smacking him in the back with the noodle. Yuri yelled and came forward, trying to attack Sebastian. He stood his ground and whacked her in the hip with his noodle.

Meredith sat back and watched the four beat each other senseless with pool toys. She was extremely satisfied with her choice of replacing Reika's weapons with beach accessories. The four were yelling, and flailing their pool noodles in the air. Yuri and Lynde tried their best but found themselves pinned to the ground finally. Reika was on Yuri, Sebastian with Lynde.

"I yield!" Yuri squealed. Reika took her pool noodle from her and let her up. Sebastian followed suit. Reika laughed as Yuri groaned, laying on the ground still. She whacked her sister with the noodle once more before returning to the table.

Yuri came to the table quickly. "Mom, why didn't you help us?!"

"Oh, sorry Yuri. I was too busy laughing."

"Mom!" She groaned out. "You're so mean!"

"I suppose you could say I'm mean." She laughed. "Or, you could say I actually have a sense of humor."

Yuri just shook her head and sat down, pouting. Lynde came and sat next to her. "Don't worry, Yuri, at least it was fun."

"You think losing is fun?!" She grumbled.

"If you thought we had a chance in hell of winning, babe, you're the crazy one."

Yuri pouted, looking at Lynde. "Maybe I am the crazy one!"

Sebastian took a seat next to Reika and wrapped his arm around her. "We make a good team, Dear."

Reika turned and smiled. "We do, you're learning well. I'm proud of you." She kissed his cheek.

"Now you're done beating each other up, are you ready for cake?" Meredith asked. In unison, they said "yes!" Meredith pulled the cake out of the box, set it down in front of Reika, put two candles in the cake, a '1' and an '8'. The cake looked wonderful, a chocolate iced cake, decorated with raspberries. Meredith pulled a lighter from her pocket and lit the candles and waited.

"Someone's gotta start singing." Reika said, looking at each person sitting at the table. "No song, no cake." She smirked, crossing her arms. "Hurry up, before there's wax all over it!"

"I think Lynde should do it." Sebastian grinned.

"Oh." Lynde's eyes went wide with fear, "No, it's okay. You can do it, Sebastian."

He smirked, "Oh no, Lynde. we want you to sing."

Reika nodded. "I think it's a great idea!" She and Sebastian loved to pick on Lynde. He was very quiet in group settings. They hoped picking on the poor boy would get him to come out of his shell some. It was working, slowly, but it was working.

Lynde gulped audibly, and looked to everyone at the table. He snapped his eyes closed and started to sing "Happy Birthday." He opened his eyes, looked again, and finally everyone joined in.

Reika blew the candles out, closed her eyes and made her wish. *'I wish I knew what was about to happen.'* She wished carefully, just wanting to know what was to come. Though she had a feeling her wish would backfire on her.

They sat, eating cake, and telling stories of Reika as a child. Most of the stories were of Reika tormenting her little sister, Yuri.

"We were getting ready to paint our bedrooms a few years ago. Reika sneaked out of her room with a bottle of red paint, and wrote 'Don't look under your bed' on my wall. That whole week, I had some pretty crazy things written there. I think the last day, I woke up with a red hand print on my face." Yuri said, laughing. "I had nightmares for months after that! Even after she admitted she wrote it!"

Reika laughed some. "You remember the time Mom got you that antique mirror from the thrift shop down the road from the house, and I told you it was haunted. I said "Yuri! Be careful, if you spend too much time in front of that mirror, you'll get possessed!" She ran crying to Mom to get rid of it. Mom ended up putting it in her room, and proved she wasn't possessed by it. Yuri still wouldn't take it back."

Sebastian shook his head. "Good God, Reika..." He laughed. "You sounded like a handful as a child."

"It got worse as she got older." Meredith said, nonchalantly. "The older she got, the more bizarre things were. She used to turn all the portraits upside down the night before Halloween. She started dressing all Gothic, kids picked on her for it. That's when the fights started." Meredith smiled, chuckling some. "That girl had one hell of a right hook at twelve."

Reika laughed. "It's only gotten better!" She winked at Sebastian.

"I don't doubt that." Sebastian said, shaking his head.

"She used to leave these cryptic messages in my book bag and locker all the time. Most of the time I think she actually wrote them in blood. Which was disgusting!"

"I got bloody noses a lot." Reika shrugged. "I had to put that stuff to good use."

"I wouldn't quite consider that good use." Yuri said, giving Reika a droll stare.

Reika grinned. "The satanic doll circles..."

"That... That actually was funny." Yuri laughed, grinning. "Well, it is now, but not back then!"

"Satanic doll circle?" Sebastian and Lynde said in unison.

"Oh Reika..." Yuri sighed, smiling, "She took all my dolls, and made them into a little satanic cult, black robes included. They were sacrificing the male doll."

Sebastian and Lynde burst out laughing. "Are you serious?!" Sebastian asked.

"If you want to see pictures, we have some."

"Why do you have pictures of that?!" Lynde asked.

"It was rather convincing..." Meredith said, shrugging. "It was very well put together."

"Now you tell me!" Reika grumbled out.

"What would you know about satanic rituals, Mrs Avel?" Lynde asked.

Meredith stared at him, her eyes dark. "A lot more than you could imagine."

Sebastian raised an eyebrow, and Lynde nodded softly. They sat in silence for a while, finishing their cake. Finally, breaking the silence, Meredith suggested they started cleaning up the picnic area.

"So, you were kind of a wild child." Sebastian asked Reika as they took their trash to a can nearby.

"I wasn't kind of a wild child, I was a real wild child." Reika explained. "Stories I wrote for classes used to get calls to my parents. I was always causing trouble, or going to the principal's office. Mom's right, it did get worse as I got older. Especially after Dad died. I was 13 when he died, and it made me more angry at the world. I already felt like hardly anyone understood me, then I was left with a void in my heart that no one could see, or understand.

Then I started lashing out." She sighed. "I've never really gotten out of the angry stage. I try my best not to be angry anymore, but it's difficult. It's something I can't always control."

Sebastian nodded, "I think you're doing really well lately with it. I haven't really seen you get angry since the first couple days at the record store."

She smiled, "You're right, I really haven't. Though I wouldn't really consider that anger." She laughed, "It was a fun day though. I haven't actually told someone to take a picture and they actually do it"

He grinned, "I couldn't pass the offer up."

"That's true, but I still haven't had anyone actually take a photo." She smiled. Sebastian nodded.

"Rei, Sebastian! We're ready to go." Meredith called out.

Reika smiled. "We better hurry before she leaves us here!" She took off running towards the car. Sebastian followed and they got into the back seat with Lynde. They drove through the small town, heading to Reika's house. They passed by the shops sitting across from the park, one was a second hand clothing store, next to it, a bar, and then an ice cream shop. Farther down the road, was the elementary school, and another park for fishing. The small pond had docks dotting the circumference of the shore.

Across the road from the elementary school was Callisto High School. Reika sighed as she looked at the tall, looming structure. It was an older style school building, three stories high made of red brick. Reika didn't miss being a student of Callisto High School. Everyday she sat alone during lunch. She spent her freshman year at the school alone. Yuri wasn't able to provide her company, because she was in seventh grade. Reika leaned her head against the window of the car. All her memories of the town were bitter. She knew one day, she would leave this town and never have to look back.

Sebastian leaned in close to Reika and kissed her cheek. "Cheer up, dear." He whispered in her ear. "We're going back to your house, and I'm cooking dinner."

She turned at looked at him. "Are you cooking the scallop and shrimp pasta?"

He nodded with a smile. "I am."

She smiled and kissed his cheek. "Thank you, Bas."

Meredith pulled into the driveway and parked the car. "Yes! Thank you Sebastian for making dinner tonight! It gives this woman a break after the baking marathon she's been on for the past two days!"

"You insisted on me bringing cupcakes to the studio." Reika chided. "You always make two cakes though. So the cupcakes were your idea, not mine!"

"I'm a mother, I tend to feed everyone, regardless of whether they want me to or not."

"They did enjoy them!" Reika laughed. "An empty pan is a sign of great love for your treats!"

Meredith shook her head, laughing. "Let's go inside." They all hopped out of the car, Yuri, Meredith and Lynde headed inside. Sebastian caught Reika by the wrist and pulled her close.

"Are you alright, Rei?" He asked, looking into her eyes. Concern was written over his face. "You've been acting a little strange today. Are you nervous about going back to school, or is there something else bothering you?"

"I'm nervous, but I'll be okay." She gave him a reassuring smile. "New people and places always make me anxious. I'm glad you're gonna be with me."

Sebastian pulled her closer, wrapping his arms around her in a tight embrace. "It's going to be alright, Rei. If you need me, I'll be there for you no matter what."

Reika held onto Sebastian tightly. There was no safer feeling than in his arms. "Thank you, Bas." She whispered. She wanted to tell him she loved him, but the words wouldn't come to her lips.

"You're more than welcome. You've been there for me many times before, without even knowing it." His voice was soft. "It's the least I can do for you."

Reika let her hold slip, so she could see his face. "What do you mean?"

"You've become my safe haven." He smiled. "I feel I can be myself with you without any worry. I don't even feel like this with my own best friend."

"I hope you feel open enough with me" She smiled, looking down. "I'm really glad to have met you."

"I am too." Sebastian smiled, and leaned in, kissing her gently. Reika embraced him, kissing him back.

"Oh god, gross!" Yuri yelled out, gagging. "Mom wants you two inside. She's complaining about being hungry." She had popped her head out from the front door.

Sebastian and Reika broke their kiss immediately upon hearing Yuri's voice. Reika cursed under her breath, as her face flushed bright red.

"We'll be in soon." Sebastian said, rubbing Reika's back.

Yuri rolled her eyes. "Fine." She went back inside.

Reika groaned. "I swear I could kill that girl."

Sebastian laughed, hugging her close once more. "It's okay, dear. Let's get inside so I can cook. I don't want your mom mad at me."

"You're right, you don't want her mad at you." She laughed, kissing him quickly, and led him inside the house. They walked through the living room, the dining room and Sebastian stopped her short of entering the kitchen. He put his arms on either side of the doorway.

"Go relax with your family." He smiled down at her. "I'll be alright by myself."

She sighed. "I like helping you though."

"You're not helping me on your birthday dinner!" Sebastian said sternly.

"Okay, I'll leave you alone." She groaned, walking back to the living room. She sat down on the couch next to her mom. Meredith wrapped an arm around Reika's shoulders. She rested her head on her mother's shoulder.

"What shall we do while waiting on dinner?"

"I don't care." Reika shrugged. "Let's watch whatever is on the TV."

Meredith nodded, turning the television on, and picked a show on haunted buildings. Reika smiled some. She loved anything paranormal since she was a child. Meredith had tried her best to keep Reika away from media on the subject, but William indulged Reika when she wasn't home. Yuri and Lynde left the living room, and went to the basement to watch something else. Leaving Meredith and Reika alone.

Sebastian occasionally popped in the room to get updates on the show, and to share his progress on dinner. On his last visit in, Reika inhaled deeply.

"Bas, it smells amazing!" She exclaimed. "How much longer?"

"I'm just waiting on the rolls to finish up." He grinned. A timer went off, and he jumped. "The rolls are ready!" He ran off, pulled them from the oven and placed them in a basket. He brought the basket into the dining room and placed it on the table. He smiled, looking over the delicious feast he created. He made a scallop and shrimp pasta with a buttery lemon sauce, a leafy salad, and rolls he just pulled from the oven.

There was still another cake that Meredith had made, though it had more raspberries and white chocolate shavings to adorn the top. Sebastian grinned, and went into the living room. "Dinner is ready!"

Meredith sighed happily. "Finally! I thought I was going to die!" She got up and headed to the kitchen. Reika followed her in, Yuri and Lynde came after.

Reika shook her head. "If a few hours after cake would be starvation for you, I'm scared to see that a religious fasting would do to you."

"It's a good thing to be an agnostic. I have no want to starve myself for better judgment from a higher power."

"No wonder we were never baptized or went to church." Reika said.

"Your father tried to have you baptized, but you wouldn't stop screaming when the pastor took you in his arms to perform the ceremony. Thank goodness we decided to have in done privately, instead of in front of a congregation." Meredith laughed. "The poor man about dropped you in the baptismal font. You were screaming like a banshee, and you ended up vomiting on him. We were completely embarrassed, we ended up leaving before the ceremony was finished. Your father never went back to church there, either."

The group joined at the table, and enjoyed Sebastian's creations.

"Why haven't you had him cook for us before?!" Meredith said. "This is wonderful!"

"Thanks." Sebastian bashfully muttered. "My mom taught me how to cook."

Reika smiled at Sebastian. "Well, this is the first time you agreed to have him cook for us all. Maybe you'll let him cook for us more often!"

"Sebastian, if you want to marry Reika, and be our personal chef after you two graduate high school, I will gladly accept you into the family." Meredith chuckled

"Let's not get ahead of ourselves." Sebastian smiled. "There's plenty of time for thoughts of marriage later. Right now, I think it's best we focus on getting to know each other even more."

Yuri groaned. "Could you guys tone down the level of adorableness, I can't handle it."

Reika shook her head. "Shut up, Yuri. We all know you're eating it up on the inside and you just don't want to show it." She felt blush rising into her cheeks. "You're right though, there is plenty of time to think of those things."

"Oh good lord, Rei." Yuri rolled her eyes. "You two are something else."

"Be happy for your sister!" Meredith glared at Yuri. "She's finally happy again. She hasn't been in a fight in months, hasn't tormented you nearly as much. Things are looking up, and you should be more supportive."

"Being the annoying little sister to remind her of how sappy and romantic she's really being is my way of being supportive." Yuri sighed. "Apparently no one understands I'm just playing my part."

Reika just sighed, trying to get the color to drain from her face. She failed when Sebastian reached over and placed his hand on her knee reassuringly. She felt her face blush even more than before, and she placed her hand on top of his. He took it, and squeezed gently. Reika looked up and smiled some.

"And you'll play your part after dinner, by doing dishes." Meredith grinned. "It's a little sister's duty after all." All Yuri could do was groan.

The little party continued on after dinner, playing games and Reika opening presents from everyone. She was very pleased to receive a couple of albums from her favorite bands from Sebastian. Yuri gave her a surplus of black eyeliner, and new eye shadows. Meredith bought some new clothes for her. Lynde gave her a card, with some money inside. She added the gifts to her stack of boxes that she was taking to the school tomorrow. Yuri and Reika had their belongings boxed up, waiting to be loaded into the car for the trip the next day.

Everyone had started to settle down for the night. Sebastian and Lynde had left for their houses, leaving Meredith, Yuri, and Reika sitting in the living room. Yuri gave a big yawn. "I think I'm going to head to bed. Good night, Mom, night Rei." She smiled, giving them both hugs and made her way up the stairs.

"Reika." Meredith said, once Yuri made it up the stairs. "I wanted to talk to you about this year. I want you to be careful. Not the violence, you've been doing well with that, actually. I'm really proud of you. Just be careful of new people entering your life."

Reika nodded. "Alright, I will." She bit the inside of her mouth before she spoke again. "I don't trust many anymore."

"Good. Keep me updated, okay?" Meredith smiled softly, but Reika could still see the concern etched in her eyes. "Tomorrow, you'll be of age and things will become a lot more difficult. Watch your back, and don't hit anyone. I can't stress that enough."

Reika nodded again. "I promise, I'll do my best." Meredith got up and hugged her.

"Good, go get some rest. Tomorrow's a big day." Reika hugged her Mother back and headed upstairs and went to sleep.

Morning came quickly for Reika. She woke up, showered and dressed. They loaded all their things in the car quickly, met up with Lynde to follow his parents to the school. It was a 45 minute drive to Locke Academy, in a city named Boroughs. Reika was surprised by the size of the campus, and even more surprised by the size of the room that her and Yuri were sharing for the duration of the year. Meredith helped them unload their things, and got their room set up.

The building Reika and Yuri's room was in, was made of gray stone, with a deep orange roof. It looked almost like a castle. The entrance to the building was almost as magnificent as the outside. The entryway had a small chandelier hanging before the stairs. The floors and crown molding and ceiling were all a rich mahogany color, the walls were cream, with exposed beams matching the ceiling. To the left was a small social room and to the right was a small library. Reika and Yuri's room was on the second floor of the building.

Reika opened the window of their room and looked out over the campus. "It's not a bad view!" She said happily. "I could get used to this!" Across from her building was another in similar style, which was the boys dormitory.

"It's a really nice school. I'm glad you two are going here." Meredith smiled, wrapping an arm around each girls' shoulder. "I love you two."

"Love you too, Mom." Reika and Yuri said in unison. Reika smiled, she did her best to shake the bad feeling she had, it was still there.

"Oh! Before I forget... I'll be right back!" Meredith said, and went outside to the car.

"I think it's going to be a good year." Yuri said, stretching her arms up above her head.

"I hope so." Reika said, smiling some. "We just have to make it good."

Yuri nodded, and patted Reika on the shoulder. "You're right there! Happy Birthday, Reika."

"Thanks, Yuri." She gave her a soft smile. Meredith came back into the room, with a small box of cupcakes.

"More cake!" She said with a grin. "Happy Birthday, Rei!" She set the box of cupcakes down on Reika's desk, opening it, and handing a cupcake to each girl, and taking one for herself. "Cheers!"

Reika couldn't help but laugh, taking the cupcake, pulling the paper off and biting into it. Her Mom always knew how to make her feel special on her birthday. After relaxing in the girls' room, they spent the rest of the day walking about the campus. The buildings were spread across a beautifully landscaped area. One building that caught Reika's eye was the campus office building. She saw there were a few classrooms inside the hulking colonial style building. It boasted four floors, made of red brick and had a black wrought iron balcony on each floor above the front entrance.

There was a small sign in front of the building which read "Campus Meeting: 5:00 P.M. Auditorium in The Campus Center." Meredith looked down at her watch, which said 4:30 P.M.

"Just enough time to get there." Meredith laughed as they went to the neighboring building. Each building on campus has the same architectural style has Reika and Yuri's dorm building, including The Campus Center. They entered the building and went to their right, to go to the auditorium. It was a warm, welcoming room, with the same mahogany and cream color scheme. The curtains on the stage were a deep burgundy, as was the upholstery of the seats.

Meredith, Reika and Yuri took seats in the balcony and waited patiently. They were met by Sebastian, Lynde and Lynde's parents. After a few moments, a man walked out on the stage. He seemed older, with short brown hair, and from the distance it seemed speckled with gray. He wore glasses on his pudgy face, and was very stout in stature. Reika looked around, all the girls were gaping at the man on stage, even Yuri was. Reika and Meredith exchanged confused looks.

"Thank you, everyone for joining me today." The man began his speech. "My name is Samuel Blake, and I am the dean here at Locke Academy. I would first like to welcome all our new students, may you find a new home within the walls of this academy. I would like to welcome back our former students, may you all prosper more than the previous years. To the parents of our beautiful student body, thank you for trusting us to educate your children. I personally see it as an honor." Mr. Blake smiled, though to Reika, his smile hardly matched his demeanor. The man who stood before her seemed relaxed, the smile he wore was that of a deviant.

"I'm certain you would much rather use these last few hours of the evening with your offspring, parents. As for the Children, You shall hear me drone on many more days, so I shall keep it short today. If you so choose to stay in the auditorium, I've arranged for a movie to show. If it doesn't suit your tastes, behind this building, our staff is hosting a cook out. Please, feel free to enjoy the amenities provided!" Mr. Blake clapped his hands together. "I have one last announcement! One of our wonderful new students has a birthday today! I would like to wish our own Reika Avel a very happy birthday!" He pointed towards Reika. "Please stand up!"

Reika felt her face flush deeply as all eyes turned towards her. She gulped hard, and stood from her seat, putting one hand up.

"May you have the most wondrous of years this year, Dear Reika!" Mr. Blake grinned. "Happy eighteenth Birthday!"

"T-Thank you." She called out, bowing her head. She immediately took her seat. The student body clapped awkwardly.

"The announcements are over for the evening! Everyone, please enjoy yourselves!" Mr. Blake said, and walked from the stage.

Reika turned to Sebastian and buried her face into his shoulder. "I hate public attention." She said, her voice muffled.

Sebastian rubbed her back. "Don't worry, it'll pass."

"Or everyone here will know who she is." Yuri chimed in.

"Shut up, Yuri!" Reika groaned.

Meredith yawned. "Stop it you two, now, what do you want to do? Watch the movie, eat food, or go back to your room?"

"I want to go back to the room." Reika grumbled.

Yuri nodded. "Yeah, that sounds good."

Reika gave Sebastian a kiss on the cheek and the three of them left for their dorm building. They watched their own movie, and relaxed. Meredith yawned heavily after they finished watching their horror movie.

"Girls, it's getting late. I've got work in the morning and you two have school. Get some sleep. Do your best this year! I know you'll do me proud!" Meredith hugged them both. "I love you, Reika, Yuri."

"I love you too, Mom." Yuri said, hugging her back.

"Yeah, I love you too, Mom." Reika said, hugging her Mom tight. "Thanks for everything. I had a great birthday."

"You're welcome, kid." Meredith smiled. "Remember what I told you last night, alright?"

Reika nodded. "You got it." Meredith kissed her forehead, giving one to Yuri as well.

"I'll see you on Thanksgiving break! You better behave!" She winked at them. "I'm off!"

They walked with Meredith to her car, and headed back to their room. Reika laid down on her bed, yawning. Yuri sat down at her desk, looking up at Reika.

"What did Mom tell you last night?"

"She told me to be careful. That things are going to be harder now that I'm an adult." She sighed. "Getting old is no fun."

"That's strange, Mom's usually not like that." Yuri sighed. "Well, maybe it's because of you fighting. She's right though, you need to be careful."

Reika nodded. "Yeah I will, Yuri." She looked over at her, then at the ceiling. "I don't want to let Mom down."
"As long as you try, I'm sure you'll do just fine." She smiled. "We better get to bed soon." Yuri hopped up, grabbing her pajamas, and went to the door. "Oh my God! I totally forgot! Mr. Blake! He's so gorgeous!"

Reika looked at Yuri as if she were insane. "You mean the middle aged guy that was up on stage in the sweater vest? No way!"

"Seriously, Rei? You need to get some glasses. He was so sexy! Though his eyes were really light colored, he almost looked blind. His hair was perfect." She groaned aloud. "He had the perfect face, God, Rei, I can't believe you don't think he's hot!"

Reika shrugged. "Maybe I do need glasses."

Yuri shrugged. "Oh well, more for me to ogle at." Yuri winked and headed out the door. Reika stayed in the room, and changed into a pair of shorts and a shirt. She laid back down on her bed, and pulled her phone out, and saw she had a text from Sebastian.

'Rei, I'm about to go to bed. Happy Birthday again!' She smiled at the words.

'Thanks Bas! :) I'm headed there too. Good night dear.'

'Good night!'

She smiled softly, then groaned. She put her hand to her head, where a throbbing ache started. "Damn." She got up slowly, shutting the main lights off, leaving Yuri's desk lamp on and laid back down. She covered her head with her pillow, and tried to go to sleep.

"Rei, are you alright?" Yuri said as she slipped back into the room.

"No, I feel sick." Reika said, her words muffled by her pillow. "Wake me up in the morning?"

"Yeah, feel better." Yuri said softly.

"I'll try." Reika muttered, finally slipping into a deep sleep.

Chapter Two

Reika felt a gentle hand rest against her cheek. "How precious she is whilst sleeping." She could feel the vibrations of a man's sultry voice next to her ear. "To have our cherished daughter home is splendid." His hot breath against her ear made her body shiver. She tried to turn away, but her arms were bound above her head. Groaning, she tried again, pulling against the bindings holding her arms against a cool iron headboard. She felt the man's lips rest against her cheek, leaving her a tender kiss.

She felt panic rise in her chest when she realized it wasn't a dream. Her eyes sprung open, yet she couldn't see anything. Encapsulated by total darkness, Reika began pulled harder against her bindings. "Let me go!" She cried out. "Why am I here?! Just let me go!"

"I'm afraid we can't oblige." Another voice whispered in the darkness, a woman this time. "You are our flesh and blood, and we've waited far too long to bring you home. We can't let you leave without a proper welcome back to the family."

"Let me go!" She growled. "You're not my family, I don't even know you!"

"I'm afraid to tell you, you're incorrect." The man said, his voice was calm in the wake of Reika's hysterics. She heard the creak of the bed, feeling his hands gently cup her face. The room was slowly illuminated, one candle at a time lighting on their own. Taking in her surroundings, Reika saw she was lying in an elegant canopy bed, with red velvet curtains. The colors in the room were rich, and dark. The candles rested on top of a rich cherry dresser. She brought her attention back to the man in front of her.

Reika's eyes were met by a pair of silver ones set in a face so perfectly sculpted. Straight black hair hung around his face, and a loving smile adorned his lips. What frightened Reika most, wasn't the strange color of his eyes, but the prominence of his incisors in his smile.

She tried to shrink back from him, but the bed beneath her wouldn't allow her but an inch. In the man's eyes she could see sorrow at her disdain. Reika whimpered, and the man pulled away from her. She got a better look at her captors, and her heart sank to the floor. Standing before her, was the woman with red hair, and silver eyes she had seen at the park. The man was tall and slender, just as she remembered seeing in the years past.

"You-" She whispered. "You've been following me for years. Why?"

"I gave you to Meredith." The woman said. "She wanted two children, I gave you to her, and I made it possible for her to have Yuri." A smile spread across her face, but it was far from tender. "I wanted my child back at 18 years old, and here you are."

The man sat down next to her on the bed, he went to touch her face once more, but withdrew. "You are my daughter." He smiled gently. "You are the daughter of the Angel of Death."

Reika's eyes widened in fright. "Angel of Death?" She whispered.

"He goes by many names, but prefers to be called Samael." The woman said, arms crossed over her chest. "As for me, I am Lilith."

"The Mistress of the Night." Samael said simply.

"Indeed it is my title." Lilith grinned. "Now, we need to discuss business."

"Business?" Reika looked at Samael. "What business? I just want to be left alone!"

"I'm afraid you only have two choices." Lilith said, coming closer to her. "You either choose to accept your life as our daughter, or your life before this moment will cease indefinitely."

"What the fuck?!" Reika groaned through gritted teeth. "You bring me here, against my will to God knows where, and tell me to either accept you as my parents or you're going to kill me?!"

"It's exactly what I'm telling you." Lilith grinned. "I haven't any objections to slaughtering my own lamb."

"Reika, my sweet." Samael said gently. "I promise you will be well taken care of in my custody. Please, choose your fate wisely."

Lilith produced a dagger from her waist, and inched closer to Reika. "What is your choice? An eternity of night, or a definite end?"

"I have to choose now?!" Reika's heart began beating faster. She hadn't any idea what she was agreeing to, but she knew she didn't want death.

"You must choose now." She peered over her shoulder at the beautiful wooden clock behind her, it read 5:47 AM. "We only have until six o'clock this morning to finish this process, or I slaughter you."

"We'll explain everything once the process is over." Samael said, trying to comfort Reika as much as possible.

"I-" She squeaked out. She swallowed hard, trying to calm herself some. Reika didn't want to die, but she didn't know what she was accepting. She felt the best choice was to accept and find out. "I want to live."

Samael placed his hand on her cheek. "You will never regret your decision, my love. Now, close your eyes, be prepared, it may sting momentarily."

Reika couldn't believe what was happening. She hoped when she closed her eyes, it would all prove to be some vivid dream. She clamped her eyes shut, and waited, holding her breath. She could feel him moving closer, his breath against her skin. She shuddered as her body tensed up.

"Would you like it if I released your arms?" Samael whispered into her ear.

"Yes."

"Do you promise not to hurt me?"

"Yes." Reika opened her eyes. Samael peered into her face, his expression gentle, kind. Something in her felt he was trustworthy, despite the dire words Lilith spoke. He touched her cheek gently, his gaze heavy upon her eyes.

He nodded. "Alright." Sitting up, Samael reached forward, and placed his hands over her's. The shackles and chains dissolved into nothing. Softly, he brought her hands down to her chest, and locked eyes with her once more. Reika was mesmerized by him, in the moment she knew she would do anything he asked of her. "Hold onto me, and relax. We have only a little time left."

She wrapped her arms around his neck as he slowly descended to her throat. She saw his incisors glisten in the rich candlelight, but felt no fear. His hair laid against her cheek, tickling her. His lips brushed against her skin, and finally she felt the sharp pain of his incisors piercing the tender flesh of her neck. She whimpered at first, but the pain was replaced with the most euphoric feeling she'd experienced. It felt as if something deep inside of her had burst, and raced through her veins.

Samael pulled away from her, and looked down into her face once again. Reika slowly opened her eyes, they had transformed from their deep velvety brown to a hazy cool silver. A proud smile tugged at the corners of his mouth. "Welcome home, my daughter. You must be famished, after being locked away for 18 years. Are you thirsty?" Reika only nodded, still consumed by the indescribable whirlwind within her.

She released her arms from his neck, her hands trailing down his arms. Once her hands reached his, Samael took one of them in his, and nodded to her. She pulled his wrist close to her and touched his skin to her cheek before she bit into his flesh.

"Very good, my dear." He whispered. Waiting patiently, Reika finally relinquished his wrist, and her head fell back against the pillows.

"I feel exhausted." She whispered out, closing her eyes.

"Rest, my dear, and we shall see you in the living world."

Samael leaned over her once more, and kissed her forehead.

Chapter Three

Reika woke up and groaned, her head pounded in blinding pain. "Fuck." She muttered, rubbing her temples. She sat up slowly, rubbing her face with her hands. Bright sunlight poured through the open window. The light hurt her eyes, she still felt groggy, and didn't dare get up just yet.

"What the hell happened?" She said softly, looking down at her hands. There was blood caked on her skin where she was bound to the bed. "It really happened?"

The door opened and Yuri walked into their room. "Reika! You're awake!"

"Yuri." She said, looking up at her. "What time is it?"

"Classes just ended. I couldn't wake you up this morning, I decided to let you sleep, you felt like you had a fever."

"Holy shit." She mumbled, crossing her arms over her chest, trying to hide her wrists from Yuri.

Yuri walked closer to the bed. "Rei, are you alright?" Yuri reached a hand out to Reika's face, wiping at the corner of her mouth. "It looks like you bit your lip, coughed up blood, or something." She held her hand out for Reika to see. She grabbed Yuri's hand.

"Are you serious?" She turned, and grabbed her pillow, and noticed a small stain on her pillow. "Oh my god." She ran her hands over her face again. "This is bad." She groaned. "Can you close the blinds?"

"Yeah." Yuri went and closed the blinds. "What's going on, you haven't been sick in years."

"I'm not sure." She looked at Yuri, wrapping a blanket around her shoulders. "I'm going to see the school nurse tomorrow morning."

Yuri nodded. "Okay, let me know if there's anything I can do to help."

Reika nodded. "I think I'm gonna go take a shower." She went to her dresser, pulling out a long shirt, and a pair of jeans. "I'll be back." She grabbed the rest of her things and went off to the bathroom quickly. She quickly noticed that the light sensitivity she was feeling when she woke still lingered.

She hurried into a shower stall, and locked the door. She turned the water on, and let it heat as she undressed. Reika kept staring at her wrists, terrified of what had happened to her after she had closed her eyes. She shook her head, trying to clear her thoughts and climbed into the shower, letting the water soothe her.

She held her hands out in front of her, staring at them. She remembered pulling at the shackles binding her to the bed, and how badly it hurt her wrists, but all that was left was dried blood caked on her skin.

"What is happening to me." She whispered out, tears falling down her cheeks, merging with the water flowing down her body. "What am I?"

"My child..." A familiar voice. "You are a demon."

Reika's eyes went wide. She got out of the shower quickly, wrapped herself in a towel and opened the stall door. "Lilith." She said, staring at the woman she had seen in her sleep. "You... you're real." She stared at Lilith, frozen in place.

"Of course I am." Lilith said softly. Though, the woman had the same red hair, and silver eyes, her clothing was much different from the night before. The night before, she was dressed in a dark dress, hugging her curves in all the right places. Tonight she was wearing a plain black skirt, and a red button down shirt.

"There's no way." Reika whispered. "I must have a really bad fever."

"No, my little one, you're perfect." Lilith smiled softly. "You'll feel different since we woke your powers last night. You'll get used to the light sensitivity soon, and you will learn sunglasses are your best friend." She touched Reika's cheek, wiping some of the water from her face.

Reika stepped back. "No, this can't be happening!" She shook her head, closing her eyes.

"It is happening, Reika, you're going to have to accept that. If you don't accept your fate, you'll die, don't forget you made this choice. There are many enemies in this world that would love nothing more to brutally murder you, and steal your power away. Though you are immortal now, it doesn't mean you can't be killed. There are always loopholes to gifts of this nature."

"What the fuck are you talking about?!" Reika yelled. "I'm not some demon spawn! I'm just some girl in her last year of high school! My Mother's name is Meredith, not Lilith! My sister is Yuri! I don't know this Samael person, and I don't know who you are! Just leave me alone!"

Lilith walked towards Reika, backing her into a wall. "Reika, this is all real. I hate to break your perfect vision of reality. She's not your real mother, I am. If you need more proof, look at my face, then look into the mirror." She put her hands on Reika's shoulders to steady her. "You need to accept it. You need to start learning your powers, or you will become vulnerable to the other evils in this world who will inevitably seek you out and try to kill you."

Reika stared at Lilith, eyes wide. Lilith lowered her hands. Reika walked back to the shower stall, dropping her towel and dressing quickly. She walked to the mirror, studying her own face. "Oh my-" She said softly, touching her own cheek, looking at her eyes. "There's no way." She turned to Lilith, who had followed her. She looked into Lilith's eyes, which now mirrored her own. "My eyes are even the same."

Lilith grasped Reika's shoulders once again. "You understand now? You really are my daughter." Reika simply nodded. "Will you go on a walk with me? We have much to discuss. Go to your room, get some shoes, and meet me back in the hallway."

"A-alright." Reika said. She went back to the stall once more, grabbing her things, and returned to her room.

"Rei!" Yuri jumped up as she entered the room again. "Are you alright?"

Reika nodded. "Yeah, Yuri. I'll be back. I need some air."

"Alright." Yuri said. "Just make sure you take your phone with you, and call me if you need anything, okay?"

She nodded again. "Yeah. I got it." She held up her phone, dropping it in her purse she had thrown over her shoulders. "I'll be back. Don't wait up for me, I don't know how long I'll be." Reika left her room, and met back with Lilith. "Where are we going?"

"We're going to my office on campus. Follow me."

Reika sighed, "Alright. Can you tell me anything while we're walking?"

"What do you want to know?"

"Everything."

"We'll start from the top when we get to the office. Samael is waiting there for us."

"I just want to know why I was chosen. You have to have many other children to have chosen from. What makes me so special?"

"You're mistaken." Lilith stated, her pace was quick as the walked down the sidewalk towards the large red brick building on campus. Reika tried her best to keep up with her. "You are our only child. There is substantial weight with your role. The way you were raised, and the discipline you applied to your arts has proven to us you would be able to handle your role."

"I don't understand what you're trying to say."

"Samael will be able to explain it to you much better than myself."

"And you're taking me to Samael right now?!"

Lilith nodded again. "We must get you started. There are many things you need to learn."

Reika shook her head, trying to keep up with Lilith. Everything was happening so fast, and she didn't know how to handle it all. She wished she could get Sebastian right now, though she didn't know how he'd react to all of it. He would probably think she had gone insane. She felt like she was losing her mind. She didn't understand why she was even following Lilith right now. She wanted to run from them, yet the part of her that was compelled to listen to what she and Samael had to say kept her feet moving forward.

They arrived at the brick building, Lilith led her around to the side entrance of the building, and went up the stairs to the third floor. They continued down the hallway to the office right at the end. Lilith opened the door, and waved Reika inside, closing the door behind her.

The office was decorated in deep burgundy curtains, similar to the ones Reika saw in her dream. The desk was dark, and intricately carved. There was a large leather desk chair facing the window. Samael was sitting in it, Reika could feel his presence without a doubt. The chair turned around slowly.

"Welcome, my heir." He smiled at Reika, lacing his fingers, and resting his chin there. "It's simply wonderful to finally meet you in the flesh. Look how beautiful you are, especially that you now have the same eyes as your Dear Father."

Reika froze in place. She didn't know what to say, or what to do. With all the training she had, all the fights she had been in, nothing had prepared her for this.

"There's something else I wanted to give you." He smirked, standing up and made his way in front of Reika "Consider it a late birthday present." He held his hands out in front of her, palms towards the ceiling. An old leather bound volume appeared in his hands. He held the book out to her. "This is vital to learning your powers. Write a question in it, and it will give you whatever answers you seek. Be aware, it has a mind of it's own. Sometimes the answers will be easy to understand and other times the messages may be cryptic. Let's just say, it can be quite obstinate, when it so chooses."

Reika reached towards the book, her hands were unsteady, trembling ever so slightly. She took it and looked at the cover, etched in red was her name. 'Reika Lilin Avel'. She stared at her middle name, and started laughing.

"Lilin." Reika shook her head. "Reika Lilin. It's so obvious."
She kept laughing, tears streaming down her cheeks.

"Will you take a seat?" Lilith asked. "We've got a lot to
explain to you."

Reika looked at Lilith and nodded softly. "Yeah." She sat
down, placing the book in her lap, and wiped the tears from her
cheeks.

"You already know what we are and our names." Samael
began to explain. "We're here to show you how to use your powers.
They are vast, ranging from mind reading, to transportation, and
many more." He returned to his seat behind the desk, Lilith took the
seat next to Reika. "We mainly make deals with humans who cannot
obtain their wish through conventional means."

"Like my Mom?" Reika whispered, looking up at Samael.

Samael nodded. "Yes, exactly. We grant wishes. It sounds
lovely, and sweet. Though, it isn't. These humans who make
contracts with us, pay a steep price."

"Their souls." Reika frowned deeply, her chest felt tight with
a whirlwind of emotions. She felt sadness, anger, and gratitude.

Meredith gave a lot for Reika. She had given her soul for the two of them. A sob slipped from her lips before she could cover them with her hand.

"You are correct. Meredith Avel wished for two children. I gave her you. You were put into her womb. I also made it possible for her to become pregnant with Yuri." Lilith said softly, it almost sounded as if Lilith sympathized with Meredith.

"What a fine job Meredith did. She raised you well." Samael smiled, his eyes gleaming. "You will make us proud."

"How could she." Reika whispered, her heart ached deeply for Meredith, for all the sacrifices she made for her. All Reika could think about was how horrible of a child she had been, and how many times she had disappointed her. She gave up everything she possibly could, and for what? For a violent daughter-turned-demon spawn who caused nothing but problems from the day she was born.

At least Meredith had Yuri. She was an angel compared to Reika. She got good grades, was rather popular despite her rather eccentric style of clothing. She was everything Reika wasn't. Reika was lucky to get passing grades. She fought, skipped classes, and got into trouble outside of the school a lot. People feared her, and rightly so. Everything about Reika was terrifying. She dressed like a Gothic girl, swore like a sailor, and had the temper of redhead.

Coming back to reality, Reika looked to Lilith and Samael. "I can't believe she gave so much up, for me, for Yuri. It doesn't seem worth it."

"That's what you have to understand, Reika." Lilith said, sitting atop Samael's desk, and crossing her legs. "To her, it was worth it. To Meredith, her trade with us was worth it because she made it worth it. She was able to love and nurture two girls the best she could. She was able to create a child with her beloved husband. Humans are after one thing in this life, and it is a legacy. Whether it be fame, or to be remembered by their loved ones for the gift of memories they bestowed upon them. Everyone wants to be remembered when they are gone. Even if it's only by one person."

"Some humans just find themselves more desperate than others and that's where Lilith and I come in. Our jobs in this realm, aside from reigning over the demons in the underworld, we are brokers. We create contracts with humans who find themselves at the very edge of desperation. They give us their soul, and we grant them their deepest desires. Whether it be fame, riches, a family, the list knows no end."

"I'm going to have to take peoples' souls?" Reika asked hesitantly. She knew it was the 'family business', but she didn't feel cut out for it. She was far from sympathetic, like most demons seem to be, but she couldn't see herself taking someone's soul for what they wanted most. She wasn't very sociable either. There were few people she enjoyed sharing time with. Reika felt that time she spent alone, was time well spent.

"Of course, My Sweet." Samael grinned. "Though, we will have other work for you. Work which is much more suited for a Demon with your talents."

"What do you mean by my talents?" Reika looked up, confused. "I am going to have to take souls." She gulped audibly. "I don't know if I can do it."

Samael smirked. "Dear Reika, you'll get used to it. I promise. The more souls you consume, the stronger you will become."

"I don't want to be stronger, I just want to finish high school without getting arrested." She muttered.

Lilith smiled softly. She walked to Reika, and knelt down in front of her and placed her hands on Reika's knees. "You really don't have to worry about High School. We're here for you now and forever. We'll make sure you get through this year. We're going to train you, and show you all you need to know." She nods slowly. "Everything will be alright. You're strong, we know you can do this."

"It's not a matter of if I can do it." Reika muttered, staring down into a set of eyes that mirrored her own. She sighed, it was all too much. Reika didn't know what she wanted to do with her life, but the more they told her, the more everything made sense. In the world Reika lived in, there were never coincidences. Everything which happened in her life, happened for a reason. Though, Reika didn't know why it happened, it did, and everything seemed to work out. "I know I could. I just want to know why I must."

Lilith nodded, "I'm sure you'll find your way soon enough." She smiled. "We're here to help you. We will guide, teach and protect you." She patted Reika's leg softly. "You have nothing to worry about."

Reika nodded softly. She knew the best choice in this situation would be to accept what is happening, and move forward. Life seldom goes the way anyone wants it to. Reika knew it all too well. "Okay. I'll do it." She looked into Lilith's eyes with a new determination.

"You do know what this means, Reika?" Samael said, standing from his desk, and circling around to stand behind her, placing his hands on her shoulders. "It means there is no turning back, from this moment forward until the end of time you will be shrouded in darkness. You will see the worst pains of the world, and will perform tasks even the worst of humans will find despicable. You will have to turn your back on everything you know. I hope you are ready for that step, Reika."

She closed her eyes, a shiver crawling over her skin in reaction to his words, and his touch. She would be fine with leaving most everything behind. She loved her family and friends, but she knew they would be alright without her. Her sister was a strong girl, and Reika knew she could survive on her own. There were two people, though, she would be sad to leave behind. Her Mother, Meredith, for all she gave her. Though, Reika felt she could never face her again, not after she had inherited the powers from the people who took Meredith's soul. There was also Sebastian. In the few short months they had spent together, she had grown deeply attached to him.

Reika opened her eyes, looking into Lilith's once more. "I can do it." She said with a sharp nod of her head.

"Wonderful." Samael said, clapping his hands together. He returned to his desk, crossing his hands and leaning his chin on them."Shall we get started with the lesson, then?"

Before she could agree, Reika found herself standing in an unfamiliar place. She was looking out across a playground, the moon and stars shining above her. She turned and looked behind her, seeing Samael standing in front of a scrawny woman on the ground in front of him. The woman looked up, her face was dirty, her hair and clothes unkempt. She was shaking visibly, her hands clasped together.

"Are you *him*?" She asked, her voice rasping out.

"I would appear to be this *him* you are referring to." He smirked.

Reika walked up towards Samael, trying to get a better look at the woman. Her eyes were bloodshot and crazed.

"Please, you have to help me. I don't know what to do. I need more, and you're the only one I could ask for help. Everyone else has abandoned me! I'm alone, and I just can't take it anymore!" The woman rattled on grasping onto handfuls of her matted hair. She rocked back and forth on her knees as she sobbed.

Reika stared at the woman, not understanding what could put a person in such a state of mind. Such crazed desperation carved into the woman's face was haunting. The only possible reason Reika could come up with for this woman's behavior was an addiction of some sort.

Samael shook his head, a smirk heavy on his lips. "Is it really worth the price, hm? To lose your soul, just for another high? So be it. I will help you, but I will take your soul." Reika felt the air around them vibrate. Samael knelt down beside the ratty woman, brought his mouth close to her ear. "I will take what belongs to me first, then you will receive your exchange."

The woman shivered, "Okay." She nodded once, closing her eyes tight, clasping her hands together hard. Samael positioned his lips over her neck and drove his fangs into her neck. The woman screamed out trying to break free from Samael's grip, but he held her tighter. Her face was full of anguish as she struggled against Samael's strong grip on her. She finally settled down after a few moments had passed, her eyes glazed over, becoming blank.

Samael released the woman and shoved her back to the ground, and dropped a syringe into her hand. "It's all you'll ever need in your life, this one dose." He turned swiftly, took Reika's arm, and they left the woman in the park.

"Lesson one, My Dear. Humans have many desires, and will become desperate for these to be fulfilled. When the struggle to fill the void in their life reaches an all time low, it is not uncommon for a human to turn to a demon for a contract. The contract is this: Their soul in exchange for their deepest wishes to become a reality." Samael explained as they strolled through the darkened streets of a seemingly peaceful town. "Souls of these people, Dear Reika, are your fuel, they are your nourishment. If you wish to become stronger, devour as many souls as you possibly can. Any parent would wish to see their child surpass them, myself included."

Reika just nodded, listening to Samael's lecture. She was intrigued by the new world laid out in front of her. It was dark, malicious, gritty, and ruthless. The feelings the new reality she was thrown into left her feeling as if she were watching a gruesome train wreck. It was absolutely unbearable to fathom, yet she couldn't turn away. The allure of the powers she inherited was great. She wanted to know more of what laid dormant, but was terrified of the consequences.

The changes in her body were already very evident. Her body already felt stronger, wounds healed faster and her reaction time was quicker. It was like she woke up to a completely new body, though almost all her physical characteristics had stayed the same, aside from her now silver eyes. She already knew she would have to cover them to avoid any students picking on her. She was already receiving strange looks for her wardrobe, she didn't want to think of what would happen if she showed her shocking new eye color.

She looked at Samael again, the reality of the situation had started to slowly sink in. She had watched the man she was currently walking with devour the soul of a woman. She had seen the essence of the woman leave her body, the light of life leave her eyes, leaving the shell of a human laying there in the park.

"She was already done living, Reika." Samael said softly. "I know what you are thinking. I can see it. When someone wishes for such an awful existence, they have already given up their want for redemption, their need for cleansing, and have accepted death. Essentially, they are already the empty body of who they once were. There is almost nothing left of people like her. Save your pity for the living."

Reika contemplated his words deeply. "Why should we pity the living?"

"Because, My Dear, they are fools. They do not know what waits for them at the end. They almost always become residents of my domain. In essence, giving up and forfeiting their soul to me or my family would be a much better end than to suffer through all the troubles of life and die out silently. They could achieve much more with my help whilst living, than to come to me after their life has ended."

"Why does living life the best they can make them fools? Most people don't know of our existence. I didn't even know what I was until you came to me in my dreams. As the saying goes: Ignorance is bliss. I can hardly pity someone who is ignorant of the world's tormented reality."

Samael stopped and glared at her. "Are you stating the world should pity you? Why should they pity someone who is all-powerful? Why should they hold any sympathy for a being whose purpose is to prey upon their weakness?" He spat the words at her.

"It's not what I'm saying." Reika said, her tone defiant. "I'm stating no one in this world is worth the pity. Every person chooses their own life, and I'm not going to be the one to pity, or to praise their life choices. I don't have time for that. I have time enough to live my own life, and learn my own lessons. Nor do I expect anyone to pity me for my position in this world. We each play a role, and if this is mine, so be it. No one deserves my pity, only my wrath if they cross me."

A smirk danced across his lips. "That is befitting of the Daughter of the Angel of Death." He took her arm once more, and lead her down the street. "Let us continue this lecture, yes?"

Reika gave a small nod as she walked with him. She felt her body being pulled, closing her eyes, she felt like she was being yanked through the skies. Upon opening them again, Reika found herself standing with Samael in his office once more, though Lilith wasn't anywhere to be found. Samael went around the desk, sat in his chair, and Reika took her chair as well.

"You must have questions for me. Please, feel free to ask them."

"How do people summon us?"

"It entirely depends upon the demon. For me, simply writing my name in your own blood on even just a scrap of paper, and calling out my name will suffice. To summon one so young, as yourself, an incantation may be used. There are plenty of generic incantations spread among the humans, all they must do is insert your name into it. If the incantation is strong, you should feel the summon immediately, if not, they must try until you do."

"Can you choose not to go to them?"

"You may, however, if they have spilled blood for your summons, you must show yourself." Samael leaned back in his chair and sighed. "Many children will try to summon me by just saying a spell with my name in it, I won't reveal myself to them. I will consume any adult's soul, but I cannot defile a child. It is a personal rule."

Reika nodded. "I understand. I couldn't do it either." She sighed. "Though I don't see how I could even take anyone's soul."

"You will get past the fright of it." He smiled. "The longer you wait, the more your hunger for one will grow. Your palette as a demon will develop soon enough."

"Am I still able to eat food?" Reika frowned at the thought of never being able to eat food again.

"Of course you will still be able to." He laughed. "You just won't grow from it. There are certain foods I adore, yet, I cannot go a day without the want for blood."

Reika thought for a moment, and remembered vaguely tasting Samael's blood for the first time. The thought left her body covered in goosebumps, it scared her, yet she craved it all the same. "This is all normal?"

"It certainly is. You will come to terms with it soon enough. Lessons shall end for tonight. Now, we shall drink."

Reika watched as Samael went around to a small cabinet, and brought out a decanter filled with a deep garnet red liquid, and two wine glasses. He set them down on the desk and poured the liquid into the glasses. The room echoed with Samael's slow, methodical steps as he rounded the room and stood behind her. His hand crept into her vision, offering her the glass of the mixture.

She slowly brought her hand up, taking the stemmed glass in her hand, afraid of what would happen if she refused. "Very good, Love, now, drink it."

She brought the glass towards her lips, the scent strong under her nose. She looked up at Samael, and moved the glass away. "This doesn't smell like anything I've ever had before, what is it?"

A grin spread over Samael's face. "A dear friend of mine made a donation to my collection. I felt it would be a wondrous experience to share with my Daughter."

She nodded softly. "Hopefully it will prove as wonderful as you say." She bit the inside of her lip, and looked down at her cup.

"It will, my sweet." He sat down in the chair next to her. "Now, let us drink!"

She looked at Samael, who raised his glass. She brought the stemmed glass towards her lips, watching him carefully. She took a sip at the same time as Samael. The rich liquid coated her mouth, her senses reeling from the unearthly flavor. She took another drink, savoring it. Samael let a deep throaty laugh escape his lips. Before she was even aware, she had finished her glass. She felt warm throughout her entire body, her head abuzz.

"How precious. My, look how flushed your cheeks are. You appear so youthful." He smiled sweetly. "You must have been an absolute delight as a child."

Reika chuckled, "Mom had her hands full with me. I was her problem child. I'm sure you would have found it funny."

"Of course you were. You are *My* daughter after all."

She looked down, frowning "Yeah, I guess you're right. It's still hard to believe my whole life has been a lie."

"You're not human, Reika. You're a demon. It's far past time to accept it. You have much to learn, Reika." He set his glass down, and took hers as well. "A change of plans is in order." He smiled softly.

"Change of plans?" She towards him, concern heavy in her eyes.

"Let us begin yet another lesson." He went to his desk once more, and retrieved Reika's book. He sat it in front of her on the desk, and opened it to the first page. "When you open this book, if you place your palm on it's first page, the pen you need to use will appear. Please, try."

She nodded, and leaned forward, placing her hand on the page of the book. She felt warmth underneath her hand, and was shocked to see an antique style fountain pen appear in the crease of the pages. The pen was black, with silver filigree, and was tapered to a sharp point at opposite end of the nib. "What a beautiful pen." She said softly.

"It is a very special pen, indeed." Samael stood from the chair, offered it to her. She took the seat, and picked the pen up to study it. "To use the pen, you must feed it first."

"I must feed it?" Reika looked up confused, and back to the pen. She touched the tip of her finger to the point of the pen, and pricked her finger on it. She frowned a little, but kept her finger on the tip, watching carefully as the filigree on the pen shifted from silver to blood red.

"Very good." He smiled. "It seems satisfied with it's meal. When you write in this book, a few things may happen. If you write questions, and it will give you answers. Granted, those answers may not be what you wish to hear. You may write things you wish to remember. You aren't limited in what you want to write in this book, just remember, the book will know what you write. There is a wealth of knowledge beneath the cover, and if you ask the right questions, it might be revealed."

She nodded slowly. "I can ask it anything I want?"

He smiled, "Yes, but start simply."

She nodded, thinking of what to write first. She laughed a little, "Well, simple it shall be." She brought the pen to the paper's surface and wrote *'What is my name?'*

'Have you forgotten so easily, miss? Your name graces my cover. How silly of you to forget your own name!'

Samael laughed. "Indeed it is still as I remember it. This book used to be mine. I'm thankful it's polite to you. I wasn't called such kind names."

She looked up at him. "What kind of names did it call you?"

"Such names are not appropriate for the current company." He smiled, a twinkle in his eye.

Reika laughed, her apprehension began to dissolve. She looked down to the page before her and noticed another line of text from the book.

'Samael is a deeply respectable demon, however I cannot help myself. I had to inform him of his stupidity more than a few times.'

Reika couldn't help but laugh again. Samael peered down at the words and shook his head.

"I think we've had enough of you tonight." Samael said aloud to the book. He closed the cover, and the pen disappeared from Reika's hand. "What nerve, to exclaim my stupidity in front of my daughter." He laughed some. "Some things never change, no matter how many centuries pass." Reika just smiled. "I think we've had enough fun for tonight. How about I walk you back to your room so you can rest for class tomorrow?"

She nodded. "That would be nice, thank you." She paused, her mouth contorted. "Thank you, Samael." She whispered out, her face red.

Samael picked the book up from the desk and knelt down in front of Reika, taking her hand. "My dear, please, you may call me what you are comfortable calling me. I have many names. Eventually, I would hope you choose one of affection, however I will not force your hand in the matter."

She held onto his hand. "As with any change in life, it will take time." She bit her lip. "It's quite a bit to take in all at once. I'll be okay though, I promise."

Squeezing her hand, Samael smiled and helped her to her feet. They were silent until they exited the building and were walking down the sidewalk.

"Was your life good with them?" Samael asked, his voice faint in the stillness of the night air. "From afar your family seemed happy, at least for a while."

"Yeah, it was good." She looked down at the ground as she walked slowly with Samael. "It was wonderful until Dad died, then things were strained. They still are."

"Death is a peculiar thing to mortals. It brings the true nature of the being to the forefront." Samael sighed. "It's interesting to watch from our point of view. As I see it, mortality is much too short for the petty arguments and hatred towards each other. Nearly all beings in this world are cruel. It seems they hold onto the evil within. Do not mistake me, I benefit greatly from those who harbor the evil, but I began viewing the world differently once I saw you in it."

"How could I change your view so much?" Reika looked up at him, stopping on the path. "You hardly know who I am."

"That is where you are wrong, my dear." Samael led her to a nearby bench, and they sat down together. "A father knows his child, whether or not they converse regularly. You weren't very old when your mother gave you to Meredith." A flicker of regret came and passed in his eyes. "I chose to watch you grow and develop into the being you are today. I wanted so badly to speak to you, to embrace you, yet I was advised not to."

"None of it was your decision?" Reika asked, she looked shocked.

"Only to be involved with your life, though it was from afar. I never wanted you to leave my sight. The decision to give you to Meredith was Lilith's decision alone."

"It all seems so unfair." She shook her head. "Why? Why did she choose to give me away, and then come back for me later? It doesn't make any sense."

"I wish I understood it myself, so I could inform you of it. It was never my intention to have you live with another family. You were- No, you are my daughter. In my mind, the safest place for you is within arm's reach, to catch you if you fall, to hold you when you cry and to embrace you in moments of vivacity. I am so terribly contrite with the situation." Samael pressed his hands together and leaned forward bringing his elbows to his knees. "I should have stopped her. Reika, I am deeply sorry for all of this, it isn't fair to you either."

Reika leaned back against the park bench. "I wish I could say it's alright, but I can't even comprehend what's happening. I went to sleep a 18 year old human girl and woke as a demon. The people

I've called parents all these years are just surrogates. My own sister isn't blood. I have powers deep inside I don't even know how to use. The way you explain it, Lilith never wanted me." She turned her body towards him, crossing her legs as she sat on the bench. "Yet, the words you speak are sincere in your want of a daughter. I believe you."

"I've only given you my word in all this. How can you believe me?"

"Sometimes it's all a person needs." She smiled softly. "I see the resemblance when I look at you, and at Lilith. My attitude and actions growing up make much more sense with the explanation of what lurked within for 18 years. Aside from that, no one speaks like you do anymore, not unless they love someone deeply. I don't think I could ever call Lilith Mother, but one day, I feel I could call you by Father."

A smile swept across Samael's lips as he turned to meet her eyes. "You make such an ancient being feel joy again. Before this moment is ruined by anything else, please let me take you back to your room."

Reika smiled. "I'm glad to have made you feel better." Yawning, she stood up. "It's been a long day, some sleep would be nice."

Samael joined her, and took her hand once more. "Forgive my boldness." He said before pulling her into a warm embrace. "I just wanted to feel my daughter in my arms after such a long time. The only piece of this moment which saddens me is how long it's taken me to have you in my arms once again."

Reika wrapped her arms around him gently and rested her head against his shoulder. "The way you speak of the moment, I wish I remembered it."

"The beauty of our lives is we have many lifetimes to create memories." Samael whispered. He let go of her hesitantly. "There is plenty of time in eternity for this. Let's get you back to rest."

She nodded, and they continued onto her dorm building in silence. Reika stopped before entering her building, Samael handed Reika her book. "Thank you, for everything tonight." She looked up at him. "I know we can't discuss everything in one night, but the answers you gave me tonight suffice for now. Thank you again."

"I was more than happy to give you some answers, dear." He slowly brought his hand to her cheek. "Go rest, we will cover more tomorrow."

Reika nodded again. "Okay, Good night." She smiled.

"Your classes start when you wake up, Reika. Please report to my office when you do." He let his hand linger on her face for a moment, before bringing it back to his side.

"I won't be in any other classes?"

"You may do so if you wish. It may keep Yuri from knowing too much. I had forgotten of her." Samael sighed. "Go and rest, we will take care of everything regarding your schedule in the morning."

"Good night." She whispered out and slipped through the door. She looked at the cover of the book once more. Seeing her name emblazon the cover made a smile appear on her lips. She cradled it to her chest as she made her way up the stairs and to her room. She tried her best to be quiet as she opened the door and slipped inside. She closed the door, and the light next to Yuri's bed came on.

"Rei, where have you been? I tried waiting up for you, but it got too late. It's almost two in the morning." Yuri said, her voice groggy. She rubbed at her eyes as she sat up in bed.

"Sorry Yuri. I tried not to wake you." Reika sat her purse on the floor and her book on the bed. "I've been in the Dean's office this whole time."

Yuri's eyes went wide. "You mean the hot guy on stage today?!"

Reika laughed. "Yeah, it was him."

"What did he want?"

"He just wanted to cover ground rules with me." She sighed. "He gave me a birthday gift as well, a journal. He said when he was my age, writing in one helped him with anger issues." Reika felt terrible for lying to Yuri, but there was no way she could disclose the truth to her little sister. Everything Samael told her made sense, yet it was all so fresh in her mind, that it hadn't sunk in yet.

"How nice of him." She smiled. "Well, I'm going back to sleep." Yuri shut her light off and turned over.

"Night Yuri." Reika said softly. She looked down at her bed, and sighed. She slipped her jeans off, and threw them on her chair and climbed into bed. She laid her book next to her pillow, closed her eyes and drifted off to sleep.

Soft petals danced in the wind, a sweet scent rushed past Reika. She was in a world she hadn't seen before. Looking around her, she saw an infinite field of irises. She ran and ran to try to find the end. Falling to her knees, she caught her breath as she tried to shake the feeling of trepidation. Standing once more, she caught a glimpse of trees on the horizon. With new determination, she pushed herself farther, finally reaching the beautifully petal adorned white hydrangea trees.

A single white petal fluttered down from the branches. She held her hand out, letting it land in her palm. She smiled and brought her eyes to the horizon once more. She spotted a river carving a path through the scenery. She came to the bank of the river, and blew the white petal from her hand. It danced and twirled through the air, finally landing on the water's surface. Once it made contact with the water, the petal turned red. It seemed strange to Reika, but she tried not to think too much of it. Instead she returned to the hydrangea tree, seated herself underneath it's shade and watched the horizon. She felt safe and relaxed.

Reika sat for what seemed like hours, legs folded underneath her, eyes closed. The sound of a river flowing met her ears, yet she didn't care. She just sat, breathing steadily. She felt at peace, despite the storm beginning to emerge within.

"Reika!" She heard Yuri's voice. Reika opened her eyes to look around but saw nothing. Her vision began to shake. "Reika!"

Her eyes shot open and was greeted with Yuri's face. "It's time to get up for school!"

Reika groaned. "Okay, *Mom*." She chided, rolling out of her bed. Opening the doors to her closet, Reika tried to stifle a yawn. "Today's going to be a long day."

"You shouldn't have stayed out so late." Yuri murmured.

"There was much to discuss last night." Reika retorted, as she pulled out a pleated black skirt and slipped it on. She put on black and green striped knee high socks on, and white button down shirt, with black accents. "Trust me, I would have loved to have been asleep." Reika grabbed her black Mary Jane shoes and slipped them on.

"Are you still feeling sick?" Yuri asked. She was adding her finishing touches to her outfit. She wore a pretty light pink handkerchief hem skirt, with a black hook and eye shirt. She had a pair of matching pink ballet flats on, with white lace tights on.

"A little, I've got a pretty bad headache and light sensitivity cause of it." She rubbed her face with her hands and went to her desk with her make up bag. Looking in the mirror, she was met with a hazy silver stare. The eyes staring back at her in the mirror sent shivers down her spine. Though she had told herself over and over again it was all real, to see the truth so blatantly was hard to stomach.

"That's gotta suck." Yuri sighed. "My first class is in 15 minutes, I'll see you later! Hopefully we can grab lunch together." She scooped up her book bag and left.

Reika sighed, letting her head fall to the desk with a thud. After a few moments, the silence was broken by the beep of her cell phone. She pushed herself away from the desk, reached for her purse, and pulled her phone out.

'Our first class isn't until 11 A.M. Do you want to meet at the cafeteria and have breakfast together?'

Reika smiled, seeing the message from Sebastian. She saw there was one more message on her phone. She didn't recognize the number.

'Dearest Reika, please go to breakfast first this morning. Meet with me afterward. In your make-up bag there are a set of colored contacts if you so choose to use them.'

Immediately she knew it was from Samael. She was grateful he had thought to give her something to make her feel less exposed. She quickly responded to Sebastian's text message.

'Sure, meet me out front of my building in ten minutes?'

She opened her makeup bag and pulled the small contact lenses container out and opened one of the wells. She placed the contact in her eye carefully and repeated the process with the other. She looked in the mirror, and smiled sadly. The eyes she once knew were back again, but they were only artificial. Reika could never be the person she was before, and it was hard to accept.

Trying not to dwell too much on everything, Reika pulled a tube of eyeliner out and applied it, as well as mascara. She ran a brush through her hair and gave herself a small nod in the mirror. She laughed a little as she went to her bed and grabbed her book, slid it into her book bag. She swung it onto her back, grabbed her purse and left.

As she exited her the building, she saw Sebastian leaning against the tree in front of it. She grinned, seeing him standing there.

He turned, seeing her and grinned as well. "Hey, I missed you yesterday. Yuri said you weren't feeling well. I asked her to have you call me when you woke up, but I guess she forgot."

"I'm sorry if I made you worry." Reika came up to him and wrapped her arms around him. "I'm doing better today."

"It's alright." Sebastian said, holding her tight. "You're forgiven since you're my escort to breakfast this morning."

She laughed. "I'm so thankful for your forgiveness, oh great one. Though I can't walk with you to class, unless it's in the Campus Office. I have to meet with Mr. Blake today. Apparently my classes are getting rescheduled." She sighed. "I hope it doesn't change too many of them."

"Did he say why your classes are being changed?"

"No he didn't." She shrugged. "I wish I knew."

Sebastian frowned, and jumped when he heard his phone go off. He pulled his phone out and read the message. "I just got a message from Mr. Blake. I'm supposed to go with you for the meeting."

Reika felt her stomach shrink at the same time as she felt happy. She hoped Samael was changing their classes so they would still be together. All she was aware of, was the fact they wouldn't know until they arrived in his office. "Did he say what time to be there?"

"He just told me to eat, and come to the office with you." Sebastian smiled and kissed her forehead. "I'm sure everything is going to be alright."

Reika smiled up at him, she felt she could face anything so long as Sebastian was at her side. "Come on, let's go eat."

He smiled back at her. "Sounds like a good plan." Reika held onto Sebastian's arm as they walked to the cafeteria.

Chapter Four

"Thank you both for joining me today." Samael said. He was perched behind his desk, chin rested upon linked hands. "I wanted to discuss something rather important with the both of you. Our school is realizing some teenagers have a natural tendency to stay up later than their peers. My idea, is to have a trial run with my senior class, at least those who have a record of tardiness, of late afternoon and evening classes. I would like you two to join the trial group."

Reika smiled and nodded. "I would like to, absolutely!"

Sebastian grinned. "That sounds perfect!"

"Splendid, your classes will begin tomorrow afternoon at three. Meet in room 203 of this building, you will need notebooks and writing utensils, the books will be provided when classes commence. Please, enjoy today as a gift from me, and be prepared for tomorrow. Oh, I would like to have a few words with Miss Avel in private, Mr. Luciano you may be dismissed."

Sebastian stood from his chair, and smiled. "Thank you, Mr. Blake for letting me be part of the trial run." He patted Reika on the shoulder and left the office.

Samael waited for a few moments before speaking. "Lessons will be tonight at nine o'clock. The subject tonight will be simple, but execution of it shall be difficult. There is also an event I am holding on the 23rd of September in your honor. I shall escort you to the event. Some of the subjects we will cover in the regular schedule of classes will help with the event."

"What is the event for?"

"In essence, it is a coming of age ceremony for you."

"Like a debutante ball?" Reika asked.

"Exactly, except we aren't looking for a suitor for you." Samael smiled. "It seems you have done well in finding one on your own. I only wish to introduce you to the world in which we live in."

Reika smiled softly. "It sounds like fun." She sighed. "Though, I'm nervous and I don't have anything to wear for a ball."

Samael grinned. "I assumed you would say something of the sort. Part of tonight will be spent finding a dress fitting for such a beauty."

She could feel heat rise up in her cheeks. "Are you sure?" She asked.

"I'm absolutely positive. I have a few friends who owe me some favors. I am more than happy to use them for my daughter."

She smiled. "It's really nice of you to do all of this, really."

"Reika." Samael stood and rounded the desk. He knelt down before her and took her hands in his. "I've waited years to spoil my child, please give me the pleasure in doing so."

She nodded. "Of course I will." She smiled. "I've missed having a Father. You're not the man who raised me, but there is something about you, it tells me I can trust you."

Samael smiled, bowing his head. "I don't think you understand how wonderful it is to hear those words. It warms me deep where I've been frigid for many years."

"What do you mean?"

"It's a story for another day. It is lengthy, and tragic." He patted her leg gently. "Just know I am ecstatic to have you in my life once again."

Reika smiled. "I'm glad too."

"Now, go and enjoy today." Samael patted her leg once again. "Just remember, nine o'clock is my time with you."

Reika nodded. "I will remember." She leaned forward and hesitated for a moment before laying a gentle kiss on Samael's cheek. "I'll see you then."

Samael touched her cheek, and stood. "Have a beautiful day, my dear."

She smiled, stood, gathering her things and left the office. Once she exited the building, she found Sebastian sitting under a large oak tree. She took her back pack off and sat it down on the ground, taking a seat next to him. "What should we do today?" She asked, laying her head on his shoulder.

Sebastian leaned his head against hers. "We could do many things. We could watch a movie, read a book together, listen to music, practice some sword work." He smiled. "Anything you want to do, I'll be glad to do it with you."

"You're right, there are so many things we could do." She laughed. "And I can't think of anything to do. I always want to practice but I'm sure I've burnt you out on it already."

"You haven't, not yet at least." Sebastian laughed.

Reika grinned. "We could, but where is there a place to practice here?"

"We might be able to practice out by the football field. They might have a gym class going though."

Reika shrugged. "If they do, oh well. It wouldn't be the first time we've practiced in front of the entire world." She sat up and looked at him. "Do you have two swords, or should I run back and get mine?"

Sebastian laughed again. "Rei, is there anything in this world aside from swords and throwing people that gets you this excited? I only have the one you gave me. We'll walk to your building and you can grab your two, it's on the way to the field."

"I hope you're prepared to scare the shit out of your classmates." Reika grabbed Sebastian's arm and pulled on him. "Let's go!"

Sebastian jumped to his feet. "You're going to be the death of me, Reika." He laughed. "I couldn't think of a better way to die."

"Don't plan on dying any time soon." She turned and gave him a sweet smile. "I still need you." They walked hand in hand to her dorm building in silence. Reika ran inside, left her book bag and grabbed two of her wooden swords and ran back outside to join Sebastian once more.

They continued walking in silence to the football field, swords in their left hands, and Sebastian held Reika's waist with his right. Occasionally, someone they passed would nod and say hello to Sebastian. Reika would smile awkwardly in their direction and put her head down until they got past them.

"What's got you acting so shy lately?" Sebastian asked. "Are you alright?"

"Yeah, I'm fine, everything here is new and so different. There's a lot to adjust to. It'll all come with time."

"I think you're doing well, Rei. You don't need to worry about anything."

"I wish I could say you're right." She sighed. "New schools always make me nervous. It used to be I would worry if the others would like me, now I wonder if I'll like anyone here."

Sebastian nodded. "Like I said, don't worry so much. I'm here, and if anyone has anything to say about you, they'll have to deal with me."

Reika smiled. "You're the sweetest, Bas. I'm glad I found you."

"Oh, but I was the one to find you. Have you forgotten?"

"You're right on that one, you did find me." She laughed. "Now you're stuck with me. Are you sure you can handle it?"

"I'm positive. If you haven't killed me yet, I think we're going to be just fine."

Reika laughed. "It's a good thing we don't use real swords to practice with." They finally arrived at the football field. "No classes, and no loners here smoking cigarettes." She grinned. "It's perfect."

Sebastian smiled. "We've got a whole field to ourselves for practice." He laid his book bag down, and they walked to the center of the field. "Let's see how much space we can cover."

Reika grinned. "Are we doing prearranged, or free form?"

"I say free form, it makes me think more. Are throws and sword takeaways alright?"

Reika nodded. "It sounds perfect! Let's make it a long fight though, and try not to hurt each other too badly."

Sebastian nodded in agreement. "We'll start on your call."

Reika stepped back from Sebastian, her sword still on her left, she waited with her hand on the hilt. "Draw." She said, her eyes were intense, boring through Sebastian's body. They both pulled their swords and pointed the tips at each others' throats. Slowly they began circling, waiting for the other to make a move. Reika raised her's above her head, offering Sebastian a shot at her body. He lowered his blade and lunged forward, trying for an upwards strike against Reika's side.

With a resounding crack, Reika knocked the blade away, hid the sword behind her and waited. Sebastian dropped his low, towards Reika's knees. In an instant,she brought her sword up, and straight down towards his head. Sebastian side stepped, and Reika rolled forward from the velocity of her missed strike. She popped back up, sword ready, and charged forward, hiding her blade once more. She swung at the side of his head, and Sebastian rolled backwards. He held his sword parallel to the ground above his head when he came to his feet to block another downward strike.

Sebastian stepped back and swung for a blow to the side of her head, but by the time he got to her, Reika was behind him. She tapped her sword against the back of his knee, and wrapped her arm around his shoulder. She leaned his head against her body and turned, making him fall to the ground once more. As he fell, Sebastian lost hold of his sword, and Reika kicked it away from him.

She knelt down over top of him, and rested the wooden sword against his neck. "Hello down there." She smiled.

"You got me." He laughed a bit. "I still have much to learn."

"As do I." She stood, offering her hand to him. "We'll learn together." She looked down at the ground, they were on the 30 yard line. "We covered a fair amount of ground." She grinned.

"It's not bad at all!" Sebastian looked around. "Oh." Reika looked in the direction he was looking in. The entire gym class was staring at them. In the front of the group was Yuri.

"Oh my God!" Yuri groaned out. "Can't you two seriously ever stop doing that crap?!"

Reika rolled her eyes. "It's better than cheer leading." She shrugged.

Yuri tried to think of something to say in return but nodded her head. "I can't fight you there. You have a *really* good point with that one."

Sebastian laughed. "You got that right!"

"That was amazing!" One of the girls in the gym class yelled out. She was tall, a slender build with long brown hair tied back behind her. She wore a black choker necklace with her gym clothes and sported black nails.

"You would think so, Ella." One of the other girls piped up. She had long blonde hair, she was petite and her face was pixie like.

"Shut up Camille." Ella growled out.

"Yeah, shut it, Camille." Yuri said, looking over her shoulder. "The girl over there with the sword is my older sister. She's not one you want to anger."

"She's your sister?" Ella asked, coming forward. "Oh my God!"

Reika laughed. "Yeah, Yuri's my little sister. She's pretty cool. Just don't mess with her, cause you're messing with me too." She winked at them and turned to Sebastian.

"It's not like she's even really fighting." Camille scoffed. "I'm sure Sebastian let her win. She can't be *that* good."

Reika stayed turned from the crowd, but her hands tensed, squeezing the sword hard in her left, and her fingernails biting the palm of her right hand. Her eyes met Sebastian's, she tried to calm herself by breathing slowly. Sebastian gave her a knowing, gentle smile and a wink.

"If you think you can do any better, Camille, why don't you give it a shot?"

"Sebastian." Reika whispered out, her eyes wide.

Camille laughed. "Like I'd fight with that freaky ass bitch." She rolled her eyes. "Anyone as weird as her isn't worth my time." "Shut up, Camille." Yuri shot her a harsh glare. "You have no idea who you're messing with. Reika is one of the coolest people around, and you don't want to be on her bad side. So you either need to shut up, or, well, shut up. It's your best option, unless you're an absolute idiot, then she might just knock some sense into you or put you in a coma." She smirked.

"Sebastian, let's go." Reika said, her hands shaking heavily. "Please?"

Sebastian nodded. He ran and got his book bag, his wooden sword and returned to Reika's side. Reika kept her back towards the crowd until Sebastian's return, then she took off.

"What, are you scared little freak?" Camille called out.

Reika turned, and in what seemed like an instant, she was nose to nose with Camille. "The only thing I'm afraid of is going to prison for maiming a stupid bitch like you."

"Um, excuse me?!" Camille growled. "Who the fuck do you think you are?!" She grabbed Reika shirt with both hands and stared her down, eyes furious. "What are you going to do now, bitch?!"

Reika looked from Camille's perfectly manicured hand on her shirt back to the girl's face. She took a deep breath and smiled at her. "Oh, so many options." She murmured, as she grabbed over Camille's hand with her opposite and twisted. Camille squealed in pain. Reika scooped her elbow up and pressed down. Camille's grip broke off and she fell to the ground. She turned to Sebastian and they walked out of the football stadium together.

They could hear the laughter of the other students in the background as Camille screamed in the midst of a tantrum. Reika smiled softly. "I didn't actually hurt her."

"I know, you did good." Sebastian kissed the top of her head as they walked. "That girl is a piece of work. She made fun of me when I first came here. I'm pretty sure I've cussed her out at least once since then."

"I hope I don't have any classes with her." Reika breathed out heavily. "I'll end up punching her in the face, and break her stupid ugly plastic nose."

Sebastian stopped walking while he laughed. "Ugly plastic nose?!" He leaned over, bracing himself on his knees. "Oh my god, Reika!"

Reika looked at Sebastian and laughed too. "It is plastic right? No one has a nose as perfect as her's."

"It might be, I don't know for certain Rei." He stood back up, trying to control his laughter. He wrapped his arm around her shoulders. "Let's go drop this stuff off and find something else to do."

"Sebastian! Reika! Wait up!" Reika turned, hearing Yuri's voice. She saw Yuri running towards her, and Ella trailing behind her. Yuri stopped right in front of them. "I can't believe you didn't break Camille's stupid face!"

Ella stood behind Yuri, her arms behind her. She looked up at Reika. "We've been waiting for years for someone to stand up to her." She smiled. "It seems we've finally found someone to do it."

"Look, don't hail me as some hero for throwing a stupid girl on her face. I'm no hero, I just don't take anyone's shit." Reika said, her voice stern. "I'm far from being a good person, don't idolize me. It's a long road to the underworld if you choose to make me your leader."

"What do you even mean?" Yuri asked.

"What I'm telling everyone is I'm not a person to make into a role model. If you want someone to look up to, look anywhere else except my direction."

"Come on, Ella." Yuri glared at Reika. "Let's get out of here." Yuri grabbed Ella's arm and started away from Sebastian and Reika. Ella hesitated for a moment, but left with her.

"Reika, what's going on?" Sebastian asked, his brows furrowed. "I've never seen you like this."

"I don't want Ella to be like me. I don't want anyone to be like me." Reika looked up at him. "Some people are unique because they want to be, they want attention. There are few who are as unique as I am on purpose. There is something about me which I can't control. I don't want someone idolizing me for it. It's a constant struggle to even attempt to keep it in check, and if someone tries to be like me, there are only two paths for them. Either they'll end up in jail or dead. I know myself well enough to keep myself away from those outcomes, others wouldn't be so fortunate.."

"Reika, I think you're doing great." Sebastian said. He placed a hand on her shoulder, and offered a comforting smile. "I mean every word of this, if you need someone to talk to about whatever is going on, I'm here. I'm not going to push you to talk, just know I'm here."

Reika nodded gently. "Thanks, Bas."

Sebastian pulled her into a soft hug. "Let's go watch a movie or something, okay?"

She nodded again. "It sounds like a good plan." She smiled and they took off towards her dorm building.

Chapter Five

"I heard of your little scuffle on the football field today."
Samael chimed, he slowly moved away from the window, to stand
behind Reika's chair. "Learning the art of self control is a very
necessary skill, and I'm quite proud of you to do so. Though I must
agree with some of my students, Camille should have been dealt a
more harsh punishment. I am considerably bias, however."

Reika leaned her head back, looking at Samael. "You think I
should have punched her instead of just tossing her away?" She
sighed. "The way I see Camille, she's expendable. She isn't worth
my time, or the energy to maim her."

Samael smiled down at her. "You're learning priorities as
well." He touched her cheek. "A beauty, as well as intelligent. How
could a Father get so fortunate to have an offspring as brilliant as the
child before me?"

"I wish I knew the answer." She laughed.

"Regardless, are you ready for our outing tonight?"

"I think so." She felt nervousness rise in her stomach. "Am I
dressed well enough for it?" Reika looked down at her clothes. She

had changed into a pair of black ripped jeans, knee high motorcycle boots and graphic tee shirt.

"Anything you wear will be ravishing. If you feel the need to change clothing, I can provide you something to your liking. For such an excursion, I believe dressing as you always do will give you the best results for a custom ball gown."

"A custom one?" Her eyes lit up.

He nodded. "Only the best for you, my child." Samael rounded her chair and offered his hand. "Shall we venture off now?"

Reika took his hand and stood. "Absolutely." The moment she stood, the world around her disappeared. Once she opened her eyes, she found herself standing in the middle of a boutique. The black walls danced with silver and pink swirls, mannequins were dressed in lavish gowns that cascaded in all the right places and the mirrors were framed in the most beautiful ornate gold frames. She looked around the store in awe.

Samael placed a hand on her back and smiled down at her. Reika smiled too, and looked to the back of the store. She saw a petite woman come out with pastel purple hair cut into an adorable bob. Her face was soft, exquisite like a fairy, and resting perfectly in her hair was a silver bow with a zombie hand perched in the center. She had a full black skirt on, petticoat included, a white top with a ruffled collar and a pair of ankle boots.

Luna smiled, her large golden brown eyes beamed with happiness. "Samael! It's good to see you! I see you brought your daughter to meet me finally!"

"Ah, Luna! It's certainly a pleasure to see you once more." His hand trailed across Reika's back and took Luna's hand. He brought her hand up gently and kissed it. "I apologize deeply for coming here so late and asking a favor of you. Our next visit shall be leisurely rather than business and yes, I certainly brought my daughter with me. Luna, this is Reika. My dear, this is my good friend Luna."

Reika extended her hand and shook hands with Luna. She smiled. "It's nice to meet you, Luna."

"It's nice to meet you too, dear!" Luna grinned and held Reika's hand still. "When Samael contacted me about making a dress for his daughter, I was shocked! I didn't know it had been so long since you were born! He told me you were finally of age and needed a perfect dress." She took Reika's other hand in hers and stepped back, getting a good look at her. "My dear, I cannot wait to make you a gown! It's going to be fabulous!"

Reika grinned as well. "I'm sure it will be, all the dresses in your boutique are amazing!"

"Thank you so much!" She beamed. "It means a lot to hear it!" She let go of Reika's hands went to the back of the store quickly, grabbed a book, sketch pad and pencils. "Let's get started!" She waved them over to the desk to join her. Reika looked over to Samael and they walked over to join her.

"What is it you're looking for?" Luna asked.

Reika looked to Samael as he answered. "Black and red is the color scheme. My only request would be something relatively easy to move in." Samael laughed. "Though, I'm not the one wearing it." He looked to Reika. "Do you have any ideas?"

"Something easy to move in would be great." She laughed. "I don't really like big puffy dresses though. Black and red are my favorite colors, so I'm very accepting of it. If we could have something with long flowing sleeves, that would be really cool!"

Luna grinned. "I have the perfect idea!" She began sketching up an idea. She peeked up from her paper. "If you guys are hungry at all, I've got pizza in the back room. I've also got a decanter of a really nice wine cocktail in the back as well." She smiled and went back to drawing.

Samael chuckled, and went to the back of the store. Reika sat and watched Luna's drawing come to life.

"You're new to the demon world, Reika?" Luna asked, still sketching away. "Don't worry too much, dear. It's not as bad as it seems on the outside, or at least how others have portrayed it. It's a rather glamorous lifestyle. I've had this boutique here in San Francisco for..." She thought for a moment, "for almost 50 years." She laughed. "It's amazing to see how fashion changes, but some of the faces stay the same."

"There are a lot of demons in the world? Humans don't know about them?" Reika's eyes were wide.

Luna sat her pencil down and looked up. "A few I know are shape shifters. They use their abilities to create a new persona, age the persona gracefully through the years and die, so to speak. Then they relax for a few years, and do it all over again." She grinned. "New faces are never really new, they are only new masks."

"That's insane!" She gaped.

"If someone says "They are the 'insert-name-here' of their generation, more than likely, it actually is the person their speaking of." Luna laughed, and looked up, seeing Samael walking back to the desk. He was carrying three glasses of wine and a plate with a few pieces of pizza on it. He sat them down on the desk. Luna smiled at him. "Thanks Samael. Isn't it true though, most famous people are the same person with a different face every few decades?"

Samael laughed. "Oh dear Luna, you are giving all the entertainment world secrets away, aren't you?"

"I certainly have to, you probably have a slew of the bigger names attending your daughter's ceremony! She's probably going to have a heart attack seeing all of them. Oh, speaking of entertainment business, weren't you in it for quite some time?"

An uncharacteristic blush developed on Samael's face. "A long while ago, in London. My name isn't known because I was a member of a playing company."

"During the Renaissance?!" Reika exclaimed.

"Indeed it was during the Renaissance time period." He smiled wistfully.

"How amazing!" Luna grinned, and put her pencil down finally. "I have one done!" She pushed the pad over to Reika and Samael to look at. Before her was a beautiful drawing of a dress with the collar of a blazer jacket, a wide belt with cords draped around the waist. The hem of the dress was asymmetrical, starting mid-thigh on one side, and went just below the knee on the other. Under the hem, was some lace, to give the skirt some body. The sleeves on the dress were long, and flared out. The middle of the sleeve was cut out and replaced with cord holding either piece together.

Reika gaped at the paper. "This is gorgeous!"

Samael smiled. "I am always amazed by your work, Luna. This is a wonderful dress. It really seems you have captured Reika's essence in the form of a gown."

"You're too kind, Samael!" Luna laughed, and took one glass of the wine. She took a sip. "I'm glad you like the dress! I'll get started on the pattern tomorrow. It should take me about a week to make. Orders have been slow this week, so you picked a wonderful time. Granted, I would have prioritized your order." She grinned.

Samael picked up the two remaining glasses and handed one to Reika. "Remember, my friend, I only give compliments where they are due. You are a wonderful designer, and it shows with the status of your boutique. The high profile people who come to you for dresses really explains the quality and pride you put into your profession. Among those customers, you have an old as time demon. I believe this says everything."

"It's hard to believe you're so old, Samael." Luna laughed.

"As old as time?!" Reika's eyes went wide. "You don't even look old enough to be my father."

Samael laughed as well. "The years have been good to me."

Reika took a drink of her wine. "They have been. I hope they are as nice to me as they have been to you."

"You look stunning for 18." Luna said, with a smile. "You will mature in the same fashion, I'm certain of it." Luna took a slice of pizza from the plate and took a bite of it. She sat it down. "One of the many perks of our kind is we can eat just about anything and not gain weight."

"We're genetically designed as warriors, so our physique is made strong and lean." Samael smiled at Reika.

"Some just actually use it for fighting and wars. Others just eat all the food they can and don't gain weight." Luna laughed. "I swear if I weren't a demon, I'd be the next reality show star, 'My 500 pound designer.' It would be a hit!"

Reika laughed. "Oh my goodness. My little sister always got angry at me because I could eat anything and not gain weight. She has to be very careful."

"Samael! You have another child?!"

"No, the girl Reika speaks of is the daughter of her surrogate."

Luna nodded in understanding.

"I'm so thankful to have Reika back in my life."

Luna smiled. "I can see it, Samael. I haven't seen you this content in years. I'm happy for you. Maybe Reika and I can become better friends!"

Reika grinned. "I'd like that!"

"Good! You can visit me anytime you'd like!"

Samael smiled and wrapped an arm around Reika's shoulder as they both took a sip of their drink. Reika set an empty glass down, leaned her head against Samael's shoulder and yawned.

"Aw, Samael, she's still developing, you shouldn't have her out so late!" Luna teased. "Take the sweet girl home and let her rest. I'll inform you of when the dress is ready."

He rubbed Reika's back. "Are you ready to return home?"

Reika sat up and nodded. "I am. I'm sorry I couldn't stay longer, Luna. It was really nice to meet you, and I'm sure we'll be able to meet again sometime very soon!"

"Don't worry one bit, Reika. It was a pleasure meeting you! I can't wait to see you in this dress! It's going to be gorgeous! I'll see you both soon! Have a good night!"

"You as well, my friend." Samael stood, taking Luna's hand and laid a gentle kiss on her hand once more. "We will see you soon."

Luna smiled, and stood. She went to Reika and hugged her tight. "It was good meeting you. You're going to be just fine, especially if Samael is your father and mentor. Not many of our kin are so lucky. You can already tell how much he cherishes you. You will flourish in this world." Luna whispered in Reika's ear.

"Thank you, Luna." Reika smiled, hugging her back. She let go, and returned to Samael's side. He took her hand and they left. Reika opened her eyes and they were in his office once more. Reika took her usual seat, as Samael strolled to the window to gaze over the campus.

"Did you learn anything tonight?" Samael asked her.

"I did, Luna was very informative of the community. I had no idea there were more like us around."

"There are many, as there are many different classifications. Luna mentioned shape shifters, most of them dwell in the entertainment industry. They are actors, musicians, artists, writers, or designers. You and I are a different classification altogether, we aren't quite demons, yet we aren't quite angels either. We collect souls of those who want something in exchange for it, yes? We also are to help ferry the souls of the dead to their proper afterlife."

"Wouldn't we be rather busy all the time?"

"Ah, we are considered conduits, we are the 'light at the end of the tunnel' in a sense. Souls of the deceased seek us out, and use our bodies to pass through to either the underworld or to the heavens. Our mere existence is enough to help them through to the other side."

"Does it hurt us?"

"It may leave you fatigued for the first few days once you're able to act as a conduit. You will learn how to manage it."

"What happens to lost souls? Do we go to help them, or do we leave them?"

"Generally a lost soul is one who's body expired before they were finished living. There are beings who are devoted to helping these souls find peace, then the souls find us and move on, however we are not those beings."

Reika nodded. "This is all so interesting. I had no idea any of this existed. How many conduits are there?"

"There are two conduits, though only one is active."

"You and I?" She asked.

Samael nodded. "I am the only active conduit from this world to the next. There is much more for the deceased to experience after passing through us. As I said before, it may make you feel exhausted at first, however you will start to feel something much different later. For myself, it was much like pride, as well as a strengthening." He came over to her and took her hands. "I would like to show you."

"How are you going to show me?" Reika looked confused.

Samael let go of Reika's hands and lowered one of his, the lights dimming with the elegant motion. In the midst of darkness, Reika saw Samael's body begin to glow with a soft silver light. At the center of his torso, was a swirling black void. Through the crack in the curtains over the window, Reika saw a wispy white light come forth and enter the void in Samael's center. The white light slowed, showing a thin woman's frame standing before him. He looked to Reika, and the figure looked to him.

The figure became more clear, a young woman, with long flowing hair and large soft eyes stared at the swirling hole. "What is waiting for me on the other side?" She whispered.

"Freedom." Samael replied in the same soft tone. "Do not be scared."

"Alright." She nodded once and reached forward, her hand was drawn into the vortex embedded in Samael's body. She brought her hand back, touched her face and returned it to the vortex. "Goodbye. Thank you Angel Samael."

Reika watched as the woman's figure disappeared into the void within Samael. Her eyes were wide. Once she was gone, the void and the light emitting from Samael disappeared. Slowly, the lights came back on.

"This occurs day in and day out, it is a constant flow of souls into me. It has been happening for so many centuries, I cannot even notice it happening anymore." Samael walked back over to Reika and knelt down in front of her. "Humans fear me because my name is synonymous with death. I am not a vicious being when it comes to the souls who wish to pass on. I will be their guide, and make sure their journey is safe. It is when humans wish to tamper with their own fate that I become ruthless. Granted, those who use my service as a last resort for selfless reasons are more than likely spared."

"It's all linked to what a person is fated to be?" Reika asked. "If they ask for something out of the selfishness dwelling within, it almost always backfires? In turn, if they ask for something because they have no other choice, it would go well for them?"

"I would like to say yes, however fate is temperamental. Each human has a different path, and the path may differ by their choices."

"Doesn't the fact that people have free will mean fate isn't a factor?"

Samael smiled. "You certainly are brilliant. It means fate is undecided, but decided. There are many paths a human can take. Each path, however, leads to the same end."

"Death."

"Yes, indeed death meets all mortals at the end of the journey."

Chapter Six

Sitting alone under the tree outside her dorm building, Reika had her book laying in her lap. She touched the tip of the pen to the blank paper. A single drop of red began swirling about the page. Reika lifted the pen and waited.

'Good afternoon Miss Lilin. What question lingers in your mind?'

Reika contemplated for a moment before writing *'Am I an only child?'*

'Indeed you are, however many lived before you, and were slaughtered long before they reached your age. You were saved by a selfish act.'

'What was the selfish act?'

'I cannot say, however I will say this: do not trust Lilith. Have a nice class tonight, Miss Lilin.'

Before Reika could write anymore questions, the book slammed shut. Reika sighed, "No wonder he said this book was an asshole." She looked up and saw Sebastian walking her way. She smiled, and slipped her book back into her bag. She got up and ran towards him and threw her arms around him.

"Hey!" Sebastian yelled, catching Reika in his arms. "What's with the surprise attack?"

"Surprises keep life less boring." She kissed him on the cheek.

"Don't get me wrong, I like when you're like this, I'm also terrified." Sebastian laughed.

"Why are you scared?"

"Because you're not normally so doting."

"You're right, but sometimes I just get the urge to hug you." She laughed, letting go of him. "We better get going to class though."

"Doesn't it feel weird to be having a gym class at six at night?" Sebastian murmured as he and Reika walked towards the campus center. "In a ballroom, no less!"

"We're probably going to be having dancing lessons. I heard there was a formal ball on Halloween this year." Reika pulled her phone out, and sighed. It was September 19th, she had four days before the ball Samael was holding in her honor. It seemed a bit late to be having dancing lessons. She slid her phone back into her pocket and looked to Sebastian. "I hope you're wearing some tough shoes, you're bound to get your toes stepped on at least once tonight."

"Dancing, as in the waltz?" Sebastian looked at her, his face showed obvious nervousness.

Reika laughed. "I'm sure they aren't going to be teaching us how to hip grind each other. It's a school after all." She yawned heavily. Everyone in the evening classes was still adjusting, yet Reika was adjusting to staying up even later than the other students and trying to maintain the same schedule. Her lessons with Samael weren't physically demanding, they were rather mentally exhausting. Her powers were developing well, it was just a struggle to keep up appearances as a regular student as well.

"You do have a point there." Sebastian laughed. "I just never expected a school to still teach ballroom dancing to students in this era."

"I'm glad they are, it's good to keep an old art alive. If people didn't preserve arts, we wouldn't have martial arts, music, or any of the many things we enjoy." She smiled. "It will be good for you."

"I never said it'd be bad, I just found it interesting they are still teaching it here."

"It's nice, isn't it?"

"Yeah, it really is."

They arrived at the campus center, and went to the ballroom. Reika wasn't prepared to see Samael standing next to the door, greeting each student.

"Good evening Reika, Sebastian. I am quite excited to be teaching a wonderful class tonight!"

"I'm sure it will be fun, Mr. Blake." Sebastian smiled.

"Please, head inside and take a seat. You may set your bags on the back wall behind the chairs."

Reika smiled and nodded.

"Reika, I'll need your help demonstrating to the class, would you mind terribly to do so?"

"Oh, not at all, Mr. Blake." She nodded. "I'll help you. I'm not sure how good I'll be though."

"Worry not, child." Samael smiled "You will know all you need to when we begin class."

Reika nodded some, but his words scared her. She and Sebastian entered the ballroom, went to the back to set their things down. She took his hand, squeezed it and they went to sit in the front row of chairs. The rest of the class filed in, and sat down. Samael entered the room and shut the door gently.

"Good evening my students." Samael smiled. "I'm certain you're all wondering why you have a physical education class in a ballroom. With a homecoming dance coming soon, I thought it best to teach the students how to dance properly." Most of the students laughed or whispered to each other, Sebastian and Reika looked at each other and smiled. "I'd like to call Reika Avel up to have as my demonstration partner." He said simply. "We have heeled shoes for our females, if they so choose to wear them. There are varying sizes set off to the side. Please feel free to take a pair. They are all brand new, and you may keep them if you so choose."

Reika looked over to the stack of shoe boxes. "May I change shoes before we begin?" Reika asked. Samael gave a simple nod.

"All of the girls who choose to wear the shoes, please go ahead and change."

Reika stood, went to the stack of shoe boxes, selected her size and returned to her seat. She took off her sneakers, socks and put on the cute pair of shoes. Samael smiled at her, and held his hand out for her. She stood, made her way to him and took his hand.

"Sebastian, would you please start the music on the stereo?" Samael asked as he kept hold of Reika's hand, and took her waist.

'Place your hand on my shoulder.'

Reika's eyes went wide at the sound of Samael's voice inside her mind, yet it wasn't audible. Slowly, she placed her hand on his shoulder as he instructed her to. Out of the corner of her eye, she saw Sebastian go to the stereo in the ballroom. Reika waited patiently for the music to start.

'Follow my every move. These dances are all about the man leading the woman.'

Reika looked up into Samael's eyes, and the music began. At first, the dance was a simple flow. Reika followed the steps with ease.

"These are our basic steps." Samael said to the class. "We will work on this in a moment. However, I would like to give you a demonstration of what you could learn if you chose to continue in this style of dancing. Sebastian, would you play track two, please?" Reika stood, nervous as to what would happen next.

'Just follow my lead. I know you will do well.' Samael flashed her a smile, and the music began to play. A sultry Latin theme echoed through the room. Reika felt Samael's hand up her back to her shoulder and down to her hand. He began moving away from her, slowly, methodically. She followed suit, her steps precise, and drawn out. Samael pulled her close and spun her around, In the midst of the movement, her leg hooked around his body. She felt her body fall backwards, and rise up quickly into another spin.

Samael caught Reika in his arms from another twirl, and slowly moved towards her. She felt him draw back and went into him. The movements back and forth partnered with spins continued. Finally, Samael twirled her about once more, in a grand display, before she landed on her feet. All her weight was pressed against Samael, as he held her close. The music stopped and Reika stood upright, taking a deep breath.

The class applauded. Reika looked at Sebastian, he too was clapping his hands, but jealousy seemed to peek through his eyes.

"Please pair up and we shall begin class." Samael said simply. The students began chattering among themselves. Samael turned to Reika and patted her on the shoulder. "A wonderful show you did, my daughter. Please, work with Sebastian. You two make a wondrous team. A teacher brought me a video of the fight you and Sebastian had on the football field. You make a perfect couple."

Reika smiled and nodded. "Thank you." She left him and went to Sebastian.

"Reika, that was amazing. I never knew you could dance."

She laughed some. "I didn't know either."

"How did you do all of that?"

"I just listened." She smiled, shrugging her shoulders.

"You're amazing, Reika." Sebastian smiled at her, admiration shining in his eyes.

Chapter Seven

The sound of orchestral music flowed down the hall and into the room Reika sat in. Luna was adding the final touches to her hair. She gazed into the mirror, silver eyes with perfectly dark make-up enveloping them stared back. Her dress was exquisitely made, and fit like a glove. Reika's raven hair was swept back from her face, a fully bloomed red rose was pinned behind her left ear, and wisps of hair were strategically placed to frame her beautiful face.

"I'm anxious about tonight." Reika whispered out.

"Why are you so worried?" Luna smiled gently. "You'll do fine tonight. Your father planned everything to be seamless and smooth."

"What's going to happen tonight?" She turned and looked Luna in the eyes. "I feel like there is going to be much more than wine and dancing."

"As far as I know, that's all we're going to be indulging in. Sometimes, they hold auctions too. There might be one tonight, but I haven't heard anything yet."

"An auction?"

"Yeah, it's usually later in the night, if there is one."

A soft knock sounded through the room. It made Reika jump. Luna patted her shoulder and smiled. She walked to the door and opened it. Reika stood up, and walked towards the door as well. As Samael came into full view, the expression on his face melted her heart.

"You look-" Samael took a deep breath, and came towards Reika, taking her hands in his. "You look absolutely stunning."

Reika smiled. "Thank you, Papa." She said, her voice meek. The past week of ballroom dancing, and lessons had brought her closer to Samael. She knew it was time to accept everything, and it meant accepting Samael as her father.

Samael's face bloomed even more than Reika thought possible. "The word I've yearned to hear slip from your mouth for years, and I hear it tonight." He wrapped his arms around her shoulders and squeezed her.

"Papa, please! If you squeeze me any tighter I might not be able to speak at all!" She croaked out.

Samael let go of her. "I am sorry, my love. I couldn't help myself. Now, we must make our way to the ballroom. Are you ready?"

"Not quite, but there isn't anything I can do." She laughed, nervously.

"There certainly is, my dear." He knelt down before her, and took her hands. "All you must do is be yourself. I will be there with you, if you need anything at all. You're a brilliant woman, and the world will embrace you just as I have." He stood, keeping her hands in his. "Let me show them the beauty of my daughter."

Holding onto his hands, she stood up and took his arm. The heels she wore brought her closer to his height. She gazed at his suit, he was wearing an all black suit, including the button down shirt. His tie matched the deep red in her dress and had a red rose pinned on his lapel.

"I'm ready." She said with a soft nod.

Samael smiled, and leaned into Reika slowly, leaving a soft kiss on her cheek. "You'll do brilliantly." Reika smiled and held onto his arm. He led her out into the hallway of the brightly lit mansion.

The walls were cream colored, with gold sconces lining the hall. Reika looked to her left and saw an ornate wooden railing. Over the railing, she could see clusters of people talking. She tried to keep her composure as she saw quite a few actors and musicians she adored. Her eyes were drawn to a gorgeous chandelier hanging before her. Despite the music playing, the sound of Reika's heels echoing through the hallway was deafening.

Samael and Reika stood at the top of a gorgeous stairway which lead to the ballroom floor. They stood, looking out over the crowd, and they all slowly began to turn their gaze towards them. The initial reactions of the guests made Reika's heart swell. Their eyes upon her in a reverent adoration she had never experienced before. She thought, maybe it was their reaction to Samael, but when she turned towards him, his eyes held the same look.

She offered Samael a smile and squeezed his arm gently. He gave her a soft nod and together, they descended the stairs slowly. Reika looked over the ballroom, trying to take in all of the faces amidst the sea of guests. She spotted Lilith in the very back, a man with black hair and piercing blue eyes. An uneasy feeling sank deep within her from the look in his glacial eyes. She returned her attention to Samael as they finished their descent of the stairway.

Samael guided her to stand in front of the crowd, and let go of her arm. She gracefully cupped her hands in front of her, and waited. He bowed deeply to the guests, and stood tall once again. He made a grand gesture to Reika, and slowly she sank down to her knees and bowed her head, her hands forming a triangle. She rose just as slowly as she had bowed down. The crowd clapped as she rose. Samael returned to her side, and took her arm once more.

"I want to express my gratitude to all of our guests for being a part of my wondrous daughter's welcoming into our world. I'm certain all of you will find her as charming as I have." He smiled gently in Reika's direction. He turned his attention back to the crowd. "So, please my friends, help me welcome Reika Lilin into our world."

Applause erupted from the crowd and Reika smiled. She still felt nervous, but was beginning to enjoy herself. She jumped slightly as the lights went out, except for one light in the center of the ballroom. Samael took Reika's hand in his, kissed it gently and led her towards the lit area. She stopped, and Samael let go of her hand.

He stood in front of her, and bowed. She followed with a curtsy. The whole formality of the waltz She and Samael were performing felt so awkward to her still. She enjoyed the smoothness and flow that accompanied her feet while dancing, yet she didn't like the stiffness of the rest of her body.

Samael and Reika danced about the ballroom together as the crowd watched in awe. They floated across the floor swiftly and beautifully. Reika began to feel more of her apprehension dissolve within the pit of her stomach. Their dance however, ended as soon as it felt it started. They exchanged their bows and curtsies then made their way to their table. The evening was full of wonderful food, and much more dancing. She had met so many fellow demons, their names were lost on her.

Reika was surprised she hadn't seen Lilith all night, though she hadn't seen Lilith since the night she brought her to Samael. Remembering what the book said to her, she tried to pay no mind to her absence. She danced once more with Samael, before taking her seat at the table for some final words from her father.

"As many of you have experienced in your coming of age ceremony, we were asked to take our first souls. We shall conclude our festivities in the ballroom shortly, and whoever chooses to join will make their way to the venue behind this beautiful mansion where an auction will be held. We have many fine *products* available tonight." Samael smiled deviously. "Thank you all, so much for attending tonight. I do hope you enjoyed yourselves deeply this evening."

Reika looked to Samael, and tried to hide the shock she felt at his words. Their eyes met momentarily, and she saw something devious lurking beneath his mercury gaze. He reached his hand out towards her, she took it. "Come my dear, we must peruse our stock, and make a selection. You are the honored guest, and get to take the first look."

"The first look at what?"

"Your first taste of the world of darkness." Samael smiled a crooked smile. Reika felt her stomach drop, as she stood with him. They exited the ballroom to the terrace overlooking a garden. After making their way down the stairs, they headed towards an octagon shaped wooden building. "There will be an auction tonight. Choose your desired morsel and I shall obtain it for your enjoyment."

They walked together, entering the building and headed towards the holding chambers. Reika was astounded by the vast contrast between the mansion and the building she was now in. The rooms she had seen inside the mansion were decadent and plush. Now, the building she walked in was dank, and smelled horribly. She held onto Samael's arm, as they walked into a room, with many prison like cells. There were many people in these cells, yet Reika was only drawn to one.

The final cell on the right, Reika saw a woman sitting on the bench hanging from the wall. She had long brown hair, half was pinned back, to expose her face. Her cheekbones were high, and bright green eyes peeked out from the shadows cast by heavy lashes. Her nose was perfectly straight, and her lips a beautiful shade of pink. As Reika slowly walked towards her, Samael grabbed her arm and she turned towards him.

"Why are all these people here?" She asked.

"They wish to make contracts with us."

"They already have a price to pay, but you're putting more of a price on it?"

"We do." Samael stated. "They are prominent figures in their world, as are we. The reason we put monetary value on our," He paused for a moment, "guests, is because of their stature in humanity. You see, my dear, we rule from the shadows, whether the world knows it or not."

"I never knew we held so many." Reika looked down. "I knew we had a lot of the Hollywood scene, but I never knew we had dignitaries as well."

"Not only in America, my dear, all over the world. The woman who enchants you so, is from Europe."

"What does she want from us?"

"She wants a more simple life, away from the fame and cameras." Samael said. "She wants to be free from the holds the Monarchy puts on her."

"She's a princess?"

"She certainly is." Samael pointed to the cell next to the princess'. "He's a judge, the one next to him, he's a cardinal."

"A priest?!"

Samael laughed. "He is. Each person on this room is seeking something, my dear, ourselves included. The only difference? We are able to procure what we desire without such repercussions as losing our immortal souls."

"We have souls?"

"In a sense, yes." Samael shrugged. "We have our essence, yet we fill our bodies with the souls of those who seek what they cannot reach to gain more and more power. If you wish to learn more from them, go speak with them."

Reika's eyes went to the princess at first, but she then turned to the Priest. She went to him, standing in front of the bars. "What is it you want from us?"

"Salvation for another. I wish to take her place in Hell, so that she may end her suffering." The Priest said, clutching his rosary between his shaking hands.

"Why would you subject yourself to eternal torment for another?"

"I love her." He whispered. "So dearly did I love her and she loved me. Though, she didn't love herself. I thought I could save her,

I thought I could bring her salvation and take her pain away. I couldn't do it. I still believe I made things worse for her. The guilt she felt was made worse by my words, and I never meant for her to feel so badly that she'd do what she did. It was my fault, and I deserve to suffer in her stead."

"What did she do?"

The Priest looked up at her, tears brimming over his lashes. "She committed suicide." He swallowed hard, trying to maintain his composure. "She went to the place we went on our first date, a beautiful cliff, overlooking a river. She flung herself over the edge. Before she did it, she carved 'I'm sorry' into the tree we had our initials carved into. I pushed her too hard in the church. Everything she knew and was, it was questioned or condemned by their laws. She was beautiful and free before I tried to save her. I didn't, I killed her. I might as well have put a knife to her throat and slit it myself."

"What was her name?"

"Leslie Clark." He said softly, the way her name rolled from his lips, it sounded like a prayer.

"And what is your name?"

"Father Nathan Richardson."

"I expect I'll be seeing you again, Father Nathan." Reika said, and turned, walking back to Samael's side. She took his arm. "I want the Father."

"Your taste is impeccable, my dear. You will possess his soul before the dawn."

Samael lead Reika out of the cell room, and into a spacious auditorium. There were chairs set on the ground floor, and stadium seating above. Reika was lead to the center of the upper level. The benches were cushioned with beautiful red cushions. She took her seat, and watched as the guests who chose to join in on the auction. Samael placed his arm around her shoulder.

She looked to him. "Papa, how am I to pay for the one I want?"

"It will be a gift, my dear. All the proceeds of this auction will be yours. I am bidding in your stead for the one you want. Are you certain on your choice, you want the Priest, not the Princess?"

"I could tell the Princess wanted something selfish. The Priest wanted to right a wrong he had made. It is a noble cause for suffering, and I am glad to deliver it to him."

"The ones who wish for selfish and wasteful things make the most satisfying treat. Remember that, Reika. You will get your Priest tonight, but next time, show no mercy."

"Mercy is for the weak, Papa. I am not." She gave him a stern look. "Giving a person what they want, in exchange for what I want isn't mercy, it's business."

Samael laughed, his face brimming with pride. "You are my daughter, after all. It's fitting for you to say such things!" He leaned in close, and kissed her on the cheek as the lights began to dim around them.

The guests' attention was brought to the stage, where the curtain rose, and the lights shone brightly. The auctioneer took the stage, one arm rose in the air, and paddles with numbers appeared in each patron's lap. A sly smile crept across his lips. His face was as handsome as the rest of the demons she had met. Perfect bone structure graced his face, and beautiful raven locks fell down around his face, to his shoulders. He stood tall against the stage in all black, a stark contrast against the light wood construction of the auditorium.

"I am pleased to see you all here." He called out. "No need for introductions here tonight. If you know my name, wonderful, if not, you need not know it." He grinned. "Let us begin."

The lights on the stage dimmed and each of the six which were held backstage came out. Three men, and three women stood before the crowd. All but the Priest looked to be very wealthy and prominent figures. She felt she would have an easy battle obtaining the Priest. The bidding began with the European Princess. She was taken fast, by a handsome man in the front row on the ground level. The auction continued at the same fast pace the Princess was sold at, and Reika realized the Priest was last.

"Finally, we had arrived to Father Nathan Richardson." The Auctioneer said. "He wishes to sell his soul so that his former lover may rest peacefully." A few people laughed in the audience. "May we start the bidding at 10,000 dollars?"

Samael raised his hand. The Auctioneer nodded towards him. "Ten fifty?"

A Woman on the ground floor raised her hand and shot a look at Samael.

"Ten seventy-five?"

Samael raised his hand once again. "Make it thirty."

"Thirty it is. Thirty-five anyone?"

The woman raised her hand. Samael scoffed, and looked to Reika. "Worry not, my dear. You will get your Priest."

"Forty?" The Auctioneer called out.

"I offer fifty." Samael said, standing up.

"Fifty-five, my lady?"

"I withdraw." She stated simply.

"Fifty it is, to Samael Blake."

The crowd clapped softly and Reika smiled some. Samael lead Reika down to the stage, Father Nathan stepped down from the stage and joined them. Samael held out two pieces of paper to the Auctioneer. "Thank you for your services tonight. The payment for Father Richardson, and payment for your services."

"It's quite strange how you put prices on peoples' souls." Father Nathan said. "I've never seen such a thing in my life, yet to be a part of it as a product was much more horrifying."

"You're more than a product. Consider it more of a contract auction than a soul auction, or a blood auction." Samael smiled. "Everything is always much bigger or much smaller than we make it out to be. You've made this auction out to be something much smaller than it truly is. It isn't as simple as you think."

"If it isn't what I see it as, than what is it?"

Samael turned around, stopping in front of Father Richardson. "This business is my life, and now will be my daughter's. Every soul is worth the same price in my eyes. The price is what they deem it worth, whether the price is a castle, or a feather, the worth of a soul is what the holder believes it to be."

"Then why do you auction people off like slaves?"

"It's more of a donation." Samael smirked. "My daughter needed a start in this world, and these friends of mine have plenty to share. The money aspect isn't about the worth of your wish, it's to make an impression on me and my kin. The people who bid probably aren't the smartest of beings, they probably think there actually is more value to each person's soul than there really is."

"So, each soul holds the same amount of power?" Reika asked.

"Yes, almost everyone's soul is the same in the end. As always, there are exceptions to these rules. If a person is truly good, or truly evil, their soul holds more power. Holy men usually are above average in their weight. Murderers carry a heavy weight, well, any violent criminal does if they don't repent."

"What happens when they repent?" Father Richardson asked.

"They become the same as everyone else." Samael said, as he turned and began walking again. "A holy man is different, because his soul is like a bright light, whereas the evil man is like a void of darkness."

"What would your soul be like, Samael?" Father Richardson asked.

Samael laughed. "If I knew, I would tell you."

"You haven't a soul?!"

"I do, but it is lost inside me among the millions I've consumed over the centuries."

"Millions?" Father Richardson asked, stunned.

"I'm sure there's many more than that." Samael laughed. "I've lost count years ago."

"How do you not lose your identity with all of those souls swimming inside of you?" Father Richardson asked.

"Have you forgotten what I had said before?" Samael grinned. They arrived in front of a stone cottage on the property which held the mansion and auction house. Smoke billowed from the cottage's petite chimney.

"All souls are the same, there are rare souls which are very good, or terribly evil." Reika interjected. "With them all being the same, there isn't much to mask his essence."

"This is so intriguing." Father Richardson said, his eyes full of morbid interest. "I never realized there were secrets such as these in the world."

"They aren't secret, it's just that no one wanted to believe them." Samael's face became dark, shadows dancing upon his face from the light of the moon. "Did they not teach you of the monk who supposedly scribed the 'Codex Gigas'?"

"It's hardly ever mentioned." Father Richardson said. "I only know because of my research before priesthood. They do speak of Theophilus though."

"Ah, the one who slipped away." Samael's smile turned bitter. "I remember him."

"Who is he, Papa?"

"He was an archdeacon who wanted to be a bishop." Samael explained. "Which is why I was surprised by your request. It wasn't for power, or for escape from your vows, but for love. It's quite noble. Obviously, I wasn't the demon who appeared to you, I appeared for the others. They all wanted power, money, or fame. You're an absolutely rare breed."

"We take vows, Samael. We help people, and I need to help her." Father Richardson said.

"Say her name." Samael smirked. "I want to hear it again."

"I need to help Leslie Clark."

Samael turned and opened the door to the cottage. "Step inside, and we shall free her from her eternal imprisonment." Reika went inside the cottage first, the furnishing was sparse. There was a cream colored couch, and matching chair which contrasted with the dark wood background. The couch and chair were facing a brightly lit fireplace. Reika took a seat on the couch, and waited. Father Richardson took a seat on the couch as well. Samael walked to the chair, turned it around and finally sat down.

Reika looked to Samael and waited.

'Give him a chance to back out from the deal. With cases where the one who is giving up is doing so for another, it's best for them to think deeply of their decision.'

Reika looked to Father Richardson. "Are you absolutely sure about this?"

"In all honesty, no." He sighed. "It's against my vows, and I know where I'll end up."

"Why not wish for something else then?" Reika suggested. "Perhaps not to save her soul, but for you to be together once more?"

"The thought had never crossed my mind." He said. "Would it bring her back from the dead though?" His face lined with distress.

"No, it wouldn't. You would join her."

"I would die?"

'Indeed the Priest would die. Though his actions would undoubtedly bring his soul to the heavens. His barter would bring her's as well. Hopefully Miss Clark loved him as much as he loved her.'

"You would, however you wouldn't go to hell." Reika repeated the information Samael had given her.

"You would be safe from the flames, my friend." Samael smiled. "You body would simply disappear after the deal has been finished."

"Let me be with her again." Father Richardson pleaded. "It is what I want."

"Very well." Reika said. The many times she had watched Samael take souls still hadn't prepared her for this moment.

'The man is a holy one, take his soul from his wrist. You wouldn't want to give him a heart attack before you take his soul.'

Reika reached over and took his wrist in her hand. She brought his wrist to her mouth, and for the first time, she felt her incisors extend out, into sharp fangs. She hovered over his flesh, and took a deep breath. Closing her eyes, she sank her teeth into his flesh.

'To extract his soul, drink deeply. This man shall die tonight regardless, so you may consume as much as you'd like. Concentrate all your thoughts on taking his essence out, and it shall be yours. To grant his bargain, think of it and it will be taken care of.'

Reika heeded Samael's words, and thought hard of taking Father Richardson's soul from his body. She could feel the transfer, but it was slow. His blood made her mouth sting only slightly, she was able to bear the sensation. After what felt like a lifetime, Reika finally felt the last portion of Father Richardson's soul leave his body and come into her's. She then lead her thoughts to reuniting him and Leslie once more. She let go of him once she had finished it all.

Father Richardson opened his eyes and looked at Reika. "Thank you." He said and began to disappear.

Reika watched, her brow furrowed. She turned to Samael. "Did he just join her?"

"He did," Samael smiled proudly, "and you took your first soul. How do you feel now, my dear?"

"I don't really feel any different." Reika said, looking up.

Samael laughed. "My child, come here." He held his hands out to her. Reika obliged, standing and walked towards him. She took his hands, and knelt down in front of him. Samael let go of one of her hands, and wiped his thumb at the corner of her mouth. "You made a mess of your beautiful face." He brought his thumb to his mouth and licked the red from it. "Quite a meal you partook in, an exquisite taste he had."

"It was good, yet, it isn't the best thing I've tasted." She said, a soft smile on her lips. She looked down. "Did I get any on my dress? Luna would be so upset if I got blood all over her creation."

"No, just you chin, and a little on your cheek." He leaned forward and kissed her cheek. "There, you're perfect again." Placing a hand on her shoulder, he sighed. "I suppose we should return to the campus, yes?"

She nodded some. "It is late."

"Let's return." Samael smiled, taking her hand and leading her through the door of the cabin.

Chapter Eight

Sitting beneath their usual tree, Reika had her head laid on Sebastian's shoulder, eyes closed, listening to the breeze rustle through the autumnal painted leaves. Reika could hear the soft sound of the Sebastian turning the pages to his book. Opening her eyes, she sat up and looked at him. She touched his cheek gently. "You've been awfully quiet today, Bas."

Sebastian looked up and smiled at her. "Sometimes you don't need words just to enjoy someone's company." He put his bookmark in his book and closed it. "Do you have something on your mind? I can see you're thinking too much, it's written in those big brown..." Sebastian stopped short, a frown forming on his face. "...silver eyes."

Reika's eyebrows shot up in alarm. "Oh no." She whispered and looked away.

"What is it?" Sebastian brought his hand to Reika's cheek, and tried to bring her gaze back to his. "What's wrong?"

"I don't know how to tell you." She whispered.

"What would make it easier?" He asked. "You don't have to tell me anything if you don't want to. Though you look like you want to."

"I want to, but I need permission." Reika said softly. "We need to go to talk to Papa." She groaned out. "I mean, Mr. Blake."

"Oh." Sebastian swallowed. "Lead the way." He felt his stomach drop. He hadn't any idea what to expect. Reika calling Mr. Blake 'Papa' was strange. Her eyes weren't their normal velvety brown color he adored. He took a deep breath and stood up, offering Reika his hand. She took it, and stood with him though she still avoided eye contact.

Reika led him to the office silently. She felt as if she were going to be sick. She had suffered massive headaches the past two weeks, trying to adjust to all of the changes after she began consuming souls. The added stress of not being able to confide in anyone aside from Samael was almost unbearable. Reika had run out of colored contacts to hide the change of her irises and had forgotten to get more.

She held her hand up to knock on the office door, but Samael opened it before her hand made contact with the heavy wooden entrance.

Reika's eyes met Samael's, *'Papa, I need to tell him.'*

Samael simply nodded. "Come in, come in!" Samael smiled and stepped back, ushering them into the room. He took his seat behind the desk, as Reika had seen him do many times before. Reika took the chair to the right, and Sebastian to the left. "I believe we have some issues to discuss?"

"I don't know how to start." Reika said. "The first thing I'll say is, Meredith and Yuri aren't my real family. I didn't know about this until I turned 18."

Sebastian seemed confused. "If they aren't your true family, who is?"

"There's a story I want to tell you first, it might explain this better than I could." Reika said. She stood from her chair, and walked over to the window behind Samael's desk.

"If it helps, then by all means tell me the story." Sebastian said, his voice was calm, but it belied the storm of emotions roaring within him.

"Do you remember the story of Adam and Eve?" She asked. "There's a one that predates it. God made another woman, someone equal to Adam. Her name was Lilith." She explained. "She didn't want to be subservient to man. She was removed from the garden. She became the consort to an Angel named Samael, better known as the Angel of Death. In their union, many children were born. One was named Lilin, however, her full name is Reika Lilin Avel." She hung her head, leaving her hand pressed to the glass. "Are you following me?"

"You're telling me you're the daughter of an angel and the first woman made by God?" Sebastian asked. The thought of her story being true was funny to him, but he felt like he could believe her deep down. "Is there any way you can prove it to me?"

"There is a way." Samael interjected. "In fact there are many ways. Sebastian. The real question in this moment is what would prove to you that, indeed I am the Angel of Death, and Reika is my offspring."

"I'm sure you could convince me with anything." Sebastian shrugged. "I want to believe you both, but I can't until I see proof."

Samael nodded with a warm, soft smile. "I will give you three options. You may choose whichever ones will convince you. Your first option is this: Reika or Myself could feed from you. Our kind feed from blood, as well as human souls. Fear not though, neither of us would take your soul, you must make a bargain for it to be taken." Sebastian's eyes lit up with a mix of terror and excitement Samael hadn't seen before. Samael grinned mischievously, and stood.

Reika turned around from the window and watched Samael. She sniffed her nose, and wiped at her eyes quietly. Samael turned, gave Reika a soft smile.

'Everything will be alright, my dear. There is no need for tears, you're far too precious to either of us to let those fall from your lashes.'

Reika smiled gently and nodded.

Samael turned his attention back to Sebastian. "You don't have to choose the given option if you don't want to. Option two is to tell me of any place you wish to see, and I shall take you there. Again, this would be free to you."

"Really?" Sebastian asked, his interest growing.

"Your third option is to consume Reika's blood, and experience the powers for yourself. It would only be for a short period of time, however you would understand greatly. Again I will say, you may choose any option. Whether you choose one, a combination of two or all options is to your discretion."

Sebastian looked down for a moment, thinking heavily of his options. He looked up at Reika first, then to Samael. "I'm going to choose all three."

Reika's eyes went wide. "Are you sure?"

"I am." Sebastian nodded. "If this is your new world, and new life I want to experience as much of it as possible. I might as well start now."

"Which would you like to experience first?" Samael grinned.

"I think I want to go from the last option to the first." He looked up. "How does it work though? I don't have any way to break her skin."

"Ah, my boy, that is where I come in." Samael held his hand out for Reika while keeping his eyes on Sebastian. Reika placed her hand in his. Samael slowly brought her wrist to his mouth, and smiled. Sebastian watched carefully, within Samael's smile he was his incisors extend. Slowly still, he rested them against Reika's beautifully pale skin. Her skin enveloped his fangs, but only for a moment. Finally they pierced the skin, and her deep crimson blood welled up and flowed down her porcelain skin.

Reika watched Samael carefully without sound. She felt his fangs recede from her and he gave the incisions a gentle lick. She bit the side of her mouth to keep her silence. He motioned for her to go to Sebastian. She walked to him, and sat on the arm of the chair and held her wrist out for him.

"How much do I consume?" Sebastian asked.

"As much as your stomach can handle. It's a fair warning, it might make you ill. I promise we will take excellent care of you if it were to happen."

Sebastian nodded, and took Reika's hand in his. He brought her wrist to his mouth, and hesitated for a moment before he enclosed his lips over the trickle of blood and tasted what he had never tasted in his life.

The moment Reika's blood touched his tongue, his body felt electrified. An unmistakable power coursed through his veins, the only explanation was it was other worldly. The sensation was divine, as was the flavor of her. Reika didn't taste of iron or salt, the flavor was a mix of honey, spices and the most wonderful nectar. He wanted more, but he could feel an ache in the pit of his stomach.

Reika gazed into Sebastian's face, watching him She ran her free hand through his hair, she licked her lips, trying to keep her silence.

'I understand what you're feeling and if you cannot keep silent, it is perfectly acceptable. When he is finished, you may feed from him. We will take him where he wishes, after the deed is done. The magic from your blood will keep him strong enough until we return. Then we shall take him to rest.'

Reika groaned out, and Sebastian pulled away."Are you alright?"

Without a word, she laid her lips across his. Reika wrapped her arms around his neck and pulled him down towards her as she sunk into his lap. Releasing his mouth, she kissed a trail to his throat. She parted her lips, her breath against Sebastian's skin gave him shivers. She lingered a moment longer before she plunged her teeth into his neck, letting his warmth flow over her tongue.

She ran one hand up, through his hair and held tight.

"Reika." Sebastian growled out. "Oh god." His hands began roaming her body, around to the small of her back and up to her shoulders, holding her tightly to him.

She finally pulled away from his neck and took a deep breath. "Bas..." She whispered out, looking him in the eyes. A small drop of blood rolled down from the corner of her mouth as she smiled.

"You really are what you say." He said softly.

"I am."

"Thank you."

"For what?"

"For giving me a chance to see you so vulnerably." Sebastian said. "Regardless of their contents, secrets are hard to share with others, you and Mr. Blake did your best to show me this."

"The show isn't over yet, Sebastian." Samael's voice called across the room. "You still have your final piece of evidence to collect. What do you wish to see?"

"There are so many choices." He sighed.

Reika stood, wiping the corner of her mouth with her thumb and returned to her chair. "Where are you thinking?"

"Luxor, Karnak, Masada, Venice, Paris." Sebastian sighed. "There are so many places, I can't choose."

Samael laughed. "We will have quite a bit of time to visit all of those. For now, shall I choose one of those for you?"

Sebastian nodded some. "That would be awesome, cause I can't make the decision on my own."

"Let's kill two birds with one stone, shall we?" Samael grinned. "The two temples are rather close to each other. Whether we want to navigate the streets of Luxor by foot, or by bus, a trip between two shouldn't take very long at all."

"I knew they were close, I just hadn't realized the two were so close." Sebastian laughed. "I dreamed about it as a kid, and when I realized my family was too poor to do anything like overseas traveling I stopped dreaming about it." He sighed softly.

"Sebastian." Samael strode towards him and knelt down in front of him. "It is never to late to start dreaming again. We all have desires we wish to achieve. More often than we would like, we stray from the path set before us, yet we always end up right where we need to be." He smiled gently. "It seems you've found yourself back on the trail."

Sebastian smiled. "Yeah, I think I have." He shook his head, his face turning grim. "Though I'm probably wrong, the path ahead of us all is a treacherous one."

"What do you mean?" Reika asked.

"I wish I knew, it's just something I feel." Sebastian looked to Reika. "I don't know how to explain it."

Samael smiled gently. "It's alright, I'll explore it for you. I believe you're having quite a extraordinary response to Reika's blood."

"Intuition is something a demon can possess?" Reika asked.

"Indeed it is." Samael turned his attention towards her. "Have you not noticed a distinct feeling about a person, or an event? Any strange tingles crawling up your spine?"

Reika thought for a moment. "I have, but only more so recently." Her brow creased in thought. "I felt it the most at the party."

"The party?" Sebastian asked, his brow furrowed in confusion.

"The night Reika was at a dance competition, it actually was a ball I hosted to fully bring her into the dark world we reign upon."

"I wish you could have been there, Bas." Reika said, her words coated in guilt. "I wish I could have told you about all of this sooner."

"There's plenty of time for dancing, Rei." Sebastian smiled softly. "I understand you couldn't have told me about this. Honestly, it all sounds completely insane, but the thing is, I don't feel sick. I've heard stories of kids who thought they were vampires, drank blood and died from an iron overdose. No symptoms is a good sign."

Reika smiled tenderly. "You're going to be fine, Bas."

"You certainly will be." Samael grinned. "Shall we make our way to the desert?"

Reika and Sebastian nodded in unison.

"One last piece before we leave." Samael held his hands out and soft flowing fabric appeared. "Reika, you'll probably be better off donning this rather than your usual attire. I only say this because seeing such a beautiful woman walking the streets of Luxor as you dress would only cause chaos."

"How so?" Reika reached out, taking the fabric in her hands. "Is it disrespectful in their culture?"

"It is." Samael nodded softly. "There is a longer skirt there, as well as a longer sleeved shirt, and a light scarf you may wear around your neck, unless you wish to cover your hair. It's best to avoid eye contact as well. If you wish, I also have a pair of sunglasses for you."

Reika sighed. "When in Rome, I suppose."

Samael snickered at her exasperation. "It's not quite Rome, but I assure you, to do as the Egyptians will make the experience much easier. Lilith refused to wear modest clothing, and there was quite an interesting reaction. She wasn't pleased with the unwanted attention."

"I understand not wanting to stand out, I'm just hoping this won't be too hot." Reika mumbled.

Samael smiled. "It'll be alright, lighter cotton is always much cooler than expected. Go ahead and change in the office. Sebastian and I shall wait for you in the hallway."

The two exited the office and stood in silence for a moment while they waited for Reika.

Samael was the first to break the silence. "Reika thinks very highly of you. I can see why she does. Even I am surprised at your reaction to all of this. I want you to know, so long as you live, I will always be a valuable ally to you." He grinned. "For you, there is no price, just whisper my name on the wind and I shall come to your aid."

"Thank you, Mr. Blake." Sebastian said softly. "I can't think of any time I would need help though."

"Please, Sebastian, call me Samael." Samael said softly. He moved forward, his face inches from Sebastian's. "I'm sure you can think of a few moments where you could use a protector."

Sebastian looked up, meeting the cool silver gaze which burned through him entirely. "I'm not sure what you mean, Samael." He looked away, nervously pulling at the sleeve on his shirt.

"I'm certain you do." Samael said, pressing a hand to Sebastian's side, on his rib cage. "One such as yourself is not as graceless as the records would have us believe."

Sebastian's face flushed red as he looked away. "Don't tell anyone."

"A word shall never slip through my lips, just know you needn't suffer."

The door clicked, opening slowly. Reika slipped out the door dressed in flowing red and black. The deep red scarf rested over her hair, and tied loosely at her neck. She gave the two a strange look. "Am I interrupting something?"

"We are finished." Samael said simply and stepped away from Sebastian. He offered Reika a soft smile. "Shall we begin our adventure?" Reika and Sebastian nodded as they followed Samael down the hall. Once outside, Samael took them to a secluded area, turned to them and offered a large smile.

"Take my hand." Samael said to the two. Reika and Sebastian followed order, each taking a hand. Reika looked to Sebastian and then closed her eyes, feeling the familiar sensation of being pulled through the cosmos. Opening her eyes, she was greeted with the fantastical image of deep blue water flowing, palm trees scattered in the horizon. Raising her gaze from the river and turning, her breath was pressed from her body as her gaze feasted upon the sight of ancient sandstone painted against a perfect, cloudless blue sky.

Grinning, she turned to Sebastian who had tears streaming down his cheeks, a look of awe strewn about him.

"Am I dreaming?" Sebastian whispered. He sniffed his nose, and wiped his face off, yet the grin still remained.

"Bas, you're not dreaming." Reika said. "Do you need me to bite you, to make sure of it?" She laughed some.

"I'm afraid to say yes to the offer."

"I wouldn't recommend any sort of contact in that nature in broad daylight in a conservative country." Samael interjected. "Now, shall we visit the temples? We haven't much time."

Taking a stairway up from the banks of the Nile, they joined the procession of tourists heading towards the entrance to Karnak. As they approached the temple, they were greeted by sphinxes adorned with ram heads lining the entrance way. Reika looked up at the pylons looming above. The sight was much more magnificent than she had ever anticipated. She looked to Sebastian, and smiled. His child-like wonderment of his surroundings was infectious. She turned to Samael, who was gazing about as well, yet his expression was that of nostalgia.

"You have been here before?" Reika asked.

Samael smiled, and looked towards her. "I remember when the mound there, in front of the pylon was actually a ramp. The sphinxes were fully intact, and the stone was adorned with bright colors, instead of being washed by the sand-laden winds. We marched through these streets to the sounds of drums, the people asking for favor from their god. Many a soul came my way from these festivities."

Slowly, as to take all they could of Karnak in, they walked past the first set of pylons. Beyond the pylons, was a single full column left standing. Others stood with it, but were far from their former resplendence. Reika wished she could see Karnak in it's original splendor, yet time had aged the large temple and she was grateful to see it as it stood.

The three made their way around Karnak slowly, taking in as much as possible and listening to Samael's stories from the temple's active days. After getting through mazes of columns and statues, they arrived at the edge of the sacred lake. Reika smiled as she looked over the vast mirrored surface. She turned to Sebastian and watched his face. He was so enthralled with the ancient beauty which surrounded him and with Samael's stories of a time they couldn't even dream of.

"The Sacred Lake of Karnak." Samael sighed out. "Simplicity is astounding in it's beauty."

"The entire temple is amazing." Sebastian said softly.

Reika stayed silent, looking to Sebastian once again. As much as he was enjoying himself, his skin looked pale, and glistened from sweat. His breathing seemed shallow and labored. He reached out, placing a hand on Samael's arm to steady himself.

Samael put his arm around Sebastian's shoulders. "Are you alright?"

Sebastian swallowed hard, shaking his head. "No, I don't know what's wrong."

"I think it wore off." Reika said, as she came and stood in front of Sebastian. "Should we get him back to the school?"

Samael nodded. "Follow me, and I will bring us to a wonderful place for our departure." Walking slowly, so Sebastian could handle the pace, they went away from the Sacred Lake, back towards the pylons. Samael led them behind a wall, and they disappeared.

They arrived in Samael's office with Sebastian slumped against him. Samael set him in one of the chairs. Reika knelt down beside the chair.

"Is there anything we can do for him?" She asked.

"I'm afraid not, he just needs rest now. He'll be fine in the morning. I'll take him to his room shortly."

"Can I stay with him?" Reika asked.

"As your father, I say yes, but as the dean of the school, I have to make you go to class today. You may come back after classes."

Reika sighed. "I understand. Where shall I meet you?"

"Return to my office after classes and I shall take you to him."

She nodded, leaned down and kissed Sebastian's cheek. She went to Samael and hugged him tightly.

Samael smiled, holding her tight. He patted her back. "Go, child. Your physical education class is going to start shortly at the football field."

She nodded. "I'll see you after class. Today, I've missed all my classes aside from gym."

"Tread lightly, My Dear." Samael warned, drawing back from their embrace, but looked her deep in the eyes. "All the females are in a combined free day class. Lilith is supervising."

"Can I please not go?" Reika asked, her eyes pleading with him.

"She is very much expecting you." Samael sighed. "I wish I didn't have to put you in such a position, yet she wishes for you to be there, and I am, unfortunately not able to deny her."

"She gives me a terrible feeling." Reika's gaze fell. The night of the ball, Reika felt Lilith's eyes drilling into her with a seething jealousy she hadn't felt before. The man who stood next to her, his intentions were malicious, and neither of the pair did anything to hide their true feelings. "As did her date at the ball."

Samael nodded. "I know of Adrian." He sighed heavily. "He is not on my list of allies. Again, I shall tell you, tread lightly. Your intuition is not leading you astray, listen and you shall prevail."

"I believe you." Reika nodded in response. "I'm still learning to believe in myself. I'll be aware at all times from now on." Reika let go of Samael, and turned towards the door. "I love you, Papa. I'll see you soon." She didn't give Samael a chance to respond as she slipped out the door and made her way to the football field.

Reika walked quickly, the flowing skirt, and shirt fluttered in the wind as she walked. A chill ran up her spine. She looked down at her feet and realized she hadn't changed back into her usual attire.

"Shit." She sighed out. Entering the small stadium, all eyes turned towards Reika. "More unwanted attention." She muttered.

"Look who finally decided to show up!" The thin, blonde Camille called out. "Mrs. Blake, She isn't even dressed properly!"

"Silence Camille and continue your warm-ups." Lilith said, staring straight at Reika. She was dressed in a stylish track suit, in her favorite shade of burgundy with black accents. "I will deal with Miss Reika alone." Lilith walked towards Reika, placing a hand on her lower back. "Follow me." She said in a hushed tone.

Reika tensed at the sensation of Lilith's hand hovering on her body. She matched her pace, and they walked to a secluded area next to the concession stands.

"I finally have a moment with my daughter." She smirked, her eyes were cool, lacking any sort of emotion. "It's such a pity I have to steal you away from him by means of institutional rules. If it weren't for this class I doubt I would have even seen you!" She sighed. "You didn't even greet me at the ball either! Come now, Child, what is this about? Do I frighten you?"

"No, I've just been learning what all of this is about. Papa has been teaching me late into the night." Reika said simply. "I've been busy trying to manage my schoolwork with Father's lessons. I'm sorry."

"Don't lie to me." Lilith sneered. "You're not sorry. There's nothing I hate more than apologies made in vain. You spend all your time with the boy, and Samael. Just remember Samael is mine. I am not one to share my belongings."

"I had no intention of stealing him away from you." Reika looked at her, confused. "He's my Father. I only want a relationship with him as that, anything other than a father daughter relationship is sickening."

Lilith laughed. "You are so naive still, child. It's not uncommon amongst our kind to have family members become mates. Just know if you take him from me, I'll take yours, and much more."

Reika tried to suppress her anger. "Understood, Lilith." She said through gritted teeth. "In turn, you must know if you harm him in any way, I will destroy you. I may still be learning the ways of this world, but I am completely aware of the wrath that I am capable of."

"A true daughter of mine." She smirked. "If only I could be proud. Instead I get to hear of you, the stupid boy and my beloved traipsing the desert without me. I could teach you many things your Father cannot. Perhaps you should discontinue your lessons with him, and schedule ones with me. I assure you, my lesson would be much more pleasurable than Samael could teach you."

"Don't think me so naive that I don't know what you are." Reika said simply. "Shall we return to the class, I'm certain the students are waiting for you."

"There is one last thing to address. What do you intend to do during a gym class wearing such a ridiculous outfit?"

"Body movements, stretching, simple body study." Reika shrugged. "Clothes don't define what I can and cannot do."

"Do as you please, it is clear you're not going to heed the words of others." Lilith snarled.

Reika turned and walked away. Though she had more fight in her than she needed, Reika knew it was not the time to continue heated words with Lilith. Instead she returned to the football field, where she began her slow movement practice.

"Reika!" She heard a familiar voice call her name out. She turned to see Yuri running towards her. "What's with your outfit? Damn, I hardly see you in weeks, and when I do, you're dressed like some middle eastern woman. You're changing so much, it's kind of scaring me." Yuri looked down as she bit her lower lip. "When will you have time for your little sister?"

"Oh, Mr. Blake took me on a trip to a middle eastern community, I didn't want to offend anyone so I dressed like this. I forgot about gym class and didn't have time to grab some clothes." Reika shrugged. "I'm sorry, Yuri. I've been so busy lately. Mr. Blake is trying to help me figure out what I want to do after graduating. I've never put thought into it, I never thought I'd make it this far. I'm just stressed."

"Reika, just try to remember you have a sister who misses you." Yuri sighed. "I know you've been stressing about a lot of things. You don't sleep well anymore. You toss and turn all night, and it wakes me up."

"I can't quite control what I'm doing in my sleep." Reika sighed. "I guess I'll try sleeping pills so I don't bother you anymore." Reika knew the medication wouldn't do anything, yet she wanted to appease Yuri's complaints.

"Whatever, Rei." Yuri rolled her eyes. "You haven't been yourself lately. What's going on?"

"I don't want to talk about it." Reika said, looking down.

"Why not? You used to tell me everything, now you don't want to?" Yuri sighed, rolling her eyes again. "You must have done something really stupid to be holding out on me like this."

"Yuri, shut up!" Reika growled. "I don't want to talk about it, so quit trying to make me! You're only going to piss me off."

"It's not the first time I've done it, so why stop now?" She glared at her. "What is going on with you?!"

"It's none of your fucking business!" Reika growled. "I don't understand why you pretend to even care. Everyone around me says it, I'm a fucking piece of shit, I'm not worth anything. So why even bother, Yuri? Really, why should you even take the time out of your day to care about someone as fucked up as me?! I'm probably going to wind up dead one of these days, or in prison, so get used to me not being around, cause I won't be around much longer."

"Where is all this coming from?!" Yuri growled out, getting closer to Reika. "Are you kidding me?! What's going to cause you to die? Are you sick? Or is someone just going to murder you because you can't keep your damned mouth shut for two minutes?!"

"That's the first thing you've gotten right so far! Yes!" Reika snarled back. "That's probably what is going to happen! Let's face it, I'm a target, and I'm one that bites back. Teeth aren't good defense against guns, Yuri. Either that, or I'm gonna end up killing someone because they can't keep their mouths shut! You're better off leaving me alone, than trying to fix a someone who was doomed from the start." Reika turned away from Yuri and stalked away from the football field. She hated when Yuri tried to pry information out of her. She never liked talking to anyone about anything, yet Yuri always tried.

A group of girls were laughing as Reika took her leave.

"Aw! Look at her! She looks like she's going to cry!" Camille yelled out, laughing.

"Would you give it a rest, Camille?" The dark haired Ella said. "She's already thrown your ass on the ground once, do you want it to happen again?"

"I appreciate your help, Ella, but I can handle this on my own." Reika said, as she turned around and came up to Camille. "Why don't you go ahead and say what's on your mind, huh? What is it you find so funny about all of this? It wouldn't be so funny if it were you, now would it?"

"It wouldn't ever happen to me, I'm an only child and I'm glad I am." Camille sneered. "My parents got it right the first time, it looks like your parents had to have a second try to get a decent child."

"Or maybe your parents were afraid of having a worse creature than you as their second child. Have you ever thought of that?" Reika smirked.

"Are you kidding me?!" Camille cried out. "Look at me! I'm perfect!"

"Oh? And how many thousands of dollars did Mommy and Daddy have to pay for that to happen?"

Camille's face transformed from smugness to sheer rage. As if the moment were in slow motion, Reika saw Camille's arm draw back in an arch, and descend upon her. A sadistic grin lined Reika's face as she caught her arm just right and drew her in. Camille tried to fight against the hold, but it caused her more pain the more she fought. Reika dropped her weight on top of Camille's arm and she dropped to the ground. Reika flipped Camille over, pressing one knee into her chest and used her other as a fulcrum for Camille's arm.

"There are so many things I could do here." Reika sighed. She began put weight down on Camille's arm. "I could break your arm, I could break your clavicle, or something on that perfect little face of yours." She continued to brace her weight against Camille's arm slowly. She could feel the tense state her muscles were in. "Maybe I could break your jaw. Having your mouth wired shut would do all of us a favor."

"You wouldn't dare!" She snarled, trying to fight against Reika's pin.

Reika grinned, her eyes wide with delight. "Oh, I would. You messed with me once, I let you off lightly. This was your second chance, and you fucked it up royally. As expected for a little princess bitch." The pressure continued to build, and she heard the joints popping gently, trying to release pressure.

Camille whimpered some. "Please, don't do it."

She laughed. "You're begging me? Oh, please, I couldn't hear you, say it again."

"Please don't break my arm!" Camille sobbed. "Please?"

"Oh, how can I say no to such beautiful cries?" Reika let go of Camille's arm, but, before Camille had a chance to retaliate, Reika struck her hard in the nose. Camille screamed out in pain and her hands went to cover her face. Pleased with her work, Reika stood and walked away without a second thought. She continued to walk, until she finally reached Locke Academy's office building. She climbed the stairs, and returned to Samael's office once again.

She sat down, and explained to Samael everything that transpired during class. She sat back, and waited for a reaction.

"I understand why you did this, my dear, however, I cannot let such things seen by the public go unpunished." Samael explained. "To appease the state and the parents of the wretched girl you did quite a number on, I must expel you from the school. It may seem like a terrible thing for me to do, however I see this event as a well placed opportunity for your training."

"I don't see how it's a good opportunity for anything. Meredith is going to come take me away, and I'm probably going to be put into juvenile detention, or jail considering I'm over the legal age. I don't want to leave."

"Even if you were forced to leave, I would still find you. I will always find you, my daughter." Samael said, trying to comfort her. He came forward, from his desk, and knelt before her, placing a hand on her knee. "I will come to take you away, I swear it."

"I know something is going to happen when she shows up here." Reika sighed. "It's not going to be good."

"I think we both can agree we wish we knew what the future held, yet it is not in our skill set to know what may come." Samael looked down. "In all honesty, I sense it as well. I cannot tell what will happen, I only know something will happen."

Chapter Nine

Reika sat outside the office building, her stomach in knots as she waited for Meredith to arrive. As much as she had tried, Reika knew nothing could prepare her for the look of disappointment she knew all too well. She leaned over, putting her head on her knees and wrapping her arms around, as to hide from the world. Only moments later, she heard a car pull up and the door slam.

"Reika Lilin Avel!" Meredith yelled as she made her way to her. "I swear, you're more trouble than you're worth!"

"I'm surprised you finally realized it." Reika said softly.

"Quiet." Meredith snapped. "Let's go." She took off towards the door of the office building. Reika followed slowly, a cocktail of unwanted emotions roiled within her. She trudged up the stairs after a quick Meredith. She was knocking on Samael's office door as Reika finally ascended the stairs. She stood behind her and waited.

The door slowly opened, Reika expected to see Samael, yet the man who stood there was, short and chubby. His brown hair was slicked back, with gray streaking it. Reika was shocked at first, but remembered this was how Samael appeared at the move in day meeting. "Welcome, Mrs. Avel, Reika, please come in and have a seat."

'Papa, is that you?'

'It is, child. Don't be scared, I promise I'll take care of everything.'

Reika sighed as she took her usual seat in the brown leather armchair. Meredith sat down and crossed one leg over the other and dropped her purse to the floor with a thud. Reika hadn't seen Meredith this furious before. She looked at Meredith, who made eye contact with her. Meredith's eyes were burning with hatred. Reika immediately cast her gaze to the floor.

"I have the unfortunate responsibility of bearing the news that I must expel Reika from Locke Academy. During an altercation located at the school's football stadium, Reika broke a student's nose and hyper extended her elbow. We have spoken to the family, and they have decided against pressing charges against Reika, they only request Reika be removed from the academy. I happen to agree she should be removed from the school, her skills are much better suited for a school with a career technical program. It seems she would benefit from a hands-on learning experience. If you wish, I could give you some recommendations."

"No, I don't want your damned recommendation." Meredith snarled. "Give me the papers to sign so I can leave."

"We have everything of Reika's packed and waiting for you as well."

"Thank you." Meredith said, her words still sharp. She quickly signed the papers, put them on the desk and stood. She grabbed her purse and then grabbed Reika's arm. "Let's go." She yanked her up from the chair and towards the door.

Reika followed Meredith, as she had no choice. Once they were outside, she whipped Reika around and stared her straight in the face. "You lost your last chance, Reika! What were you thinking?! This was the last school in the area you could attend! Now what?!"

"I don't know." Reika tried to look away, but Meredith grabbed her chin and forced her to look into her face.

"Do I take you home and have you do home schooling on the computer? I have no idea! You've really fucked up this-" Meredith stopped short, her eyes went wide. "What's wrong with your eyes?"

"I don't know." She said again.

Meredith's hand dropped from her chin, and she stepped back. "No. What did you do? Are they contacts? Please tell me they are contacts!"

"They aren't." Reika looked away from her.

"Oh..." She stumbled backwards. "Oh god... You-you're one of them?!"

"Yes."

"Why did you do this?!" Meredith sobbed. "You were supposed to be my child."

"I am your child. You raised me." Reika said softly.

"No you're not." Meredith shook her head. "You're their child. You were never mine. I can't do this. I can't keep you. You're no child of mine. They've destroyed you! Don't bother coming home!" Meredith turned and ran towards her car.

"Mom!" She called out. As much as Reika didn't want to go back home, she didn't want to lose the one woman who had endless faith in her.

Meredith turned and looked at Reika. "I'm not your mother, you are no daughter of mine. The only child I have is Yuri." She got in her car, turned it on and drove away.

Reika stood, watching the car drive away in disbelief. She sank to her knees and looked to the ground. Despite the people she still had in her life, she felt completely alone. Meredith and Yuri were her only form of support for the longest time, life without them was unfathomable. Yet, there Reika sat, with the unimaginable happening right before her. She felt a hand touch her back.

"When are you leaving?" Sebastian's voice said softly. He knelt down next to Reika and put his arm around her.

"I don't know where I'm going." She said softly. "She left me."

"Reika..." Sebastian pulled her into a tight hug. "I'm sorry."

She put her arms around him his waist and buried her face in his shoulder. "She knows what I am." She said, her voice muffled.

"Everything's going to be alright." Sebastian whispered, as he rubbed her back. "You have me, and Samael. We'll take care of you."

"Everyone leaves me at some point." She whispered int Sebastian's shoulder. "Please don't be one of them."

"I won't." He squeezed her tight. "I promise."

"Is she alright?" Samael asked, joining them.

"As alright as she can be, I suppose." Sebastian said. "Meredith just left her here. Rei didn't really say why though."

"She couldn't handle the truth that who she thought was her firstborn is actually not her flesh and blood. The child she raised is of another. She feels sick to know the one she made her pact with, created a loophole." Samael sighed. "If it had been my choice, she would have never left my side, but it was fate for her to be in Meredith's care."

Reika sighed, sat up, letting go of Sebastian and wiped her eyes. "She probably would've rather me chosen death over this life." She shook her head. "I was born to be this, death is not an option."

Samael smiled some. "No truer words have been spoken. This existence isn't effortless, you're strong, Reika, so very strong. You will be alright, in time. All occurrences and wounds will take time to heal. This cannot be denied, just know I will always be here for you. Now, if you'd like, I have something prepared for you."

"What is it?" She asked.

"Your new home."

Reika nodded gently. "That would be nice." She sniffed some, feeling another tear roll down her cheek. She wiped it again, and looked at her hand, seeing the ruby droplet fall from her fingertip and dye a single red circle on the concrete. "Papa, is this normal?" She looked down at the ground, then touched Sebastian's shoulder where his black shirt was wet. Her fingertips were stained red. She wasn't aware of all the reddish hue covering her hands until now.

"You're perfectly fine. It is how a demon's tears fall, nothing more." Samael explained. "Let's get you inside."

Sebastian helped Reika to her feet, but her balance wavered. Without a word, Sebastian scooped her up in his arms.

"Bas, you really don't have to." She said, holding onto his neck. "I would've been fine."

"Let me be your strength for once, Reika." Sebastian said softly. "I don't get this chance very often."

She nodded, and laid her head against him as he followed Samael up the stairs and to his office once more.

"How do we get there from your office?" Sebastian asked.

"It's quite simple really." Samael, grinned and placed his hand on the closet door for a moment. A symbol began to glow from underneath the palm of his hand. The light from it got brighter and brighter, blinding Sebastian. As soon as he closed his eyes to shield them, the light abruptly went out. The sound of the creaking hinges swinging open greeted his ears and he opened his eyes once more.

Through the open doorway, Sebastian and Reika saw a decadently adorned hallway leading to a sitting room dressed in deep burgundy and gold. Both were amazed at the scene before his eyes. Samael held the door open, and ushered Sebastian, who still held Reika through the door.

"I promise you there is much more amazement awaiting you here than just this hallway." He grinned. "Though, it's quite a wonderful hallway."

"This is beautiful." Reika whispered out.

Samael led them through the house, through many more beautifully adorned hallways and rooms. It was so much for the two to take in. Finally they arrived in front of a ornate door, and Samael turned the crystal knob and opened the door. Inside was a wrought iron canopy bed, with bright red crushed velvet curtains tied back with silver ribbons. The rich cherry wood of the antique dressers and desk tied the black and white Victorian style walls together.

Reika looked around, she was in awe of the room, but she felt a heavy dose of recognition. "Was this the room you and Lilith had me in, when I made my transformation?"

"It was." Samael said.

Sebastian sat Reika on her feet. She walked slowly around the room. She touched the covers on the bed. "It's so beautiful, all of it. It's like everything is from a dream." She laughed. "It doesn't help that I first saw all of this in my dreams, but it's all a reality now. If only Lilith's threats were only a dream."

"She threatened you?" Samael asked, his eyes broke out in a blaze of ire.

"Reika, why didn't you say anything?!" Sebastian asked.

"It's part of why I was so angry when I broke Camille's nose. She was going on about how I never spend time with her, and how I need to watch how much time I'm with you, Papa. She told me that you belong to her, and if I take her away, she'll take Sebastian."

"Do not trust her. Words which slip through those rouged lips are nothing but gilded deceit. You are best staying far away from that woman." Samael said, his eyes still an intense anger burning within him.

"Is she serious?" Sebastian asked.

"She's losing her mind, and I suspect she has an ally believing her words." Samael explained.

"How do you know?" Reika asked. She sat down on the bed, and listened carefully.

"I have a friend of my own who hears much of what is spoken." Samael smirked. "You both will certainly meet him soon. I've heard words from him that late in the night, whilst Lilith roams her garden alone, she whispers words of utter nonsense or has horrendous fits of rage."

"That's bizarre." Reika looked down. "Does she still have access to this house?"

"Not anymore." Samael let out a relieved sigh. "Darius, the friend I had mentioned helped me create a protection barrier against her. Of all things I am skilled in, runes are not one of them."

"Are there other protective barriers in place aside from runes?" Reika asked. "I'm certain she'll find a way around those, even if it meant recruiting someone else to enter."

"There are only four people able to enter this house without having the misfortune of death come upon them. Three of those beings sit in this very room." Samael smiled.

Reika smiled, but tried to suppress a yawn. The day hadn't been physically exhausting, but the toll on her mental stamina was tremendous. Reika tried her best to ignore the pain that crept from the shadowy corners of her mind, yet the undeniable pain of abandonment shocked through her body. She crossed her arms over her chest, sniffing back sobs. "They're both idiots." Reika whispered. "They're stupid to abandon such a person."

"I understand it hurts." Samael said, crossing the room. He sat down on her bed, placing a knee gently on her leg. "You're such a wonderful being, Reika. Please, don't let this scar you."

Reika shook her head. "I can't let it." She said, her voice still just a whisper.

"Get some rest, child." Samael said, pulling her into an embrace. "There is something in the drawer of the table here which will help you get some sleep." He leaned back, still holding her shoulders and kissed her forehead. "Sebastian and I will be across the hall if you need anything."

Reika nodded, and laid back on the bed. Samael went to the hallway, as Sebastian came to Reika's side, to give them a moment alone.

"Are you going to be alright?" Sebastian asked. He sat down on her bed, and took her hand in his. "Do you need anything before I leave?"

"For you not to leave." She held onto his hand tight.

"I know." He whispered. "Samael wants to talk to me though. If I can come back, I will."

"Can you open the drawer and get what Papa was talking about? I'll need the help to sleep."

"Of course." Sebastian smiled gently, as he retrieved a small glass bottle from the drawer. The contents of the bottle was black, and had a slight shimmer as it passed under the light. Sebastian handed it to her and rested his hand on her leg.

"Thanks." Reika said softly. She sat up, laying the bottle on her pillow and wrapped her arms around his neck. "I love you." She whispered into his ear. "Sebastian, I really do."

"I..." Sebastian stuttered. "I love you too, Reika." He felt his face flush red, as his heart raced. "Get some rest, I'll come back later on." He said and kissed her. He let go and went towards the door. "Hey, Rei?"
Reika raised her gaze towards him, her face was just as red as his.
"Yeah?"

"I really mean it."

She smiled. "I know you do. It's alright, go and talk to him."

He nodded and slipped out the door. Reika turned, grabbing the small bottle from her pillow, unscrewed the cap and took a drink.

She set the bottle on the nightstand and laid down. Closing her eyes,

she slipped into a deep sleep.

Chapter Ten

Opening the door to the room across the hall from Reika's, Sebastian felt nervousness rise in him like it had never done before when he went to speak with Samael alone. He took a deep breath, steadying himself and entered the door across from Reika's. The size of the room was the same as Reika's, but the furnishing was much different. Equipped with a elegant yet simple sleigh bed made out of a deep walnut, with matching dressers and a desk, the room was decorated in a deep emerald green, with gold trim. Across from the bed were two black leather chairs near a small bookshelf.

Samael was seated in the leather chair farthest from the door. "Come in, please join me."

Sebastian walked over and took a seat in the remaining chair. "Is everything going to be alright?"

"In time, yes." Samael nodded. "I have seldom seen any situation resolve itself overnight. I've been thinking greatly on something, and wish to ask you about it."

"What is it?" Sebastian felt his stomach drop. He knew Samael didn't want to have small talk, and he knew he wasn't prepared for what was to come.

"Reika loves you dearly, and I can tell your affections are shared. I could never bring myself to be the one to destroy true love. In fact, I would much rather encourage it. If you choose to stay with Reika, she will continue on her life long after you die as a human. It is inevitable, however, I can give you the option of becoming one of us. If you choose, Reika would be the one to collect your soul and give you an eternity with us. If you choose not to, I will give you protection. You will become a target for those who consider us an enemy."

Sebastian's eyes went wide. "You mean it? There has to be a catch. What's the catch?"

"There really isn't one." Samael laughed a little. "Well, you would become my son. I am not certain if that is a downfall or an upgrade. From what I understand of your life, I would think it a welcomed change."

Sebastian looked down, and sighed. "You don't have to know much to know you're right. It would be difficult to adjust to, but I'm absolutely sure it would be a great change."

"When you are ready, speak with Reika. Regardless, consider me a father figure if you wish. I will be glad to take on the role for you."

Sebastian smiled softly. For him to hear someone be so willing to offer him guidance in his life was purely touching. His own father was far from the title. "Thank you, Samael. I really would like that." He looked up, and swallowed hard. "Do you think Reika would be alright with the idea of me becoming one of you?"

"Reika is full of surprises, I wish I could give you a defined answer, yet it is lost on me."

Sebastian laughed. "You're absolutely right with that. She's unlike anyone I've ever met in my life."
"Ah, boy, you see, she is unlike anyone I have ever met either, and I've been alive a few more years than you." Samael laughed too.

"Only a few?" An incredulous look spread across Sebastian's face.

"The mind doesn't age unless it's user wants it to." Samael smirked. "This body may have seen roughly four millenniums. The world population doesn't follow the lunar calendar anymore, I've lost track."

"I couldn't imagine anything you've experienced." Sebastian sighed, smiling wistfully. "It must have been amazing."

Samael sighed as well. "It was, yet again, there are many memories I wish I could forget. The world is shrouded in mystery and death with only glimpses of the true beauty within. As a man whose sole purpose in this world is to personify death, the beauty has been lost on me on many occasions. Seldom have I felt pure joy. Many years, no, centuries I've been alone. The only person I had was myself. The years passed slowly, yet near the end I had come to an understanding. To be happy with one's self, the world cannot shake you."

"It can't shake you?" Sebastian asked. "What do you mean?"

"The world cannot break you down. You will exist as you were meant to, and nothing can change that. You will be able to reach your dreams, and hang from the stars as the world passes you by. It may seem like you are at the same point in your life, but you aren't. You are only ascending. Soon, you will realize the stars you are grasping are the same size as the world your feet were planted on. Then you are met with a scary thought: what would happen if you let go?"

"I don't know what would happen." Sebastian said, he was intrigued by Samael's speech.

"My boy, you would soar." Samael smiled. "Those who reach the heavens, and never let go may unfurl the wings hidden deep within."

Sebastian smiled. "There's only one way to go, and that's up." He thought for a moment. "Do demons have wings?"

"Some do, most do not." Samael looked up. "I do have wings, though I don't use them much anymore. With the technological advances, using them would draw too much attention."

"Does Reika?" Sebastian asked.

"I'm not certain of that." Samael thought. "It is possible. Lilith did not rise with wings however."

"What is her story? How did she come about?" Sebastian asked. "I've heard so many legends, it's impossible to know which one is the truth."

"Each story contains a fragment of truth." Samael leaned back, staring at the ceiling. "The true story is quite interesting. I opened my eyes, and saw the most beautiful scene before me. A gorgeous oasis, lush forests and cascading waterfalls. Curiously beautiful animals inhabited the area and there I laid. I hadn't any clue of where I was. I knew who I was, I knew language. I was aware of many things, my location was not one of them.

"The world was pure, new, and untouched. I heard gasping in the distance. I thought myself alone, and I was. Until Adam and Lilith breathed their first breath."

"You saw him?" Sebastian asked.

"I can't answer that." Samael smiled mischievously. "Who I saw with Adam and Lilith, is still a mystery to me. What was before me, was a man and a woman laying on the ground, near the bank of the river coursing through the forest and a bright light hovering above them. My role in this world is not natural, and even I haven't any idea who controls all of this. They were created in a union,

Adam wanted to consummate that union. He brought himself on top of Lilith and she screamed, throwing him off.

"The light had spoken, trying to convince her everything was alright, yet she refused. She did not want to be used, and tortured by the hand of her equal. The light told her to leave. She stood and began walking towards where I was. I knew exactly what to say, and it is when I created my first pact."

"You just knew? What was your first pact?" Sebastian was sitting on the edge of his seat, absorbing all he could.

Samael's eyes lit with bittersweet reminiscence. "Before my eyes, was the embodiment of feminine perfection. The words slipped through my mouth. I said 'I would accept you as my equal, and let you live forever. I only require one thing in exchange: the soul you were just given.' She said nothing, she brought her arms around my neck and kissed me. There was a fierce fire burning within her, and it is still coursing after four thousand years. It seems though, insanity has taken hold of her mind."

"How did that happen? You would think the first woman would be impervious to any sort of disease." Sebastian asked.

"The human race was never meant to live forever. It's true the earliest ones lived for a very long time. Occasionally, when a human became a supernatural being, they lost their sanity for many reasons. I started seeing the signs of it about a hundred years ago. Despite my attempts to cease it, they were in vain."

"You still love her despite all she is doing?"

"Unfortunately." Samael sighed. "Though, it's enough story telling for this evening. I have an appointment to keep, and I shall see you tomorrow. You may stay here tonight. If you choose to leave, just exit this room, and return to the door you entered in. It will take you to my office and you may proceed to where you need to go."

"Thank you Samael." Sebastian smiled. "Your story was amazing. To hear the truth about something speculated by the world, from a person who was actually there. I'll never forget this."

"I will tell you many more stories throughout the years." Samael smiled. He stood and patted him on the shoulder. "Relax this evening, and if you stay here, please keep an eye on Reika, as I'm sure you would."

"I'll be here." Sebastian smiled. "I'm looking forward to these stories."

"For some, I wish I could say the same. Good night, Sebastian." Samael said as he slipped out the door. Sebastian sat alone for a few moments. He pulled his phone out from his pocket, seeing a missed text message from Lynde.

'I just heard your girlfriend got expelled from school. Yuri is being pulled out of the school and is going back home. I am too. Have fun with your criminal. Lose this number.'

"So much for a best friend." Sebastian groaned at the message from Lynde. He tossed the phone on the chair next to him, leaned forward and put his head in his hands. "I have everything I need in her though." He whispered to himself, and stood. He went to the door and made his way to Reika's room once more.

# # #

"Don't even say what you're thinking, Lilith. I do not care to hear it." Samael said. Lilith took hold of his arm, walking fast across the campus. "I honestly don't give a damn what you are feeling over this relationship. Your jealous rage is quite tangible in this moment. Give it up, it isn't going to get you anywhere."

"How dare you speak to me like that!" She hissed, tightening her grip on Samael's arm. The pain hadn't really ever bothered Samael, however tonight was different.

"How dare *I* speak to you like *that*?!" He growled, breaking his arm out from her grip. "I don't think you understand the extent of this situation! Do you even realize putting Reika with those humans has caused many more problems than if you would have left her in my care?! Of course you hadn't! You have only thought of yourself in the centuries we've been together! Do something for someone else for once! There is a world full of people out there, Lilith! I hate to be the one to destroy your charade, but you aren't the center of the universe like you seem to believe!" He stormed off.

Lilith stood, watching Samael walk away from her. She was shaking, rage filled her small body. She took off after him, and grabbed his arm once again. Samael turned. "What do you want now?!"

"You're being unreasonable Samael!" She glared at him, grabbing his other arm. "I did what I had to for the both of us! She would have become too strong and would have killed the us if I didn't give her away."

"Somehow, I can't seem to believe you. Oh, I really wonder why this doubt has risen up. You are a treacherous snake, as you have always been. Release me." He stared down at the woman in front of him, a woman he used to know so completely. Now, She was no more than a stranger.

"What would you do if I didn't let go?" A corner of her mouth curled up in provocation. "Are you going to hit me? Throw me to the ground? Oh, that isn't in the repertoire of Samael." She clicked her tongue. "I guess there isn't anything you can do... Now, is there?" She cocked her head to the side, and gave a smirk.

"I don't think it is very wise to tempt me. I've kept my hands to myself for many years, and now you're testing my resolve?" He stared at her, his eyes dim. "You're a fool, Lilith." He moved his arms in a swift motion, and broke free from her grip once more. "I don't think you'll be so fortunate with the next occurrence." He disappeared before she could say anything more. All he wanted was to decimate her. Samael was so infuriated by Lilith for what she had done, and felt like a fool for believing things would change for the better once Reika had come back to them.

He sighed, looking at his surroundings. He had appeared in a forest far away from Lilith. He cloaked his presence as to not be tracked down by her. He sat underneath a tree, leaning his head back, looking at the canopy looming above.

"Darius, this would be a splendid time for you to come forth." He said softly, closing his eyes momentarily. "I know you can hear me, Darius Gregory." The sound of leaves rustling greeted his ears. He opened his eyes to a whirlwind of leaves before him. The leaves settled, and before him stood a man with dark honey blond hair pulled back to a braid at the base of his skull. Darius was sporting dark jeans, biker boots, a halfway buttoned white collared shirt and a leather blazer. His deep green eyes set into a perfectly masculine face stared down at Samael.

"You called me here, Samael? What's troubling you? You rarely call upon me unless there is something bothering you. In fact, I believe it's been about 18 years since we have met alone. It's the girl, or Lilith, isn't it?"

"You know me all too well, Darius. It actually is both of them. I'm very pleased that the girl, Reika, is back in my life." He rubbed his hands over his face, and raked them through his lengthy black hair. "However, Lilith is troubled by the relationship I've established with our daughter. She is completely engulfed by jealousy. She has lashed out at me over and over since Reika's birthday. I'm not one to strike others, but she is pushing the boundaries. It's difficult to restrain myself with her."

"This sounds like classic Lilith." Darius sat next to his friend. "I certainly will keep my ears open of any plans she might be constructing. At the moment, I haven't heard of her plotting anything as of yet. We can't underestimate her, you know this all too well."

Samael turned his head towards Darius. "You haven't a clue, Darius. She's been obsessed over Reika since she made the decision to give her to the human couple. I've kept my emotions buried since that day. I believe you are the only being who knows my feelings about this whole situation fully. Lilith knew I was upset over her giving Reika away, but not how badly."

"I certainly do know. It has happened to me as well, granted the end result for my own was far worse than this."

"You are correct and I am sorry." Samael sighed. "I'm just at the end of my patience with Lilith, yet there isn't any way to rid myself of her. I've never felt such resentment and such euphoria at the same time. I never conceived I could love someone as deeply as I love my little girl. She is so strong, brave, intelligent, and beautiful. I only wish I could have been the one to raise her, and not Meredith or William."

"Do you think she would have been the same brilliant star in your life if you had raised her?"

"What do you mean?"

"All of what has been instilled in her has been because of the human couple who raised her. Do you think you could have done their job better?"

"I," Samael stopped and thought for a moment, "I'm not certain."

"I am glad you have her back. However, I think that was how it was always meant to be. If you hadn't sought after your daughter for so long, you wouldn't feel the same way now."

"You always put situations into perspective for me, and I greatly appreciate it." Samael muttered, looking up at the leaf camouflaged sky once more.

"Ah, yes. How humbling it is to see such a being as yourself ask me for advice. Really, Samael, it is quite flattering." Darius smiled softly. "Keep Lilith close, but guard yourself, my friend. She certainly is readying something devious. I would be worried if she weren't."

"I only wish I knew what she is plotting."

"Sadly, I do not know that much. The full details are out of my realm of knowledge." Darius sighed softly. "How is your daughter adjusting to this new lifestyle?"

"On the equinox, she claimed her first soul, that of a righteous priest. Her choice was wonderfully made. The others available that night were bland, she made an excellent choice. Though, I worry for the compassion she bestowed upon him. I pray she isn't so gracious to all her clients."

"For you to pray, she must be a gentle soul." Darius smirked.

"She has compassion, yet I believe with the proper clients calling upon her, the vicious part of her will emerge. Lilith threatened her, her human sister fought with her, and another student taunted her. The student ended up with a broken nose and almost had a broken elbow. The girl has to go through four to six months of rehabilitation for her arm. Students who witnessed the event said Reika was uncharacteristically cruel. There is hope she will show no mercy to those who do not deserve it."

Darius smirked. "I think Father Samael need not worry of his precious daughter. His blood courses through those veins. She will be fair and just when it is needed, but will be cruel and ruthless as the situation commands it."

"What is it you are sensing, Darius?"

"The one named Lilin possesses great strength within, and hardly does she realize what she holds." A throaty, dark laugh resonated through Darius' body. "If Lilith were intelligent, she would not waste her time making threats towards her. Lilith will never be able to fulfill them."

"Reika barely knows how to use her powers." Samael sighed. "How can she use the power she has, if she doesn't understand it?"

"Look to nature." Darius said, spanning his arms out before him. "Many female animals in the kingdom are fierce protectors. Moose, bears, or hyenas. If you put any of these females in a situation where they protect their young, they become unimaginably strong. What threat did this unfortunate woman deliver to Reika?"

"If Reika were to even take me from Lilith, she will take Sebastian." Samael sighed. "This is absolutely ridiculous."

Darius laughed. "She indeed is an idiot. Lilith and Reika are cut from the same cloth. If only Lilith were to look in the mirror, and see the ferocity within herself when it comes to you, Samael, would she then understand her daughter. Yet, there is a difference between the two of them, the difference is your blood. Whilst Lilith has to consume your blood for it to be within her, Reika already possesses it. You said she broke the girl's nose and almost broke her arm?"

"From student accounts of the fight, Reika took the girl down, had her arm bent against her leg, and taunted her with the things she could do. The girl begged, she let go of her arm, and punched her in the face, breaking her nose."

"The slow torment is much like your style." Darius smirked. "The quick strike is quite a Lilith thing to do. She has both traits within her. I don't think Lilith realizes by making threats towards Reika, she is inevitably lighting a match in a room full of explosives."

"That is certainly a bright way of explaining it." Samael laughed. "I guess no one taught her, if you are willing to play with fire, you must first be willing to get burned." He paused, cocking his head to the side. He looked to Darius.

"You heard the boy's call." Darius answered, without needing Samael to ask the question. "It seems Reika has developed a fever."

"Will you come with me?" Samael asked.

"I will." Samael disappeared, Darius followed.

Reika laid in her bed, her face flush, sweat rolling down her cheeks. Sebastian sat next to her, trying to tame the fever with a cold, wet clothe against her forehead. He looked terrified for her. When Sebastian heard the two enter the room, he looked up.

"Good, Samael, you're here." Sebastian stood up quickly. "I fell asleep for a little bit, when I woke up and went to check on her, she had a horrible fever. It hasn't gone down at all. I don't know what would've caused it."

"She needs to feed." Darius said softly. "One soul in roughly two months isn't enough for her." Darius' eyes met Samael's. "She is undoubtedly fiercely powerful."

"She needs a soul?" Sebastian asked.

Samael nodded. "She does. I suppose I need to round up a couple humans and bring them here." He sighed.

"What about mine?" Sebastian said. "I'm already here, She can take mine."

"Are you sure you fully understand what it all entails, Sebastian?" Samael stared at him, his face grim and cold. "It means never ceasing to exist, unless someone kills you in a rather gruesome manner. It means leaving everything that humanity has taught you behind. You will never see the friends or family you have cultivated in this life ever again. You will become a destroyer, a thief, a low life. You will become what humans fear and idolize most. The life of a demon is akin to eternal night.

"If you choose this, there is no turning back. You can never reclaim the human life you had before. You must prepare yourself for that. I want you to understand what this all entails. You will have to drink blood, ensnare souls of the living who will give them up to you for their wildest dreams to be fulfilled. Are you certain this is the life you want to live?"

"I haven't stopped thinking about it since you offered it to me. I'm ready." Sebastian nodded. His eyes were filled with determination, and adoration.

"I only made you the offer yesterday." Samael chided. "I know, however, there is nothing I can say to stop a man determined to help the one he loves." He strode over, and stood in front of Sebastian. He placed a hand on his shoulder, Sebastian stood up and looked him in the eyes. Samael took his face in both of his hands and looked deep into his eyes. "Are you absolutely certain you want this?"

The resolve never faded from Sebastian's eyes as he nodded. "I'm sure. I would do anything to save her."

Samael smiled softly. "I believe you." He patted Sebastian's shoulders once more, and went to Reika's side. He gently placed a hand to her face. "Reika, it's time to wake up." He said softly.

Her eyes fluttered open for a moment. "Papa, I'm..."

"I know you are. I've brought a client to you. He wishes to be one of us, are you able to fulfill this wish for him?"

"Yes, I can." She whispered, closing her eyes. "Bring him to me." Sebastian walked forward and knelt down beside the bed. Samael took his hand, and put it in Reika's, she slowly brought his wrist to her mouth. Her eyes still closed, she bit into his wrist. The familiar warmth of blood washed over her tongue. Using what strength she could, she set her thoughts to stripping the soul from the man before her. She could feel the strength coursing through her, all the emotions attached became a part of her. The flow of emotions told a story, one of anguish, depression, and finally, a resolution in love.

The taste of the love within the soul she savored was sweet, like pure honey poured into her mouth. She brought her other hand up, entwining her fingers with the fingers of man she fed from. Reika felt an abrupt end to the story his blood told, she knew the soul was her's now. She began the process of giving him his wish. Reika willed him to become a demon, yet she wished for him to retain the sweetness that was so unique to his soul. A drude, they possessed more magical powers than most, and were, at least to Reika, delightfully mischievous.

Just as Reika fed on blood to survive, the drude would as well. She pulled away slightly, knowing her work was done, she licked the wound, and kissed it gently. She opened her eyes and, tears immediately began pouring from her eyes. "Sebastian. Oh my god, no." She whispered. "What have I done?"

Sebastian's smile faded to a face of sheer disappointment. "I wanted this, and wanted you to be the one to have my soul. You needed it, Reika, you were so sick. I just wanted to help you. I thought you would be happy." He voice started strong, but cracked and turned to a whisper with tears streaming down his cheeks. "I'm sorry. I just wanted to save you, like you've done so many times for me."

Reika stared at Sebastian's face in disbelief. "I'm not worth it." She whispered. "I'm nothing but a monster, and I've turned you into one too. How could I?" She turned to her side and curled up, sobbing. Sebastian turned away with his head drooped in defeat. He slowly made his exit from the room.

"What have I done?" She whispered over and over, through her sobs. "I'm a monster."

"I brokered the deal." Samael said softly. "He was ready."

"It doesn't matter if he was ready! I wasn't ready to do that to him!" She hissed. "He was pure and perfect! And I destroyed that! Is that what I'm destined to do?! Destroy everything I touch?! Everything I love?!" She yelled, ripping the covers back, and bolting from the bed. "I don't want to hurt the ones I love. I want to protect them. What's going to happen now, if Lilith gets a hold of him?! He's going to be killed, and he won't even be an afterthought to this fucking world!"

The door opened slowly. "You're wrong." Sebastian said through his own tears. "I wouldn't be an afterthought. I'd live on inside of you. You would think of me every day if that happened. You wouldn't let me die, not permanently at least." He wiped his eyes. "I've seen you fight, Reika. You're determined to protect what is yours, and I know you wouldn't let me slip away. I trust you, and I love you. You just have to trust yourself. I knew what I was getting myself into, and I'm happy with this decision."

Reika slowly walked towards Sebastian. "Bas, I love you too, please believe that. I just didn't want you to be ruined by this. You're such a wonderful person, I'm just scared this will change you."

"If it does change me, it will only be for the better." Sebastian whispered, taking her hands. "The hell I've been through can't compare to this. In fact, this feels like heaven to me."

A sob escaped Reika's lips, as she slipped to her knees. "I never knew... but I can feel it." She looked up to him, with red tear marks over her face. "Why didn't you say anything?"

He knelt down in front of her. "I didn't want you to worry." He gave her a smile, but his eyes were consumed with painful memories. "I was scared to tell anyone."

Darius looked to Samael, and Samael nodded. They slipped quietly out the door to give the two privacy.

"You don't have to tell me now." Reika said, her voice hoarse. She put her head in her hands. "I should have known. The signs were there."

"Reika." Sebastian said, his voice just as soft. "You should know now, that you gave me a strength that I never had before. Not only were you someone who loved me, you were mentoring me in an art, you gave me comfort without even realizing it. You're no monster, you're an angel."

"I don't feel like an angel."

"It doesn't matter if you feel like one or not, Reika. You are one, at least to me. You're the daughter of an angel, it's good enough for me to call you one." Sebastian touched her cheek. "Please don't be upset, I'm sorry, but I'm glad too." He pulled her into his arms and held her close.

"It's okay, Bas." She whispered against his chest. "Just keep yourself safe, please. I don't want to lose you. I don't know what Lilith is capable of, and if you were to die, I'd be lost."

"Reika." Sebastian said softly. "Enough of these scenarios because there is only one thing that will happen. We're going to survive whatever comes our way. I know it's terrifying, but you have to believe. You and I, we're not going anywhere but up. We'll see this through to it's end."

She squeezed him tight. "I believe you."

"It's not enough to just believe in me, believe in yourself." He whispered. "I need you to believe you can do this."

"But I'm scared." Reika balled her fists in the clothe of Sebastian's shirt. Her body was trembling. "I know I can do it, I'm just scared."

"What are you so afraid of?"

"Losing myself in the process."

"We are ever evolving, Reika." Sebastian pulled back, and looked into her eyes. "We are tested and tried, but it shouldn't change who we are deep inside. We remain the same at our core, it's our outer appearance to the world that changes."

She nodded some. "You're right." A small smile crept across her lips. "You're absolutely right."

Sebastian offered her a hand, and they stood together. He again pulled Reika into his arms and embraced her. "I know you worry about everything, dear. Please, let me do it for you, for when you are weak, and burdened with too much for your own heart to carry, let me be the one to help you shoulder it. Together, nothing is too heavy for us to handle."

Reika held onto his arms, and looked into his eyes. "How did I manage to find you? I'm grateful for the day you walked into my life."

"I'm doing my best not to sound horribly creepy right now." Sebastian muttered. His face turned bright red. "I had a crush on you long before you even knew my name."

"Why didn't you say anything?!" Reika laughed.

"I was scared you would kick my ass!" He shook his head. "I walked around town, and I'd see guys picking on you, I always wanted to say something but I just couldn't. I was so weak back then. Though I never had to. You always laid them out before I could even build the courage to move my feet."

Reika gently smacked him on the shoulder. "It would have been nice to have back up! Sometimes I was fighting three or four guys at once!"

"You amazed me every time you fought. For the longest time I had only seen your back in these fights. I hadn't even seen your face until the day you walked into the record store. You had be mesmerized before I had seen your face, but when I gazed upon you, all of you." He scooped her face up in his hands. "I knew I couldn't live without you."

"How could you fall for someone you've never seen completely before?" She asked.

"How could I not?" He smiled. "You're fierce, and wild. Nothing can tame you, and I wouldn't want you any other way."

She smiled, looking down as tears came to her eyes. "You're amazing, Sebastian."

His hand gently caressed her face. Sebastian caught her chin and tipped her head back up, and laid his lips upon hers. "I would be none of this without the help you gave me. You didn't even realize you were giving me the courage to live by just being yourself. You gave me the means to save myself." He whispered, the words resonating over Reika's lips.

Her eyes fluttered open, and were greeted by Sebastian's. She watched in awe as his eyes began to swirl, the vibrant green began to stir with a liquid silver. She felt a sadness engulf her as she watched, afraid to lose the beauty of his green irises, but they stopped swirling, leaving his eyes a wispy, marbled silver and green.

A smile spread across her mouth, and she reached up, touching his brow line. "You should see how remarkable your eyes look right now." She bit her lower lip. "How lucky I am to have such a handsome man before me."

"You just had to be yourself." He leaned forward, capturing her lips once more. "There was no luck needed." He whispered.

"Bas." She whispered back. "What are you thinking?" She intertwined her fingers in his silky long black hair.

"I'm thinking of a few things. I don't know which one you'd rather hear." Sebastian's voice was rough, yet sultry.

"Surprise me." She whispered, nibbling on his lower lip.

Sebastian groaned, pulling away, his lip slipping through her closed teeth. He could feel her fang nicking the inside of his lip. He pulled her close to him, wrapping one arm around her waist. He brought a finger to his lip, touched it gently, and looked at the blood coating the tip of his finger. "I want to taste you again." He said softly.

Reika smirked, she took his hand and brought his finger to her lips. She licked it clean of his blood and led his hand to rest on her collarbone. "Take what you wish of me."

Slowly, his hand ran up her neck, caressing her skin gently. "I couldn't be happier to oblige." He whispered his voice husky in her ear. He leaned in, and laid his lips upon her supple skin. He sucked and nibbled, kissing his way around her neck. Reika ran her fingers through his hair once more, holding the strands tight. She sighed out heavily, relishing the sensation of Sebastian's lips exploring her neck. A gasp resonated through the room as he plunged his new fangs into her milky white skin.

"Have your way with me." She whimpered out, cradling his head to her neck.

"Oh, I intend to." He said, coming up for a gasp of air before returning to her exposed throat.

Chapter Eleven

'What is this insatiable feeling deep inside me? What do I need to fulfill it?'

'My lady Lilin, I fear my pages will boast a fiery red tint if I tell you what it is you need.'

'Why is this happening?'

'It is simply your nature. You see, you are born of a Succubus, and of an Archangel. One would expect nothing less from a young woman of your parentage. Enjoy yourself, yet remember the promises you have made to Sariel.'

'Sariel?'

'Excuse me, Lady Lilin. Sariel is Sebastian. Your union in blood has made him son of Samael.'

Reika's stomach churned at the reminder of her consumption of Sebastian's soul. Still battling the disgust of her actions and her elation to have Sebastian for an eternity, she closed the book. Her eyes met those mystical silvery green pools.

"I need to go on a mission." She said softly. "I wish to go alone."

"Would Samael be alright with you going alone?" Sebastian asked.

"I don't think he'll mind. I'm also going to visit our friend, Luna." She blushed slightly. "I have much to discuss with her."

"Oh, do you now?" Sebastian smirked.

"She's a fashion designer, Bas!" Reika laughed some. "I promise, I'll be back soon." She leaned over her chair at the table in the lush library of their new home. The room was decadent, deep mahogany bookshelves covered each wall, filled to the brim with old leather bound volumes. On the wall, in the center of the room, was an arch shaped stained glass window of a dark angel, underneath was a cushioned seat.

Sebastian took her hand and squeezed gently. "You be careful." He stood and kissed her lips gently, followed by a peck on her forehead. "I love you."

"I love you too." She smiled brightly at him. She squeezed his hand back, slipped her hand from his, gathered her book and returned to her room. She laid the book on her bed, and went to he dresser, and pulled out a pair of black skinny jeans with eyelets and leather lacing up the sides, a deep red corset and a white button down shirt for underneath. She changed quickly and slipped on her favorite pair of boots.

Standing in the center of her room, she turned her thoughts to those who wished to give their souls away. It was the first time she had gone to broker deals on her own. She had taken the Priest's soul, and Sebastian's soul. She had gone on many missions with Samael, yet she hadn't taken any souls. Reika felt ready, and she had just located a soul. As she was about to leave, there was a knock at the door and it opened.

"My Dear, I wanted to speak to you." She heard Samael's voice.

Reika turned and smiled at him. "What is it Papa?"

"Are you about to leave?" He asked. "Sorry to keep you, I was curious to see if you would like to go on a collections mission with me."

She nodded. "I'd love to."

Samael held his hand out to her and she took hold of it. "I overheard you speaking with Sebastian. I'm sorry to have intruded, but I am glad I did. I'm not quite sure you're ready to venture on your own for these missions."

"Will I still be able to go see Luna?" She asked.

"What is it you need?" Samael asked. "We may go see her."

"I was meaning to speak with you about it today, and also have you speak with Sebastian." Her cheekbones flushed a soft red. "It seems silly considering our situation, how we're immortal. Sebastian wanted to speak to you about it first, but I can't get around my reasoning for seeing Luna without telling you what he wished to tell you himself."

"Sebastian is in his room, correct?" Samael asked. "Then I shall speak with him myself so we can honor his wishes. I shall return shortly." He kissed her forehead and went towards the door.

"The last time I spoke with him he was in the library. Though it's possible he's in his room now."

"I'll check the library if he isn't in his room." Samael smiled and left the room. He crossed the hall and gave a soft knock on Sebastian's door.

"Yeah?" Sebastian called from inside.

"It is Samael."

"Come in."

Samael opened the door, and entered. He saw Sebastian sitting in one of the leather chairs in his room. "I just spoke with Reika, and she mentioned you wished to speak with me."

"Oh, yes. I did want to talk to you, I just didn't know it was going to be this soon." Sebastian said, becoming visibly nervous.

"Do not worry so much, Sebastian. I promise you I am not a person easier angered." Samael took the seat next to Sebastian. "Speak freely with me."

"I know it sounds silly, considering we already have eternity together, and that marriage is very much a human thing. I want to ask Reika to marry me, and I wanted to ask your permission."

"She seemed to know already, yet you haven't asked her?"

"I told her I wanted to, but I needed your permission first." Sebastian looked up with a soft smile. "I also told her if I were to get permission, she'd not know when I'd ask her."

"Marriage is indeed a human affair, though I've known many who do marry. The ceremony is much different than any the humans hold." Samael smiled. "You're already halfway through the ceremony now. I approve this with all of my being, Sebastian. Your asking proves I am correct about your character. I only have one condition, I would prefer if you took Reika's surname."

"I am perfectly fine with it." Sebastian nodded. "I'd rather not carry my Father's name any longer than I have to. Samael, thank you."

"No, Sebastian. Thank you." Samael patted him on the shoulder. "I'll explain more of the ceremony to you later on. For now, I have business to attend to. I will have something for you when I return."

He nodded. "I'll be here."

Samael smiled and left the room. He returned to Reika's room. As he entered, he saw her sitting on the side of her bed, with her hands folded together, looking at the floor.

"Is everything alright?" She asked.

He came and sat down next to her, placing an arm around her shoulder. "Everything is splendid. Some day soon, you shall have a surprise greet you."

Reika's face beamed in delight. "So, everything did go well."

He nodded and kissed her on the forehead. "It did, we can still go see Luna if you wish. She is very nimble-fingered with her work, so there isn't any need to rush these things."

"I understand that, I just want a dress for the night he actually does ask." She laughed some, her face blushing deeply.

"It's quite alright." He smiled. "Shall we begin our adventure? I wish to see you in your natural state, your first real mission. You have seen how I operate my deals, now I wish to see how you handle this."

Reika nodded some, her eyes determined. "It was part of my plan today. I wanted to collect souls and then speak with Luna."

Samael smiled some. "I'm proud of the initiative, but also worried over it. I fear you're not skilled enough to do this without guidance. I could very well be wrong, however, I much prefer you in my watchful eye."

"I'm sorry." She muttered.

"Never be sorry for acting upon your instincts to hunt. Come to me next time, and we will stalk the night together."

She nodded. "Next time I will make sure to find you."

"Perfect." He smiled. "Let us get on with the show." Samael stood and offered her a hand. She took it and stood with him. They stepped away from her bed and Reika closed her eyes. She felt the familiar pull into darkness. Once she felt the comfort of solid ground her her feet, she opened her eyes once more.

"Welcome to New York City." Samael said.

The sounds of the bustling metropolitan area hit Reika's ears like a wave from a tsunami. Eyes upturned, Reika gasped at the overwhelming phenomenon of feeling so small. The stars were hardly visible in the segments of the night sky she was able to see past the monstrous buildings surrounding her. She looked back to

Samael, trying to digest the dizzying feeling that consumed her. "How do people enjoy living in a place like this?"

"A special sort of soul can only inhabit these lands. I've found most are unhappy with themselves, and need to surround themselves with others who make them feel superior. Those who lack the feeling of superiority tend to call our names in the starless night. They rally us into the darkened alleys, and filth of the abandoned subway tunnels to wish for what they envy most. We gift them with what they seek, oh yes, however we receive the steepest payment. What idiots we have lurking within these dark corridors."

"We've encountered many wicked beings, yet there's only been two who gave their souls so willingly for someone else." Reika sighed. "Is this world really so far from the light, that they are willing to sacrifice eternal life for something so petty?"

"I believe you already know the answer, my dear." He nodded gently. "In recent times, especially with advances society has made, the preservation of the community lost out to the preservation of oneself. Think very hard about this, when was the last time you've seen a neighbor do something kind for another just to do so, without wanting something for himself?"

"I don't think I've ever seen it." She sighed. "I've seen people steal before they even ask for help, but never anyone offering to help those in need."

"Think now to your personal experience. Were others more interested in laughing at you, rather than understanding you, and attempting to help you through times of loss."

"They laughed at me, always."

"Compassion is lost on humanity. Everyone believes they are correct, or they are owed something. This is the most incorrect mindset to live with. There isn't much I can do, or say, because it makes my belly full, and my strength plentiful."

Reika shook her head, and shivered some. "You're absolutely right."

"Are you chilled?" He asked. "Would you like my jacket?"

"Oh, I'm alright." She said, crossing her arms.

Samael took off his jacket, and draped it around her shoulders. "I'm certain you need it more than I."

"Thank you."

"Now, we have much ground to cover. The streets are crowded, we will travel by the back streets to our final destination. Stay close, regardless of the fact we cannot die, I would much rather not spill any unnecessary blood tonight. If the opportunity presents itself, I will seize it."

Reika took hold of Samael's arm and they began their descent through the alleyways of New York City. The sounds of the city still assaulted her senses. Though they moved away from the chorus of car horns, and bustling pedestrians, the crescendo of scuttling vermin and howls of stray dogs greeted her.

"Where are we going?" She asked quietly.

"We are headed to a construction site where three people have summoned us." Samael said softly. "Don't be afraid, Reika, your victims will sense it."

She nodded once and took a deep breath. "Alright." She walked with new conviction through the polluted back streets of the city. They walked through a seemingly endless maze of brick walls. Finally, they turned onto the street, and before them loomed an unfinished tower. Samael and Reika crossed the street nimbly, avoiding the endless oncoming traffic. They silently slipped into the building and in the distance, Reika heard the chanting of two males and one female.

"With the blood we offer, we ask you to join us tonight. The price we pay, steep, our requests slight. Samael, Lilin, we call upon you with these words. Grace us with your presence, let our wishes be heard."

Over and over, they heard the words echo through the empty space. Reika stopped, and listened. Samael continued forward, the sound of his slow footsteps were in time with their chants. He began clapping. "Thank you for such an enchanting introduction. Shall we begin? What is it you wish for?" Reika made her way to Samael's side. Her eyes were met by three filthy and decrepit figures.

"Thank you for coming here." The woman said softly. "Thank you so much."

Reika rolled her eyes. "Save your appreciation for someone who actually cares. I'm only doing this for myself, not you."

"We've lost everything." One of the boys said. "Our house burnt down, our whole family is dead. All we have is each other now, but we can't survive on each other."

"I am certain there are," Samael paused for a moment, thinking, "ways for you to do so, but I am also certain of the fact you may not want to hear them." He smirked. "Pardon me, continue with your tragedy."

"We've been on the street for three years." The same boy continued. "I want 50 million dollars in a bank account with my name on it in exchange for my soul."

"Are you certain your soul is worth so much?" Reika asked.

"I know my siblings' well being is worth that much."

"So be it." Reika nodded sharply. "You will receive your desire. What about you?" She pointed to the second boy. "What do you want?"

"I want a three bedroom apartment for us." He said softly. The boy's empty gaze never left the floor. "Somewhere we can live comfortably."

"Young lady, what is your desire?" Samael asked.

"I want to be famous." She said, resoluteness shone on her soiled face. "To make enough money so my family will never have to deal with anything this terrible without monetary support again."

"Shall I take the boys, or the girl?" Samael asked Reika.

She looked up to him, a devious smirk formed over her face. *'Let me take the girl and the boy who wishes for riches he is not worth.'*

'You may have both. I shall continue business when you visit with Luna.'

Reika pointed towards the girl. "You, come with me, and boy, if wish for bank account, you best follow as well." She turned and strode to a secluded area. She sat down on a large unopened paint bucket. She watched the two shuffle towards her. She smirked some. "Who wishes to go first?"

The girl stepped forward. "I'll go first."

"What is your name?"

"Jessica."

"Kneel down, Jessica." Reika watched carefully to the girl's every move. "Give me your hand." She held her open hand out to Jessica, and hesitantly, she placed her's in Reika's. "You wish for fame, yes?"

"I do." Jessica nodded.

"What do you want to be famous for?"

"I want to act." She said softly. "I've tried for years, but have only gotten a few small roles."

"It will be done." Reika nodded. "First, I get my payment. Are you completely sure you are ready?"

"Yes." Jessica nodded.

Reika pulled her hand towards her mouth, and bit down hard into the girl's skin. She heard her whimper. A rich, throaty laugh vibrated through Reika's being. She wrenched her soul from her blood. The process was slow, and difficult, as if the girl was fighting her every step of the way.

'Papa, what is this? Why is it so difficult. Sebastian was simple, as was the priest, I've barely gotten hold of her soul.'

'She is hesitant. There is no turning back now, not once the blood is spilled, and the verbal affirmation has been made. Continue as you were, and it will be alright.'

She turned her thoughts back to the girl. Before, Reika was soft and kind in her stripping of this girl's soul. Now she knew she had to be forceful. Reika felt a mental tug, as she pulled harder and harder. The girl's muscles tensed, and finally she felt the soul break free. Opening her eyes, she could see the shock on the girl's face, and quickly she gave the girl her wish. She let go, and wiped her lower lip with her thumb.

Reika watched her face carefully. Within seconds, the shock diminished, and the unfinished building was filled with a blood curdling scream. The girl clutched her chest as she sank farther into the floor. Reika felt the corner of her mouth pull up slightly, though her eyes never lost the cold stare that bore through the girl before her. She felt no sympathy at the cries echoing from the girl's throat. Standing from her seat upon the paint bucket. She strode over to the boy who stood behind the girl sobbing on the floor, his feet frozen in place.

"Are you ready, boy?" She asked. "You wanted riches, in your name in a bank account. Are you positive this is what you want?" She cocked her head to the side. "I don't want to have to wrestle with you as well."

He swallowed hard. "I... I'm ready."

"Come forward."

The boy stepped forward with clumsy footfalls. He held his hand out for Reika. She grabbed hold of his hand, and twisted him around. His back to her, she wrapped an arm around his waist and held him tight to her body. Her other hand grabbed hold of his hair, and tilted his head back. "Are you ready to become a millionaire?"

"Yes." His voice barely came out.

"What is your name, millionaire?"

"Aaron."

"Enjoy your new life, Aaron." Reika smirked, and bit into his neck. She began the same process as before, uprooting the soul from the body. The boy held in Reika's arms squirmed, yet she wrapped her arm around him tighter. His soul lifted much easier than the girl's was. Reika made his wish so and let go of him. Without a sound the boy dropped to the floor, and Reika walked towards the door. Samael was waiting for her, she took his arm and exited the building.

# # #

The chime of the shop bells rang as Reika walked into Luna's boutique. She looked around at the beautifully dressed mannequins in awe, just as she had done the first time she visited. She looked to the door that lead to Luna's office and saw her lavender topped head peak out through the door frame.

"Reika!" She yelled and came out from the back. "It's so good to see you!" She grinned. "What brings you in?"

"There's quite a bit going on right now." She laughed. "My boyfriend is working on some big engagement party sort of thing, and I wanted something amazing to wear. I don't know when it will happen though. I really loved the dress you made me for the ball so I figured I'd ask you to make something else for me. Which also means, I'm going to need a wedding dress of sorts."

"Oh!" She clapped her hands together once, lacing her fingers. "An engagement and a wedding dress?! That's so exciting! Do you want traditional, or something far from it?"

Reika smirked and tilted her head. "My dear, do I seem like a traditional bride?" She winked.

"Abstract it is!" She laughed, and went to her desk. "Would you like something to drink? I've got plenty of options. I also have pizza."

Reika laughed. "You always have pizza!"

"It's an addiction." She grinned. "Would you like anything, I'll grab it and then we can get to work."

"Something to drink would be nice. I'm not picky. I came here after I did some brokering."

"Ah, I know exactly what you need!" She went to the back, and brought back a mug. "Hot chocolate with a kick!" She winked.

"Holy shit!" Reika exclaimed. "This is amazing!"

Luna winked. "It's a secret recipe. I'd love to tell you, but I can't. You'll just have to enjoy it here. Luckily we live forever, so you can come have it anytime you want!" She laughed softly.

"I'll be here quite a bit again. I might as well become a live mannequin here!"

"That would be so cool!" Luna clapped her hands together, the metal of her many rings made a click. Reika smiled. "I have a couple designs I've drawn up that you might like for an engagement dress. Take a look." She handed Reika a few sheets of sketch paper. Reika looked at each sketch carefully. Her favorite was a red, black and white handkerchief hemmed dress. The skirt was puffy, like a tutu, yet it was still dark enough to suit Reika's taste.

"This one!" She held the paper up. "This is perfect!"

"I knew you'd like that one." She grinned. "I drew that one up after I finished your dress for the ball. I enjoy having you around, kid. You bring out a bunch of ideas in me."

"I'm glad I can be of assistance!" She winked. "Really, though, these are all great ideas. It's just that last one was my favorite."

"Consider it yours! I'll be working on some ideas for your unconventional wedding dress soon. Goodness, I am so excited for you! I can't wait to meet this boy of yours! He better be good to you!" She gave Reika a stern look. "Is he?"

"He's absolutely wonderful to me." She smiled softly. "He gave up everything for me. Absolutely everything, and I never asked him to do such a thing. I'm sure he had many other reasons aside from me to give his soul up for eternity to me, but if that isn't pure love, I don't know what is."

"When did this happen?!" Luna asked, enthralled. "How did it happen?!"

"I don't know how it happened. Papa said I came down with a fever, and I needed to consume or I'd die." She sighed. "I'm so young, it's possible for me to die from starvation. Sebastian was the closest human, and he wanted to become one of us. He told Papa he was ready, and he accepted his contract on my behalf. I took his soul in the feverish state. I could feel every emotion attached to his soul, unlike any I've ever consumed before. It was beautiful, and heartbreaking. To feel everything he has felt was incredible. All the pain from his past was gut-wrenching, and the love, especially for me, was so intense. I didn't know someone could love me as much as I loved them."

"It's very possible for such a thing to happen. You're fortunate, indeed to find the one for you so early on in life. Not many are able to find their mate so quickly. You must have had him mesmerized in an instant."

Reika blushed. "It was hilarious when I first met him."

"Oh, do tell!" Luna said, and took a bite of her pizza.

"I was going to get an album from the little record store in my hometown. I was really good friends with the owner, so he would special order me anything I wanted. I was at the register, paying for my order, then in walked this green eyed boy, with his black hair all messy, dressed in black and green. I turned to look at him, and his jaw dropped. I got really nervous, he was really fucking cute. So, instead of talking to him, I hurried out of the store.

"The next week I had another order come in, and I went to pick it up. Again, he walked into the building, those big green eyes staring me down. I was annoyed, because I wanted him to actually talk to me! So, I turned and told him if he wanted to stare at me, to take a fucking picture."

"What did he do?" Luna asked.

"He actually took a picture!" Reika laughed. "So I went to grab his phone away from him, to delete the picture, but he sent it to his best friend. He sent a text with it saying 'This is the most beautiful girl I've ever seen.' So, instead of deleting the photo, I put my phone number in, and told him to text me sometime. I hadn't even gotten a block away from the store, and I received a message from him. From that day forward, we've been inseparable."

"That is so cute, Reika!" Luna gushed. "It's too bad he doesn't have a brother. Can you show me a picture of him?"

Reika pulled her phone from her pocket and found a picture of the two of them together. She handed her phone to Luna. "This is us before everything changed. His eyes still have that beautiful emerald hue in them, but it's mixed with the silver we have. It's so haunting, and gorgeous." She sighed. "I'm so lucky to have such a wonderful man."

"You have two wonderful men in your life. You are indeed a lucky woman, Reika."

"Papa is amazing, you're right to include him." She smiled. "To answer your earlier question, he doesn't have any siblings, sadly."

"Well isn't that a shame! Does he have any friends?" She winked.

"He used to." Reika sighed. "My sister is dating his friend. He's kind of lame though, very plain."

Luna wrinkled her nose in distaste. "Well then, I guess I'll keep on my search on my own."

"Sorry I couldn't help. Have you ever met any of Papa's friends?"

"I don't think I have." She shook her head.

"I only saw a glimpse of one of his friends. He might be someone to look into."

"Maybe." She smiled. "I'll have to ask him one day."

"Hopefully you find someone!" Reika smiled.

"I hope so too. Until then, I can keep myself content with human musicians." She giggled. "Oh, how gorgeous they are!"

"It might just be the photo editing." Reika shrugged.

"Maybe, maybe not." She shrugged. "Some are super gorgeous in person, others, not so much."

Reika shook her head and laughed. "I wish I could stay longer, but I have to meet back up with Papa to discuss some more business. I think I'm going to have to take Sebastian for his first hunt soon."

"That should be fun! I'll give you a call when I have something ready for you! Reika, congratulations, love. I'm really excited for you! I better be invited to the wedding!"

"Oh, Luna, you'll be invited to the wedding, the engagement party and anything else festive in between!"

"Rest assured, I'm going to be planning you a bachelorette party!" She winked and tossed her hands up in the air, confetti appearing.

"Oh my, Luna. I'm going to be in big trouble."

She cackled. "You haven't any idea! Go on, though! Don't keep your father waiting too long!"

Reika smiled. "Alright, alright! I'll see you later!"

"Bye dear!"

Reika stood, and walked to the door. She turned and gave Luna a wave as she exited the quaint little boutique. She walked down the street, and felt a presence behind her. She turned her head to look, yet didn't see anything. She walked faster, and tried her best to maintain her composure. The heavy wind whipped against her body, Samael's jacket only shielding her from a small portion of the chilly autumn wind.

"Dear child, why must you run from me? How do you not know my touch yet, regardless of which medium it comes to you in."

She heard Samael's voice call to her, but she still didn't see a single person on the street.

"Papa? Why don't you show yourself?"

"I needn't show myself, love. I'm here to protect you."

Reika frowned. The feeling engulfing her did not feel protective at all. It was thick with hatred and malice. "This doesn't feel like you, Papa. Show yourself." She said, turning in a circle.

A hand came out from thin air and gripped around Reika's throat, slamming her into the brick wall behind her. She grabbed hold of the hand, and tried to free herself, but struggled. Finally, the man appeared, his icy blue eyes were the only thing Reika could see. She struggled for breath.

"Watch your tracks more carefully, stupid child. It was unimaginably easy to track your whereabouts. It's saddening I was told not to hurt you too badly." He loosened his grip on Reika's throat.

"You bastard. What the fuck do you want with me?!" She hissed as she twisted his hand away from her throat and moved away from him. "Who sent you?"

"There are many things I want from you, none in which I will ever tell you aside from your death." He smirked, rubbing his wrist. "As for who sent me, it should be painfully obvious."

"Lilith." She said under her breath. "Who are you?"

"My name? I'm Adrian." He laughed. "I was with Lilith at the ball. Enough of the chatting, you'll see me again very soon."

As quickly as Adrian had appeared, he disappeared. Reika rubbed at her throat. She disappeared as well, going to the hallway leading to Samael's study. She put her hand on the door, but heard voices on the other side.

"How do you expect us to keep our son in a school where you house criminals and aid the insane?" She heard a man's voice ask. "Are you wanting our son to become one of them?"

Reika was shocked. She knew she had been gone for quite some time, she just didn't know she would arrive during a meeting between a students' parents and her Father.

"Sebastian is a very good student, and shows no sign of becoming what you speak of my students. In fact, none of my students are criminals, nor are they insane. What information you are speaking from is severely inaccurate."

"The girl he's dating, she's absolutely insane. Her mother is terrified, she took her daughter home without any notice to the school. She's still on the run. Maybe she's dead, I'm hoping so. My son doesn't need to be surrounded by people like that."

"Your home would be a better solution to the matter? Where he would receive no human interaction whatsoever? If you believe this to be better, I think you are gravely mistaken in your parenting."

"How dare you question my authority over my own child! You just said Sebastian was one of your better students, how could you make a contrasting statement?"

"Perhaps it's his lack of involvement of his parents that makes him such a wonderful student."

"You're out of line!"

"How is it so, that I am out of line, when I only have the interests of my students at heart, yet your only concern is of your son being away from a girl who isn't even around anymore. You seem to have faith in ghosts, Mr. Luciano."

"Ghosts?" She heard the man, and Sebastian both ask.

"Reika Avel was pronounced dead this morning. She was found in the river down the road from here. No foul play seemed to be a part of her death. She must have gotten tired of running and wished for a peaceful end."

"Dead?!" Sebastian cried out. "She can't be dead!"

"I wish I could have told you in a better way, Sebastian." Samael said softly. "If she is your concern, Mr. Luciano, rest assured she is not anymore."

"This changes nothing." Mr. Luciano said. "He is still coming home with us."

'Bas, I'm not dead. I'm right behind the door.'

'I didn't think so, but I have to pretend to be heartbroken.'

Reika tried to suppress a laugh at Sebastian's comment.

"Mr. Luciano, I think you're making a grave mistake to remove your son from one of the top schools in Ohio." Samael sighed. "There isn't anything I can say to stop this from happening, though, is there?"

"Not at all." Mr. Luciano said.

"I am sorry, Sebastian. I wish I could do something for you. Forgive me for failing you as your teacher."

"You're not at fault here." Sebastian said softly. "I wish I could change it as well."

"Too bad, boy." Mr. Luciano said. "You're coming home whether you like it or not."

She didn't hear another word from Sebastian. She sighed heavily, unsure of what was to happen after Sebastian was taken home.

"Just sign these papers, and he will be released from Locke Academy." Samael said sadly. She heard the frantic scribbles on the sheets of paper and the chair legs screeching across the floor.

"Come on Sebastian."

Reika heard the door open and the two left, slamming the door in their wake. She slid to her knees, the palm of her hand still pressed against the wooden door. She felt the shock wear from the attack on the street outside of Luna's boutique, and sadness washed over her with Sebastian's leaving. She knew he had no say in being withdrawn. Though he was 18, any student was still considered a minor by almost any official until a diploma has been received.

Trembling, Reika tried to stand and go back down the hall to her room, but the door opened before her.

"I knew you were there." Samael said softly. He knelt down and took Reika's hands. "I'm terribly sorry I couldn't do more for the boy. I hadn't created an end for the human Sebastian Luciano. His parents can do whatever they please legally. I cannot stop them, as much as I want to."

"I wish there were some way to fix it." She said with a wavering voice. Her throat still felt tight, where Adrian had choked her. "I wish there was an end to all of this insanity."

"I wish there were as well, yet there isn't one within reach. Soon enough, Reika, we will have one." He brushed her hair away from her face, laying it behind her shoulder. Samael gazed at her neck. "What happened to you while you were gone?" He said, his tone changed completely. Samael was calm, trying to comfort Reika until he saw a bruise on her neck in the perfect shape of a hand.

"Adrian attacked me." She said softly. "I didn't even see him coming. He tried to pretend to be you, and came out from a mist. I only saw his hand, and I tried to free myself. It took me a little bit to get free." She sighed. "He used your voice, but his aura was malicious. I knew it couldn't be you. I came back to tell you and Sebastian's Dad was already here. I was too late."

"You were right on time, Reika." He said gently. "You heard what happened, instead of having to be told what happened. We will retrieve Sebastian as soon as possible. As for Adrian, he will be handled accordingly. My Dear, we must keep you safe. I cannot let you travel alone anymore. I wish I could allow it, but I cannot let you slip into the hands of Adrian, or Lilith. It's much too dangerous."

"He said I wasn't hiding my trail very well. He said he tracked me very easily." She shuddered. "What do I do? I can't go anywhere if he can track me."

"I will have to teach you this." Samael sighed. "I apologize for not teaching you more about your abilities. We have an abundance of time, yet I've neglected this subject rather heavily. There is no better time than the current to tackle these transgressions. Do you have your volume in your room?"

"I do."

"Perfect." He smiled. "Retrieve it and meet me in the library." Samael gently touched Reika's cheek. "I will have something for you to heal the bruising on your throat once you arrive."

"Thank you, Papa." She said softly. Samael kissed her forehead, and helped her to her feet. "I'll see you in a few minutes." She turned, heading down the hallway to her bedroom. She entered, and went to her desk to grab her book, but was side tracked by the piece of parchment laid upon her pillow.

My Dearest Reika,

I wanted to write to you as you went on your journey tonight with your father. I wanted to tell you many things tonight, but our time was cut short. Most days, I am not so well with words that I can speak my mind to you. It's nothing to do with you, because you are a wondrous being who has captured me so completely I could never hide anything from you. I've never been verbally savvy, speeches were terrifying experiences in school.

All of this is beside the point. I wanted to tell you, regardless of your feelings on being a monster for what you have done to me, I can never view you as such. You indeed are the daughter of an angel, and you have inherited the title as well, even if I am the only person to call you such. You, in your very Reika way, have been a saving grace in my life. You may not think you have done much for me, but you have.

I've stopped quite a few bad habits because of the freedom you have made me feel. I feel no need to do horrible things to myself anymore. I don't feel I need to be intoxicated, or in pain. You have become a cure to my aches, and my new poison. If you are the death to me, it is because of my own doing. You have been the death to my human self, due to my prerogative. I couldn't be happier to lose my former self to you. I also cannot express my elation to be able to bind my new self to you, for eternity.

I hope you find a wonderful dress as you visit your friend. I am searching for the perfect ring to adorn the finger of such an angel. The search is tedious but it is only worth it because it is for you.

My father is coming to the campus tonight, and I fear the worst when he is involved. I suspect he will take me home, and if he does, I wanted to leave you this note. I will email you when I am home, and call you when I am alone. I'm rather worried over what will happen when I return to Callisto. I know regardless of what may come, mother will take care of me. If the worst happens, I know if I call your name, you will come. I can't see anything being this bad, but at least I know the option is available. I love you more than these words can convey, Reika. I know you know this, but I need to tell you just once more before I leave.

With abundant love,

Sebastian

Reika's hands trembled as she read the letter Sebastian left her. She felt hot tears slip down her cheek as she consumed the words. The lack of his presence was already leaving their home cold and empty. She laid the letter back down on her pillow, and wiped her eyes. She grabbed her book and left the room. She sniffed back her tears and regained composure before entering the library.

"Are you alright?" Samael asked.

"Sebastian left a letter on my bed before he left. It was really sweet. I'm just sad he's gone." She sighed. "I want to go to his house and get him back, but I know I can't."

"It would be too dangerous to do so. It would be a fatal blow, and all of our kind could be exposed. You cannot risk it."

"I understand. I won't do it, but I really want to."

Samael sighed. "I understand as well. He is missed already. Let us not dwell on something we cannot fix currently. Shall we begin our intensive lessons?"

Reika nodded. "Let's do it."

"We need to begin with shielding your aura, which might come easy to you. In this school, I have always noticed there is at least one student who tries their very best to disappear in the crowd of students. It is the same intention in your mind which is used to shield yourself as an immortal. You draw yourself inward, and no one will locate you."

Reika's lips twitched, causing a subtle smile. "Much like something else I have studied. Let me see if I can try this." She closed her eyes, focusing her mind on drawing everything inward. She opened her eyes and looked to Samael, maintaining her focus.

"Very good." He nodded. "There are times when you need to maintain this, and there are times you need to let your aura burst through, and fill as much space as possible. Battle is a time when you would need to use such a skill."

She nodded in understanding. "It is a very useful skill. If I had known it were so similar to what I have learned elsewhere, I would have been using it already." She smiled.

"It's quite alright, now you know." Samael smiled back. "Let us continue. It's very possible for you to possess the ability of shape shifting. I want you to start by concentrating on the color of your eyes. What color are they now?"

"They are silver." She said, feeling strange being asked a question with an obvious answer.

"What is your favorite color?" Samael asked.

"Red." She said simply.

He smiled. "It is mine as well. However, concentrate your thoughts on making your eyes show as your favorite color. Do not feel discouraged if you cannot."

Reika concentrated deeply on the idea of her eyes being a deep crimson color. She didn't feel any change happen in her body. She looked up from the floor, to Samael. "Is there any change at all?"

He shook his head. "There is not." Samael smiled softly. "Do not let this sadden you. I am glad to know you cannot change your appearance. You are much too beautiful to do so."

"I am glad I can't either. I think I would forget what I really look like after a while."

"Thus my relief you haven't inherited all of my abilities. We will attempt something else. Do you believe you have the ability to have premonitions?"

"Tell the future?" She asked. "I'm not really sure if I can. How can we even test this?"

"Divination is easily tested." Samael ushered Reika to a table, and pulled a chair out for her. She took her seat, and Samael took the one across from her. He waved his hands, and a crystal ball appeared, set upon a beautiful pewter stand in the shape of angel wings. "All you must do, is gaze into the orb, and tell me what you see, if you see anything."

Reika nodded some as Samael scooted the orb closer to her. She put her hands up, as if she were cupping the orb in her hands, like the warmth from a flame. She gazed, unsure of what would happen.

"Empty all thoughts from your mind, Reika, as if you were meditating." Samael said softly, and finally left her to gaze.

Reika stared blankly at the orb in front of her, the crystal remained silent with it's images. She was about to look away, when she saw something appear. She leaned closer, watching intently. In the orb, she saw herself laying in a bed made of birch, with soft white and yellow linens. Her face was pale, with only her cheeks red in a feverish haze. Reika hardly recognized the person laying in the bed as herself.

She watched from another realm as Samael entered the small room with a bowl and a clothe. He set the bowl on the table next to her bed and wrung the clothe out. He sat down on the edge of the bed and placed the clothe on her forehead. Reika watched as Samael stood, and turned away from her. She saw tears slipping down her father's face, a sight she had never seen.

The orb went clear as quickly as the vision had appeared. She looked up from her vacant crystal ball and to her father's face. He was smiling with pride.

"It seems you have the gift of foresight."

"I wish it were a happier vision." She said softly.

"What did you see?" He asked, his face immediately shifting to concern.

"I was laying in a bed in an unfamiliar room. I was sick, my eyes looked dark, sunken. I was pale, and had a fever. I looked horrible. You were there taking care of me."

"What did the room look like?"

"It was really bright. The furniture was made from birch, and the room had yellow accents."

"The cottage." Samael said softly. "I have a cottage in a remote location. Why would we travel there?"

"I wish I knew the answers, but I only know what I saw." She sighed.

"I will ponder upon this. For now, let us continue to see what we can find out about your abilities." Samael said. "A crystal ball is a wonderful tool for you. You may keep this one as your own. I wish to test for elemental manipulation." He waved his hand, and the crystal ball disappeared and in it's place was a glass of water, a lit candle, a potted plant, and a miniature windmill.

Reika looked at the four objects. "Water, fire, earth and air." She laughed a little at the windmill.

"There is a fifth element, which we consume. That is spirit." Samael explained. "You have the ability to control spirits in the manner of removing them from a willing being, or at least those who have consented. Once consent has been made, it is a binding contract and cannot be released from it, except on the rarest of occasions. I have a suspicion, if you are able to control any of these elements, it will be fire."

"Why do you say that?"

"My dear Reika, you indeed have a fiery personality. It would only be appropriate for you to be able to control such an element."

She laughed. "I think you're right."

"Please stand, we will test these quickly." Samael said. Reika stood, and Samael stood beside her. All the objects disappeared except the windmill. It moved across the table slowly, on it's own and stopped in front of Reika. "Place your hand in front of the windmill. Think of how you want this windmill's blades to spin by a gust of wind only you can produce."

Reika nodded softly and held her hand out as she was instructed. She thought of wanting to see the windmill spin. She took a deep breath, trying to keep her mind steady, yet it did not work. Reika sighed and stepped forward. She blew a hard breath at the windmill, making the blades spin only a small fraction of the full rotation. She smiled in satisfaction.

"Well, I don't believe you are a wind user." He laughed. "Maybe we should try water next." The windmill was replaced by the glass of water. "With this, extend your hand again, and bring your thoughts to making the water rise from the cup, and spill over."

Again, Reika took Samael's direction and extended her hand. She thought of having the water climb from the glass and spill over the edge. Yet again, she didn't find success in her attempts. She sighed. "I'm not a water manipulator either."

"This is not such a bad thing." Samael smiled. "Usually, those demons who hold the ability to control water are heavily ridiculed. Especially if they reside on land."

"Are you saying there are actually demons who live underwater?"

"They do exist, though I have never seen them. Anyone who is an air elemental would be able to travel and see such creatures, or those who own submarines or diving equipment. They only reveal themselves to others of their kind."

"How did it all start?" Reika asked.

"One woman had called upon me and wished to become a mermaid. To create such a mythological creature, I needed to make her immortal. Once, she had been spotted by a sailor. The sailor spoke to his friends of this great beauty he had spotted in the ocean. The word spread across the land like a tidal wave and I received many requests from others to become creatures of the sea. They created communities, and eventually became more visible on the sea. To keep their secret safe, the women of the community would band together, and lure these old gruff sailors in the rocks they would lounge on, and sink their ships. As they were drowning they all would consume their souls."

"If souls are to be taken from a consenting human, then how were they able to take them from the dying in such a way?"

"They waited until their absolute final moment, and as their soul was released, they took it as their own rather than let it travel to the portal to cross into the other side."

"Oh." Reika said. "That makes sense, but it's so crazy! Learning all of these things are real, is just absolutely insane."

"I will tell you many more stories about creatures in fairy tales that really exist." Samael smiled. "Just give it time, and they will continue to come forward. Now, let's try earth." The glass of water upon the table was replaced with a small potted ivy plant. "I want to see if you can make this plant grow larger."

"Same method as before?" She asked. Samael simply nodded. Reika closed her eyes, extended her hand and held her palm open, thinking hard about how she wanted the plant to grow.

"Intriguing." Samael whispered.

Reika opened her eyes and looked at pot before her. The plant before, was an ivy plant, but the one in the pot now was a small rose bush with a single black rose in full bloom. "How did I manage that?"

"It turned into what I believe is your symbol." Samael smiled. "You have a very narrow ability in earth manipulation. Which is to change a plant into what you wish it to be. It is quite a talent to have for landscaping, yet it is useless in a combat situation."

Reika laughed. "Of course I would have a power that is completely useless, but really interesting."

"I'm certain you will find good use for this one day." Samael took the plant and moved it to sit underneath the large stained glass window. He came back to the table and the candle made it's appearance. "Once more, we shall try these things. I wish to see if you can do anything with fire."

Reika nodded her head. She held her hand out once more. She focused her entire mind on making the flame grow larger. It didn't take much to feel the flame had grown from it's modest size to about two feet in the air. She opened her eyes, and watched the large flame dance in the air. She smiled and thought it would be neat to see the flames in the shape of a rose, and the flame began to arrange itself in the shape of one.

"Very impressive, my dear!" Samael exclaimed. "Indeed you are a fire wielder! I would expect nothing less from you. I too, hold the ability of fire manipulation."

Reika smiled. "I'm glad I have something useful in my arsenal, aside from some sort of super gardener ability."

Samael laughed. "You have many things which are considerably useful in your back pocket. Strength comes in a variety of shapes. There is a great possibility if you work diligently, you could hone your skill with the earth and use it for your arsenal. It is not impossible."

Reika nodded. "Perhaps. What else are we able to test?"

"We have already tested your ability to speak by telepathy. I do not believe you are able to read minds of others, or you would have said something already." Samael explained. "Be thankful you aren't a mind reader. It is terrible."

"Are you?" She asked.

"No, however I know a few who are and they lament the ability deeply." Samael shook his head. "I could not imagine how maddening it would be to hear everyone's thoughts who surround you. If human, I would sell my soul to get rid of the ability."

"My own thoughts alone are cause for insanity." Reika sighed. "I'm glad I don't have that either."

"Now, if you are given the gift of foresight, there are many books upon the shelves of this library that may be of use to you. The book I gave you can give you the list of books to read, if you so choose to perfect your skill."

Reika nodded. "I'm sure I'll have plenty of time to do that since Sebastian is gone." Her voice was soft. She sighed, walking over to the large stained glass windows, and gazed through a small pane of clear glass among the design. The moon hung low in the sky outside, Reika saw the bright light from the full moon shining through the trees beyond the windows. As many times before, she wondered if Sebastian was gazing at the moon at the very same moment she was.

"He'll return to us as soon as possible." Samael joined her by the window, and placed a comforting hand on her back.

"It's not the fact of him returning or not that concerns me." Reika said softly. "It's the condition he's returned in that has me so worried."

"Consequences have been established." Samael said, a smirk barely pulled the corners of his lips. "I assure you, if he is hurt, something will occur. Though the only foresight I possess is that of my own reactions to situations. A multitude of lifetimes will teach you your habits in a way you can only understand once you experience it." He laughed some. "Indeed, humans and like creatures are habitual."

Reika smiled. "Everyone is in their own way." She nodded. "I'm still developing my habits, I suppose."

"Choose wisely." Samael sat down on the padded bench beneath the stained glass. "For if you choose poorly, it could very well be the ending of your life, or someone you love. If you decide to have a child, make sure you limit yourselves. You do not want to experience the heartache of their demise at the hand of one much holier than us."

"Is there really a limit to how many children a demon can have?"

"In a sense, yes." Samael sighed. "If they cannot be controlled by the parent, and run rampant, slaughtering in their wake, intervention will be called. The end of such call is devastating, for both humans and our kind."

"What do you mean?" Reika asked. She didn't quite understand what Samael was trying to say.

"The angel Michael would be sent to slaughter the demon children if they cannot be controlled. Which, I had no issue doing such. Lilith seemed to have a different way with these children, reigning chaos on mankind with them. It was repulsive when we saw the aftermath of it all. I do not rejoice in the unnecessary deaths which the world produces. The world may see me as the worst evil which dwells, but they are mistaken. There is one that holds more darkness within than I. He, truly is the king of evil, where I am of death.

"There are two sects, Reika, of creatures who are considered evil. The demons which I reside over. We are the ones who seek out those who wish to rid themselves of their eternal gift, and give them what they wish. Our lifeblood is their lifeblood. We consume their souls, and their blood. Often, we are mistaken for vampires, though they are part of our family, they do not consume the souls of man, only what courses through their veins.

"Those who do not belong to our species are called satyrs. They are the ones classically depicted with the hooves, and horns." Samael explained. "They have evolved, and are able to cloak their features, as to walk among the humans. They are the ones tempting, and taunting them to do dastardly crimes. They too feed from souls, but they must only be evil. So, as a farmer would grow his crops for harvest, the satyr whispers these intentions in the ears of their victims, until time to cultivate the fruits of their work."

"Before, you said there were very few who were considered evil, or holy. Why is that?"

"Most humans in this age, are more consumed by materialistic items, than an old tome written about holy men. Very few make time to educate themselves on what will meet them at the very end of their days. Those who do, pass through the portal unscathed, and those who choose to listen to the satyrs, are those who reside in what humans consider hell. However, those who have died before they meet the end, are the ones who speak to us."

"How does someone die before they meet their end?"

"They simply give up." Samael explained. "They are the ones who decide they cannot achieve their dreams without help, the ones who have prayed for what they wish for, but never receive it. They do not receive such requests for many reasons. By the hands of the almighty, the wishes they pray upon cannot be granted. They are selfish wants, and defy the powers of those they ask these wishes of. The only ones who are able to grant these wishes are those who will receive payment for the services, which you already know about."

"The demon brokers." She said softly.

"Yes." Samael nodded slowly. "We have used many a name, but I do like the sound of broker much better than any other name. It is much more dignified."

"It does sound more professional. What other names were used?"

"Merchant has been used a few times." He explained. "Rogue, occultist, alchemist. There are many names, but they all mean the same thing."

"How did broker become the name of what we are?"

"By the clothing of choice all demons decide to wear on these missions." Samael smirked. "Most chose black suits, for they were much more distinguished than the other options."

"Other options?"

"Military uniforms, armor, colored suits." Samael sighed. "I was quite pleased when the black suit became a standard in every man's wardrobe. I was never a lover of wearing colorful garb, or none at all."

Reika's face blushed. "How long did you have to go without clothing?"

"It was a long time ago, and not for very long. It was a very uncomfortable experience."

"I'll refrain from asking why it was uncomfortable."

Samael laughed. "It's wise of you to do so."

She shook her head. "What else might I learn tonight?"

"What do you wish to learn?" He asked.

"Many things, I just don't know where to begin."

"Ah, I have an idea." Samael smiled. "You are aware we can summon objects, like those I had on the table tonight. For those who do not understand how these things work, it seems difficult, for you, child, it seems these magical abilities are like second nature. Think of an item you wish to have at this very moment. It could be anything. Think of it adorning the very table which is in this room and see what happens."

Reika thought about what she would like in front of her. She closed her eyes and pictured it in her mind. A smile rose on her lips and she opened her eyes. Laying on the table was one of Sebastian's jackets, with a small bottle of his cologne in the pocket. She had only seen him wear the jacket once, but she knew she wanted it for comfort. She walked to the table and picked the jacket up and put it on. She turned to look at Samael who smiled.

"I must say, you surprised me." Samael said. "I was expecting a weapon, or jewelry, but you picked something far more valuable. You are a remarkable woman. You show a deep appreciation for life, and love. I could not be more proud as your father."

She blushed. "Papa, it's just a jacket."

"It is much deeper than just an article of clothing. Who it belongs to is important. Why you chose it. The scent in which it carries. What comfort it will bring you. It is much more than something to wear, but I must warn you, if you do wear the jacket anywhere, always mask your aura. You must blend yourself into the background of the world, become completely invisible. If anyone were to smell his scent upon you, I cannot fathom what could happen if you were to slip into the wrong hands."

"I wish I could say I would kill them all, but I don't have that much faith in my own strength compared to another being. After my run in with Adrian, I'm scared I'm not strong enough to handle what is to come." She bit her lip. "And what I saw in the crystal ball tonight tells me I'm not."

"It very well could have been another bout of sickness brought on by malnutrition." Samael suggested.

"Now, I have a question. I can communicate telepathically, and it is verbal. Am I able to do it the same way, only with images?"

"I wish I knew the answer to this. I have never been able to do such a thing with another being. It is possible, but very rare."

She shrugged her shoulders. "It was worth asking. My point with it though, is I didn't look sick in what I saw. It looked different, but I don't know how. Maybe it was poison."

"We mustn't dwell on this, Reika." Samael sighed. "I again wish I had the answers you seek, but I am not the holder of the book of life. I merely ferry the living into eternity and grant the wishes of those who walk dead among the prosperous."

Reika nodded. "I understand. I ask, because you never know the answers someone's mind may hold."

"Ever a student, Reika." Samael smiled, wrapping an arm around her shoulder. "You bloom every single day."

"I am trying." She whispered.

"You aren't trying, Reika. You are succeeding." He pulled her close and hugged her tight.

Chapter Twelve

The scent of roses filled the air whipping around Lilith. The hem of her black dress rippling in the breeze, as she strolled through a garden full of deep red and black flowers. The sky was stained shades of red and orange by the setting sun. A black gazebo waited at the end of the path she walked. She took a seat in the gazebo, and gazed out over the garden.

"Adrian." She said softly. "I am very impatient, you better show yourself quickly." A hand brushed the hair away from her neck, Lilith turned and looked. Her eyes met a pair of sky blue orbs, set into a sharply angled face. His rich honey skin tone caused his eyes to shine brightly like stars set in the night sky. His black hair was styled perfectly, and combed away from his face. He wore a white button down shirt, the top few buttons left undone to give a preview of a sculpted body and a pair of dark jeans.

"I am terribly sorry, I hate to keep a lady waiting." He whispered into her ear. "How may I make it up to you?"

"There are many ways you can make it up to me." Lilith said, turning her face towards his, only inches apart. She smirked, looking into his eyes. "However, business must be handled first, then we shall talk about your quittance."

"Ah, yes. The information you planted for the boy's parents to find worked well. I would think you would already know his parents had removed him from your academy."

"I did." She nodded. "I wanted to make sure you were doing your duties properly." She smirked once more. "It means I now need to make a home visit to a former student."

# # #

Sebastian lay in darkness, staring at the shadows dancing across the ceiling. He felt troubled. He closed his eyes momentarily, only to hear the sound of what seemed like branches tapping against his window.

"Boy, I know you're in there. Open the window and let me in." A feminine voice cooed from outside the glass.

Sebastian's heart stopped. "Lilith."

"Very good, you remembered me." Lilith chuckled softly. "I have something I wish to tell you. Now, would you let me inside so we can talk? It's rather chilly out here."

"No." He said immediately. "I'm not letting you in my house. Get the fuck out of here!" He growled out.

"You'll change your mind eventually. I know you will." Lilith said, before disappearing.

A sigh escaped his lips, and he draped his arm over his face. Before he could relax, he heard the door fly open, and the lights came on.

"Who the fuck were you just talking to?!"

"I wasn't talking to anyone." He said, knowing that if he explained that a succubus was just outside his window, he'd probably be carted to a mental ward.

"Don't you dare lie to me!" Brian growled out, grabbing Sebastian's arm, and pulled him out of bed. "Tell me now, who you were talking to, or I swear to God I'll beat your ass senseless! Was it that man your Mom's been fucking while she's at work?"

Sebastian looked at his Father, his eyes void of emotion. " It wasn't anyone and you couldn't hurt me any worse than you've done before. Have you forgotten that you've been hitting on me since I was little? There isn't much more you can do to me."

"You've deserved every bit of it, you filthy little bastard!" Brian got close to Sebastian's face. He could smell the whiskey on his breath. Sebastian turned his face away and coughed, the smell overwhelming. "You should be grateful I let you live."

"I don't know what I deserve in this life, but it sure as hell isn't your fist in my fucking face night after night." He said, taking a step back, giving himself space to breathe. "I don't know very many that do deserve a life like that."

"You deserve every bit of it." He said, a twisted grin spread across his face. "You've been a thorn in my side since you were born. You've ruined everything good I've ever had. Now I'm stuck with that stupid bitch, because she got pregnant with you. You're the root of every problem I have. Maybe I should just kill you, and then I'll be free. I won't have to see the disgusting reminder of how unfaithful my wife was."

Sebastian just sighed, he'd heard all of it before. "You'd be better off killing yourself, if that's what you're thinking. Killing me would land you in prison, not freedom. Kill yourself, and you'd be free of everything, including your own fucking insanity."

"I still want to live." He growled, drawing his fist back. "I just want to see you die. I want to see your blood soak into the floor, to hear your last breath expel from your pathetic body."

Sebastian groaned, watching, as if in slow motion, his father's fist being propelled forward. He took a step away, grabbing his arm, and twisting his arm away from his body, and

striking him in the ribs. It didn't seem to phase the man, his other fist swung around, striking Sebastian in the back. He let go of Brian's arm, and staggered backwards, watching his movements carefully as he tried to catch his breath. He circled around, seeing Brian's fist coming for his face, but he was too late. He felt the familiar shock of impact and ache as he hit the floor.

"You're lucky." Brian said, standing over him. "I don't feel up to killing you yet." He landed a hard kick to Sebastian's side. He shut the light off, and slammed the door shut.Sebastian pushed himself to his uninjured side, trying to stay conscious. *'I hate him. I can't wait to be out of here and for that bastard to die.'*

'If you'd just let me in, you wouldn't have to wait.' The familiar feminine voice chimed in his head.

'You're back, or am I imagining things? Jesus, Lilith, get the fuck out of here.'

'I can't leave, not while you're hurt. My daughter would be quite upset with me if I had let you suffer alone. I can help you.'

Sebastian groaned, placing a hand on his head. *'I'd rather suffer alone than be in the company of a snake like you.'*

'Then do so. I'll come back later.'

Sebastian laid on the floor for what felt like hours. Finally, he heard the rumblings of his father's snoring. Still aching, Sebastian waited a little longer before moving. The light peeked through the edge of the curtains over his window. He tried to pull himself up from the floor, but only got as far as sitting upright. Lilith's threat of returning later worried him more than his Father's. The hard floor caused his body to ache even more than he thought possible. He grabbed hold of his headboard and pulled himself onto the floor.

He adjusted himself so he was laying again on the side he hadn't been kicked on but heard something crumple underneath him. He lifted himself to pull the paper out from underneath.

My darling Sebastian,

How I adore you so. Your letter was beautiful, and I'll cherish it as you're away, just like your jacket. I figure I'll apologize now. Papa was teaching me how to summon items. I wanted something that smelled like you, and would bring a similar warmth to my skin. Home feels terribly empty without your presence. Even Papa has commented on it.

I'm sorry I'm not nearly as good with words as you are. I wish I could tell you in a more beautiful way that I love you dearly, and miss you so much that I can barely stand it. We will do whatever it takes to make sure you come back to us alive. I won't let you slip away so easily. You are mine, and I am yours. I will do anything for you, just call for me.

Be safe, my love. We will be reunited one day very soon. Please take care of yourself and don't forget to eat.

With all of my heart,

Reika

Sebastian smiled sadly at the paper in his hands. He laid it on the small table next to his bed. He felt something warm touch his back and he jumped, causing pain to shoot through his body. Slowly he reached behind his back, and grasped a warm glass bottle. He brought the bottle into view and chuckled to himself. He was holding a plain wine bottle, filled to the brim with deep red liquid. He immediately knew what she had done.

"Reika, you shouldn't have." He said, his voice barely a whisper in the stagnant air. He sat up straight and unscrewed the cap of the bottle and inhaled the scent deeply. "You really shouldn't have." He brought the bottle to his lips and took a large gulp. He sighed out happily and put the cap back on the bottle. Sebastian hid the bottle beneath his blankets and laid back down in an attempt to sleep.

"Sebastian?" He heard a soft woman's voice through the door. "Honey, are you okay?"

"I'm fine, Mom." He said. "I just want to rest."

Theresa Luciano peaked into the room, her soft blond wavy hair framed a withered, yet beautiful face. Bright green eyes full of sadness peered out from wispy brown lashes. Her petite frame slipped in the room and closed the door silently. "You really should let me take a look at you though."

"Mom, I said I'm fine." He said, not looking up from the point on the floor he fixated his gaze upon. "I just want sleep. I'll feel better when I wake up."

"Bas, you might have broken ribs and your cheek looks horrible."

"What are you going to do about it?" He asked. "We've been over this before, you can't do anything for broken ribs except let them heal. What? Do you want to poke at them to add insult to injury? Their not even broken, just bruised. My face is fine too, just another bruise. I've been through this enough fucking times to know what is wrong with me. So just leave and let me rest."

"Bas, you don't have to pretend to be strong around me." She reached for him trying to help.

"You don't get it." He said through gritted teeth. He put a hand up blocking her from touching him. "I don't want your help. You let this happen for so long, and kept it a fucking secret. It's so messed up. I don't know how a mother can let her son get beaten as much as I do, and sleep at night."

"That's not fair, and you know it." She whispered.

"It's not fair?" Sebastian shot her a lethal glare. "What isn't fair is the fact that I've begged you to get us help, and you ignore me. The fact that I've done my best to protect you from him, and you can't even return the favor. What's going to happen when he stabs me, Mom? Are you going to break out your sewing kit and hope for the best? I shouldn't have come back here. One of these days the police are gonna find my body floating face down in the same damn creek they found Reika in, and you expect me to be reasonable with you about how it's not fair for me to lay blame on you too. Your hands aren't clean of the blood that's been spilled."

"It's not fair for you to say any of this because you're not the only one who suffers by his hand."

"Yeah, you're right on that one." Sebastian scoffed. "However, I'm the only one who's had the fucking balls to stand up to that piece of shit. I'm the only one who's called the cops. Each time it's the same. You fucking lie and cover his ass. You make me out to be a liar and you want me to talk about fair? What's going to happen when he actually pulls a knife on me, or a gun? What are you going to say if I turn it around on him and end his life to save my own? Are you still going to protect him, or are you going to finally fess up and tell the goddamn truth?"

"He said he'd kill me if I didn't say all of that. He said things would be better if I just went with what he said."

"How did that go for you?"

Theresa looked down.

"Apparently not well."

"Everything is better when you're gone." She whispered.

"You're so fucking right about that." He smirked, his eyes full of hatred. "I can live my life without broken bones and bruises all over my body. And you two can play happily ever after. Maybe you should just let me leave."

"He said if I let you go he'd kill me." Her voice still the same soft whisper, her eyes never lifting from the floor.

He rolled his eyes. "He's just waiting for the day he can try to kill me. Just know you'll go down as accessory to murder, or you'll be in the ground right next to me." He sighed. "I tried to save your life, and as far as I see it, you're already dead. There's no point in trying to save a walking corpse. All because you're afraid to make one phone call, to make one move to better yourself."

"Fear has kept us alive for this long."

"Just barely!" Sebastian could feel his anger rise up once again. "What kind of life is this?! Look at me!" He shook his head. "I can barely even sit up, and you expect me to be happy that we're alive? This is a godforsaken nightmare, Mom."

"We have a roof over our heads, and food."

"And we have broken bones, and tattered souls. That isn't a life worth being thankful for."

"Not many people have what we have, Sebastian."

"You're right about that. Not many people have to live in fear of dying by the hands of someone who is supposed to be their protector. There aren't many options, and I'd much prefer an alternative to being taken out of here in a body bag."

"You're not leaving here in a body bag." She said. "You're being ridiculous."

"Are you fucking kidding me? He just told me last night he wasn't going to kill me yet." He stared at her, his eyes huge. "Yet, mom, yet. Which means not today, but someday. You expect me to just sit here and wait for my death like a prisoner?" He shook his head. "You have me mistaken for someone else."

Theresa turned around and left the room. Sebastian laid back once more, sighing out. His aches were finally starting to fade. He reached over, and took his bottle out once more and took a drink carefully, as to not spill the precious contents. He closed the bottle and put it back in it's temporary hiding place.

'Thank you, Reika.' He thought.

'Let me know when you need more. You can't go without. Let me know when you are alone for an extended period of time. I'll come to you with something Papa wasn't able to present to you before you left.'

'I will let you know. I miss you.'

'I miss you too. I love you. Are you doing alright?'

'I am now. What you sent is helping.'

'You're hurt.'

'How do you know?'

'I can feel it. Are you alone?'

'He's asleep and Mom hasn't left for work yet.'

'As soon as you're alone, please tell me.'

'If I'm awake I will.'

'If you need rest, don't worry. But please, take care of yourself.'

'I will. I love you, Reika.'

'I love you, Sebastian.'

He felt a tear slip from the corner of his eye and travel down his cheek to soak into his pillow. The reality of being separated had finally settled and his heart ached more than his side ever had. He wept silently, until he succumbed to sleep.

# # #

Reika sat alone, pouring over a book she had found in the library. She had taken to studying about foresight. Since the day

Samael had introduced her to the concept, and placed a crystal ball before her, she was not able to see another vision. It had completely frustrated Reika to the point she had wanted to toss the orb many a time. She closed the book and pushed it away from her. She laid her head down on the table and sighed.

It had been two weeks since she had last seen Sebastian. Her tears finally caught up with her. In the weeks past, she had spent it studying and working with Samael. She hadn't taken the time to rest. She spoke to Sebastian occasionally, when he was able to, yet he hadn't had a moment alone so she could visit him.

She gave into her tears, letting her body shake with them. She heard the door open quietly, but chose to ignore it. She turned her head away from the door. A gentle hand found a way to her back.

"You're allowed moments of sadness." A voice she did not recognize said. "Do not be ashamed to have them."

She looked up, seeing a man with blond hair, braided down his back. He wore a black leather jacket, and jeans. His green eyes were warm and friendly.

"Darius, correct?" Reika asked softly.

"Yes, you are correct." He nodded. "I'm sorry to have frightened you. I heard you from the hallway, and wanted to check in with you." He took a seat by her. "Samael said we will be headed out to practice some combat. Are you up to it?"

Reika nodded some. "It would be a welcomed change rather than being here in this library. I enjoy studying, but my mind isn't where it needs to be for reading. I need something more hands on, and combat training would be great."

"Are you positive you're ready for it?"

She nodded. "I am. I'd much rather do that than sit here for another two weeks."

Darius nodded. "I don't blame you. I'm not much for books either. I found the best teacher is experience. Reading a book about the subject is good as a supplement, depending on what you are studying. Foresight is a rather tricky subject, you need to read to understand the process, but you must let your mind wander and learn it's own way. I was told you studied martial arts and that it helped you with this anger issue you had growing up."

"It did." She nodded again. "I still have a temper, though. I never fully got rid of it."

"I'm sure you think it's a failure on your part, for not letting go of that part of yourself, just remember who your mother is. You are who you are because of your parents. You take after Samael quite a bit, however I see that fierceness Lilith holds inside of you. You have a fiery passion within, just as she does, only you use it properly."

"How do I use it the right way?" She looked confused.

"You protect yourself and those you love. Your violence, and anger is never senseless. I know you've had altercations where you are ruthless towards the assailant. Samael tends to do the same thing. I'm sure he will never allow you to see himself in such a way, but know he is capable of such acts."

"I've never seen him like that before." She looked up, thoughtfully. "It would be interesting to see."

"It was frightful to see, even from my standpoint. He takes a great care to not do such things, but I promise you this: if anyone hurts you, or Sebastian for that matter, there will be unfathomable amounts of hell to pay." He smirked.

"I'm surprised he hasn't gone after Adrian yet."

"Do not be surprised. He is waiting for the right time to strike." He stood and offered his hand. "If you would like, we could meet with your father, and we shall proceed to training."

Reika nodded. "Are you going to be my training partner?" She asked, taking his hand and standing.

"Yes, Samael said it would be too difficult for him to spar with his daughter, for fear of hurting you. He asked me to train with you. I hope you don't mind."

"I don't." She smiled. "You seem like a good teacher."

"I'm very harsh." He smiled. "Just do your best, and I'm sure everything will be fine."

"I'm sure it will be fine." She nodded. "I'm no stranger to training, but everyone teaches differently. It will take a little bit to get used to the change, but it will all go just fine."

Darius nodded. "It will be just fine." Silence fell between them as they walked to the sitting room and met Samael.

"You've finally arrived." He smiled softly. Samael gazed at Reika's face and took his thumb to her cheek and wiped softly. "Your face is stained with tear marks, my dear." He looked at her with sad eyes, and cupped her face in both hands. "I am deeply sorry you are distressed. What can I do to help you?"

"Just continue to be yourself." She whispered, placing her hand on top of his. "It's all I need right now."

Samael kissed her forehead and pulled her into a tight embrace. "You may come to me with anything, child. Please, do not hesitate." He whispered in her ear. "I will always be here for you, and never want you to be scared or experience solitude."

"Papa, don't leave me." She whispered. "I'm trying my best right now to be strong. I'm scared, and I miss him."

"Reika, you need not be strong every hour of the day." He said, taking her face in his hands once more. "Know that if you wish to rest your head, or need to let your tears flow, I will hold you, and wipe them all away. I am your protector, I am your strength when you cannot muster it on your own. Reika, I will always, always be here for you. I will not leave your side. I promise you, my dear."

"I just don't want anyone to see me cry." She said softly. "I have to be strong, it's who I am."

"There is strength in letting your tears flow." He said softly. "It shows you have strength enough to embrace your emotions fully. Do not be ashamed of it Reika. You are strong, and this is not a moment of weakness. If you need let these feelings go, we shall sit and let you."

Reika looked down, and sighed. "I'll be alright." She looked back up after a moment and smiled gently.

Samael nodded, and kissed her forehead gently once more. "I believe you. Shall we begin training now?"

She nodded. "I'm ready."

"Take our hands and we shall bring you to the training grounds." Samael said.

Both Samael and Darius held their hands out. Reika took them and she felt the familiar void of space. When she opened her eyes, she was welcomed by a beautiful forest around her. In front, she saw a clearing up to the top of a large hill. At the top, was a quaint rustic cabin, and a small barn. She smiled. "I've always wanted to do hill training." She said softly.

"We will go to the cabin, and you must change." Darius said. "We start immediately."

Reika nodded, and she started up the hill at a faster pace, getting ahead of Samael and Darius. "Have you heard any plans for an attack here?" Samael asked. He kept his eyes on Reika as she ran up the hill.

"I have not." He sighed. "The only things I have heard are after they happen. Unfortunately, they are keeping rather silent about their movements."

"How uncharacteristically intelligent for Adrian." Samael snorted. "He is usually too boisterous about his plans."

"I think it's Lilith putting the idea in his head. Sadly, the woman still holds a shred of her wits."

"Not for long." Samael shot Darius a look, then returned his eyes to Reika's form. She had met the top of the hill. "She's nearing the end of her mental capacity."

"How tragic." Darius said bitingly.

"It depends on how you look at it." He said softly. They finally reached the top of the hill and walked into the cabin and Reika stood still as night in the center of the small living room. When she heard the doors opening, she turned to look at Samael.

"Papa, this is the place." She whispered, her face full of horror. "This is where someone will try to kill me."

Chapter Thirteen

The forest was eerily silent as Reika stalked through, hidden. Occasionally a gust of wind rushed past her, but she felt no other presence. With a sword attached to her belt, she was practicing the ability to keep her aura cloaked while sensing any others.

Reika kept her right hand on the handle of the sword as she continued silent footfalls through the trees.

'Who am I to be tracking?' She thought to herself, looking to the sky, and adjusted her course. Her eyes looked down, and she saw a broken twig. She looked around to see if there were any others, and sighed softly when she wasn't able to find anymore. Reika stood and continued her path.

For what felt like hours, she scoured the forest floor for any sign of a trail. She hadn't found anything. Reika changed her direction and headed towards the cabin once more. She stopped and looked to the sky. It was hardly visible through the leaves, yet the lack of sunlight in the middle of the afternoon was unsettling. She heard a loud crack of thunder and jumped, startled by the suddenness of it.

Reika regained her composure and continued forward once more as the rain began to drizzle over the leaves of the tree. She stopped once more, feeling someone's aura around her. She looked around, and saw nothing but tried to find the source of the aura.

The crack of a tree branch resounded through the area. She looked to her feet, and found it was not her. She took off in the direction of the sound, her hand still firmly held on the hilt of her sword.

Another crack echoed through the trees, but was hidden by another clap of thunder. Reika raced through the woods after her target. She finally spotted the dark, hooded figure, and she ran after them. She caught up to them and drew her sword.

"You can't get very far now." She said softly.

The figure turned, and Samael's face peaked out from beneath the hood. "Very good, Reika." He said softly. "Darius has given me instructions for you. I will return to the cabin, you are to navigate your way back through the forest. Continue to shield yourself, for you are silent through the woods." He smiled. "I will see you at home." He said and disappeared.

Reika sheathed her sword and surveyed her position in the woods. She maintained the cloaking of her aura and began her path towards the cabin. The rain still poured overhead and thunder and lightning continued to roll overhead. She sighed, trudging through in wet, cold clothing.

An hour had passed, and the storm grew stronger. Reika picked up her pace, trying to get home faster. She was in view of the break in the trees when she spotted a figure in front of her. She darted towards the dark figure, placing her hand on her sword once more. Once she got closer, she realized it wasn't Samael or Darius. She crept behind them, grabbed their collar and threw them backwards.

"Who are you, and what business do you have here?" She growled.

An unfamiliar woman peered up at her with big, scared eyes. "I'm lost." She whispered. "I saw this cabin and thought I could get shelter until the rain stopped."

Reika glared down at the woman. "I don't believe you. Why are you here?"

"I just told you!" She groaned out. "Don't you get it?" The woman was getting visibly agitated by Reika's question.

"No, I don't." Reika said, her eyebrow raised in suspicion. "I've been in these woods for hours, and I haven't seen you. You're not lost. You know exactly where you are."

The woman's demeanor changed from agitated to untrustworthy. There was a devious glint in the woman's eyes. "You're much smarter than they give you credit for." She said.

Reika took a step back, and drew her sword. She pointed it at the woman's neck. "Who sent you?"

"You already know the answer to this." The woman stated. She put her hands up, in surrender. "Why even explain. They want you dead, and I'm here to deliver a message. Give up. You're never going to win against them. You might as well join them. If you don't, all the people you care for will perish." The woman's eyes were a melting pot of emotions, but the most prominent was fear.

Reika remained calm. "Underestimation is ever a sign of a fool." She rested the tip of her sword against her chest and slowly dragged the edge against her skin, leaving a cut in it's wake. "You can tell that to your superiors, if you want to live."

"I do want to live." She said softly. She cringed as the blade made it's way across her skin. "Please don't kill me."

Reika stopped the blade around the navel, letting it linger. "If you wish to live, you need to leave now. If not, I will end your life." She turned the blade and made an upward slice, cutting the woman's flesh a bit deeper above the navel. Her eyes were dark. "Tell them if they send more here, to make sure they come to join their pathetic little pawns in death."

"All of this is noted." She whispered. Her voice was hoarse, her body trembling.

"Leave now." She stepped back again. The woman disappeared without another word. Reika did a full turn, making sure she was alone again and quickly made her way back to the cabin. She sheathed her sword, took her belt off and entered the cabin. She sighed heavily. Samael and Darius were sitting in the living room and looked at her.

"You returned later than we expected." Darius said.

"I would've been back sooner if there weren't an actual threat lurking in the woods." She explained.

"What do you mean?" Samael bolted up from his chair and came towards her. "Are you alright?"

"I'm fine." She said. "I'm just cold. There was a woman at the edge of the forest, about to come to the cabin. She was here to deliver a message to me."

"What was this message?" Darius asked before Samael got the chance.

"They will kill everyone I care about if I don't join them."

"How did you respond?" Samael asked.

"I left a mark on her, a gentle cut from throat to navel." She smirked. "I told her to tell them if they wish to send their pawns, to come themselves so they can die the same death. Next time I will not be so merciful."

Samael nodded. "A fine response."

Darius smirked. "Very nice work, however, we need to increase the veil here."

"The veil?" She asked.

"We have a protective veil over our land. We need to increase the parameter, and strengthen it so it cannot be breached." Samael explained.

"How do you go about that?" Reika asked.

"It is a strong magic I have yet to teach you." Samael explained. "We have yet to try incantations with you. It might be a splendid time to do so."

"It is a good idea." Darius smiled. "Where do we begin, though?"

"With a very small one." Samael stated. "You have experienced the effect of such words when we are summoned to broker with the humans. There are many variations to the invocations used to summon us. Really, the only part of an incantation which matters is the intent of your words."

"I could read something unrefined, and I could summon someone to me, so long as my intent is obvious?" Reika asked.

"Yes, you could use your own incantation or one written by someone else." Samael nodded. "Any would do."

Reika nodded. "Does that hold true for any of these veils? Can we just use intent, or must the words be specific?"

He nodded in response. "I will show you later tonight. For now, you need to get out of the wet clothes, and relax."

Reika nodded. "That would be wonderful."

Samael led Reika to the bathroom. "I drew a hot bath for you, and there is wine on the counter if you so choose." He smiled. "Relax, my dear, you did well today."

"Thank you, Papa." Reika said softly, handing him the belt with her sword.

"Does your blade need cleaning?"

"Yes." She nodded with a giggle. "I seemed to have stained the tip red."

"I will attend to it." He gave her a single nod. "Go and relax."

Reika smiled. "I will." She closed the door, stripped down and went to her bath.

#

Sebastian sat at the desk in his room, looking at the calendar he had pulled off the wall. He sighed. It has been a month since his parents pulled him from Locke Academy. The days were growing longer, and desolate. Each day was filled with another moment of anger from his father. Most days he hadn't been hit, but his side still ached from getting kicked multiple times in the past month.

The wear on his spirits was tangible. All Sebastian hoped for was an end to the suffering. Since the day he was brought home, he hadn't had a day to himself where he could call Reika to him. He was only ever able to contact her for more nourishment. He lied, telling her he was alright and that his father wasn't beating him. Sebastian knew she would worry, and he didn't want her sick with it. Lilith was on the move, and he knew Reika needed to train rigorously for the final day of this war.

Opening his desk drawer, Sebastian withdrew his journal. He smiled softly, knowing there were only a handful of entries yet all of them were about Reika. He cracked the cover, and looked at the first entry.

May 20th,

I saw her again. The girl with the most beautiful black hair I've ever seen. There's something dangerous about her. She carries herself with a deadly aura. Most turn their backs on her, or walk faster to get away. They look down when they see her, but I've always wanted to peer into the face of that deadly beautiful woman. Today, I finally did, and I was greeted by dark brown eyes set into the face of a goddess.

I was at the record store when I first saw her gorgeous face. Around town, I had caught glimpses of the mysterious beauty, I was always intrigued, yet she was elusive. I could never catch up to her, or even see her face until now.

I don't even know her name, but she's stolen a part of me. She can keep it forever, so long as I can have a part of her in return. There she stood, dressed in all black, despite the heat of summer crawling into this godforsaken town. I couldn't help but stare. When her face turned to look into mine, she glared at me. She asked if I wanted to take a picture. I asked her why. She told me it'd be better to take a picture, because if I didn't stop staring she would gouge my eyes out. I couldn't help but smile. She shook her head, brought her hand up, and gave me the middle finger.

I don't understand why, but I was drawn to her completely. Call me a fool, but a woman who can put me in my place is the most gorgeous woman alive. It sounds completely backwards, considering my home life. I need to get to know her. I want to know her name. I've asked a few people, yet they only call her 'Goth Girl'. I know what I want to call her, but I think calling her by name would be better first, than to jump right to saying 'That's my girlfriend'.

Sebastian closed the journal, and bit the inside of his cheek to keep from crying. He missed Reika terribly.

'Reika, are you listening?'

'I'm always listening for you, Bas.'

'I miss you. Are you doing alright?'

'I am. I miss you too. Are you alright?'

'I was just thinking about the day we met.'

He got up and laid down on his bed, and heard a knock on the door.

"Sebastian, Brian is gone for a couple days. I'm going to work." Theresa called out.

"Okay, I'll see you later."

"I love you." She said and left. Sebastian let out a sigh of relief when he heard the car pull out of the driveway and he was left in complete silence.

'I'm alone.'

'I'll see you in a moment.'

Sebastian sat on his bed, and waited, with his eyes closed. He felt the mattress dip next to him. Arms wrapped around him gently and he opened his eyes, and there she was. Sebastian pulled her into his arms tight, and held her. His emotions were reeling, and his heart felt as if it could explode.

"I'm so happy you're here." He whispered in her ear, inhaling the scent of her hair.

"I've missed you." Reika said, her voice soft. She pulled back some, but Sebastian held strong. She smiled and laid her head against his shoulder, enjoying the security of being in his presence.

"Reika." He whispered. "Take me with you."

"I will." She said, she pulled back, looking into his eyes. "Let's go now."

He nodded. "Okay." He stood up, and grabbed the journal from the drawer in his desk. Sebastian turned to her and smiled. "Let's get out of here."

Reika held his hand and she took him away from the nightmare of his parents' house. She opened her eyes and they were back at the cabin. Reika smiled at Sebastian. "Welcome back." She hugged him again.

"Thank you Rei." He said softly, hugging her tight. "It's beautiful out here."

"Reika, are you back already?" Samael said, as he came out from the small barn. He smiled brightly as he saw Sebastian. "Ah, I see. Welcome back home, Sebastian. How do you fare?"

"I'm sore, but I'm whole." He smiled.

Reika looked up at him. "You're sore?" She glared at him. "Where and why are you sore?!"

"My ribs." He sighed. "Brian kicked me there a few times."

"And you didn't call for me?!" Reika's eyes roared with ferocity Sebastian hadn't seen.

"I didn't want you worrying about me."

"I worried about you day in and day out regardless." She huffed. "You're now telling me that he still beat you after we got you away. You haven't any idea how badly I want to go back there and destroy him."

"Trust me, I do." He nodded. "I've wanted to for years."

Reika's expression softened. "You're right." She took his hands and squeezed them. "I'm just glad it didn't get any worse than what it did." She blinked away tears. "Though, I can't say I'm happy they got that bad. You don't deserve to be treated that way, Bas. You're an amazing person, don't let his words destroy who you really are."

Sebastian pulled her in and held her. "I won't." He said, kissing the top of her head. "If I were to let him, he would win. I can't let him do that."

"I admire your strength, Sebastian." Samael said. "Now that you are here, we shall create your end, so you may begin your eternity."

"It's already begun." Sebastian said, he looked into Reika's eyes. "The moment I set eyes on Reika, eternity began."

#

"The boy escaped his parents' home." Adrian said softly.
"The wretch we sent with the message for Reika has been weeping
in her room since she returned. She's crying about some infected
wound, and how she's afraid of doing her next assignment."

"Why is she afraid?" Lilith sneered. "She was not even hurt
badly. The stupid child showed mercy on her. She shouldn't be
crying in her bed, she should be rejoicing." She rolled her eyes. "She
is a waste of our time, have her disposed of immediately." Lilith was
laying in her garden, plucking the petals from a red rose, and
scattering them on her blanket. Adrian was kneeling next to her,
handing her flowers when she had finished ripping the petals off the
stems.

"As you wish." He nodded. "There's something else."

"What ever could it be?"

"They have increased the veil around the cabin, we have no
way of infiltrating for another attack."

"I suppose I'll have to make a visit myself." Lilith looked at Adrian. "Apparently my people cannot do their jobs properly, so I must take it upon myself to have it done right."

"I am terribly sorry for this."

Lilith turned towards him, sitting up, and grabbed his jaw. "Remorse is for the weak." She hissed. "I never wish to hear you show weakness again. If I do, I shall tear your tongue from your mouth." She pushed him away. "Leave, and take care of that sniveling wench. Make sure you do it correctly. I don't want to have to clean up another mess."

"What are your plans when you arrive at the cabin?" Adrian asked, rubbing his face.

"It isn't any of your concern. Go do what I've asked of you." She waved her hand.

"As you wish." Adrian said, and walked away with a sigh. He made his way to the quarters where Lilith had her servants live. He opened the door to the girl's room and smiled at her. "Oh, my dear, I have lovely news for you."

"Are you going to help me?" She whispered.

"Oh, yes." He sat down on the edge of her bed. "I'm going to release you from your service today."

"No." She whispered, her eyes getting large. "The last time someone was released, they were-" Her voice trailed off.

"Yes, they were." Adrian nodded, his smile still glued to his face. "You are to join them." He reached down, and retrieved the dagger from his boot. He tested the sharpness of the blade against the tip of his finger. Pleased with the beading of blood atop his finger, he plunged the dagger deep into the woman's heart, all whilst she screamed out in protest. He twisted the blade, and waited until she stopped moving. Adrian pulled the blade out of her chest, and leaned down, kissing her lips. He took a deep breath in, as she exhaled her last breath.

He wiped the blade against his leg, sheathed it, and left the room. "All in a day's work." He said cheerfully to the others in the hallway. "Quit staring, and get back to work." He shouted as he exited the boarding house.

# # #

Darius sat with Reika in the living room of the small cabin. She was gazing into her crystal ball. Frustrated still by her lack of visions, Reika looked up to Darius. "The last vision I had was of this place." She sighed. "I don't understand why I haven't seen anything new yet."

"Because, young one, the universe isn't ready for you to see it."

"What do you mean?"

"Everything happens when it is meant to happen. Everything is seen when it is ready to be seen." Darius gave a lopsided smile. "Be happy though, I can hear all of the world's thoughts and actions. It can be quite troublesome."

"I wouldn't even want to imagine that." Reika looked at him, eyes wide. "All that buzzing inside my mind, I'd probably throw up."

"When I first awoke, I had that problem." Darius laughed, "Though, it was much more silent back then. There weren't as many beings populating the planet, therefore not as much chatter."

"How many were there?"

"Humans, there were only two in the beginning." Darius smiled, his eyes full of nostalgia. "There were many other beings who weren't human. Those were the voices I heard the most."

"Darius, what is your purpose in the universe?" Reika asked. "I know mine, but what do you do?"

"I am considered a watchman angel." He smirked. "Though, I think they may have gotten the angel part wrong."

Reika just shook her head and laughed. She gazed down at the ball before her nonchalantly. As it had before, the ball began swirling and an image appeared.

Reika knelt on the ground in the woods, arms wrapped around Sebastian. They were both bloody and battered. She was sobbing, holding him tight. His arms were weak, and he brushed her hair away from her neck and bit into her flesh.

Reika looked up to Darius. "That was rather strange." She sighed. "The first vision I saw myself sick, in bed here at this cabin. This time I saw-"

"Sebastian hurt, you as well, him laying on the ground." Darius interjected. "You were holding him, and he fed from you."

"How did you know?" Reika asked, shocked.

"I can see as well." Darius sighed. "I will tell you this. The battle shall be fierce, the pain will be immense but you will be victorious. Do not let this inflate your ego. Always be watching, always be alert, for you never know what lurks in the shadows with you."

"Though I may be hiding in the shadows, I am not the ultimate darkness." Reika said softly. "I am only death, waiting for those who reach out to grasp my hand."

Darius nodded softly. "Indeed you are death, yet you are much more."

"What do you mean?"

"You are born of the union of two creatures, one of death, one of desire." He gave a lopsided smile. "You are not only death. Within death, is the lust for living. The only way one can live is to embrace death, rather than fear it."

She smiled softly, and nodded. "Embrace death to appreciate life."

"This is what you embody." Darius said softly. "Look at Sebastian. Just as who you are, you inspired a being to face his fears, defy adversity, and become more powerful. Reika, this world needs a being like you in it. You are not going to meet your end anytime soon, do not fear. Who you are, and what you are are necessary to this world. You are not going to perish. You are needed, and you are perfect as you are."

Fighting back tears, she nodded gently. "You're right."

"I know I am." Darius smirked. "I would not have told you if it were not true. Honesty is the most important piece in dialogue."

Samael entered the room, and placed a hand on Reika's shoulder. "Come, my child." He said softly. "Sebastian wishes to show you something, and after we shall do more training in combat."

Reika nodded and got up from the table. Darius joined them and they went outside. Before Reika could catch a glimpse of what was beyond the door, Samael placed his hands over her eyes. Reika reached up, and touched his hands. "Papa! What are you doing?!"

"It's a surprise!" Sebastian shouted happily.

Reika tried to look around, but Samael kept his hands firmly planted on her face. "Where is he?!" She shouted. "Is he climbing trees?!"

"Lead her out farther." Sebastian said.

"Why must we go farther out?" Reika asked, as she walked with Samael farther away from the cabin.

"When I say go, you know what to do." Sebastian yelled again, laughing some.

"What the fuck is about to happen?!" Reika groaned.

"You'll see." Samael whispered in her ear.

"GO!" Sebastian shouted.

Samael let go of Reika, and all she saw was Sebastian falling from the sky. He grabbed hold of her and they went back towards the sky. Reika screamed, holding tight to Sebastian.

"Calm, Reika." Sebastian whispered in her ear. She was holding his waist, and looked behind him after they finally slowed. "Do you see now?"

"You have wings." She grinned. "You can fly!"

He held her close. "I can fly!" He spun them upside down, as Reika laughed and screamed. He stopped, keeping their altitude in the sky, letting Reika see the forest from overhead. She was in awe of it all.

"This was your surprise?" She whispered in his ear.

"It is." He said happily.

"This is absolutely amazing." She said, her eyes opened wide, trying to take in as much of the view as she possibly could.

"Hold on tight." He whispered and took off once more. Reika held tight as they glided over the trees together. After many turns and twists, Sebastian brought them safely to the ground and let go of her waist.

Reika stepped back, and took in the full view of him, he stood wearing black cargo pants, a pair of combat boots, with no shirt. Behind Sebastian, were a pair of black leathery wings, much like a bat's but larger. She gaped in awe of him.

Sebastian looked down, and rubbed his neck, laughing awkwardly. "Does it look bad?"

She shook her head. "No, they're beautiful." She smiled. "It's amazing. I wonder if I can fly." She whispered to herself.

Sebastian walked up to her and put a hand to her face. "Even if you can't alone, we can together."

Reika jumped when she felt someone's finger hook into the back of her shirt, and cut the fabric down to her waist. "What the hell?!" She growled, whipping around and glared at Darius. "What did you do that for?!"

"We are going to see if you can fly!" Darius flashed his mischievous grin at her.

"You think I'd have wings?" Reika asked, looking to Samael.

"If you take after your father more than your mother, which you do." He grinned. "Yes, you would. Considering you were the one to grant Sebastian this life, and he has wings is also a very strong indicator you have a set waiting to unfurl."

"You have wings." Reika said, smiling. "Can I see them?" She asked.

Samael looked to Darius and smiled. He took his jacket and red shirt off, and handed them to Darius. Reika gazed over Samael's chest and arms. She had never seen him in anything less than a blazer and button down shirt. Without anything to cover his upper body, Reika could see many markings scattered across his skin. She was greatly intrigued by them all, but her attention to the markings was broken when Samael's wings opened.

A huge set of deep scarlet wings outstretched behind Samael, blocking the light from Reika. They settled, and Reika gaped still.

"Child, close your mouth." Samael said, stepping towards her. He outstretched his hand and gently closed her mouth for her. "Kneel down." He said softly.

Reika complied, and slowly sank to her knees. Samael stepped behind her and knelt down, placing his hands on her shoulder blades. Slowly, she felt her skin heat up and Samael withdrew. He came around, and knelt in front of her taking her hands. "It may become painful." Reika nodded, and grasped his hands. She felt the warmth on her back spread and intensify. She tried her best to stay composed as she squeezed his hands tighter.

Sebastian inched closer, watching. Reika bit the inside of her mouth, she could feel her skin getting tighter, as if about to burst. She lowered her head and groaned, as they heard a snapping sound.

Slowly, her wings began to grow, pure black feathers, in the same magnificent shape as Samael's, only proportionate to Reika's size.

Reika looked up at Samael, her eyes wide. "Holy shit." She muttered and looked over her shoulder. "I actually have wings!" She moved them gently and turned back, her eyes even wider. "This is freaky!"

"My dear." He laughed gently. "You were quite alright when I explained to you all of your duties as my daughter, yet what disturbs you the most is having wings?"

"Papa! I have new appendages!" She looked at him, dumbfounded at his statement. "I have wings! Granted it isn't every day a girl finds out her father is the angel of death, but wings sprouting from your back sure as hell doesn't happen like that either!"

"Well, now that you have unleashed them, it can indeed happen every day." Samael said, with a impish smile.

Reika stared at him for a moment and began to laugh uncontrollably. Samael too joined in the laughter. After a few moments, Reika wiped her eyes and took a deep breath. Samael offered his hands to her with a smile. She took them and they stood. Reika stepped back and beamed at Samael.

"Well, how does this work?" She turned, asking both Sebastian and Samael. Sebastian walked towards her, and took her hand.

He looked to Samael. "Could I show her?" He held her hand tight.

Samael smiled. "I will say yes, under one condition. I need a moment alone with Reika first."

Sebastian nodded and let go of Reika's hand after he squeezed it. He began walking towards Darius. Reika watched his back, and his wings shrank, then laid across his back, dissolving into his skin. She looked in awe as she saw a miniature version of his wings almost tattooed across his back. "How amazing." She whispered.

Sebastian turned and winked. "You're not so bad yourself."

Reika gaped at him, and couldn't find any words to respond with. Darius and Sebastian slipped inside the barn during Reika's silent moment. She shook her head, and turned to Samael.

Samael held his hand out to her. "There is something I wish to give you."

She took his hand and they began walking. "What are you wanting to give me?"

"I gave Sebastian a necklace, for protection. It's function is similar to your cloaking ability, yet it works without the mental energy needed to maintain it."

Samael brought her to a bench sitting in front of the barn. He placed a hand on her back, and she felt her wings shrink down, and disappear. She shuddered at the feeling. She watched as Samael's disappeared as well. "I feel things are going to become quite tense in the coming days. I want you to be prepared. You have the sword I had created for you. You need armor. Though a demon may be hurt and it not kill, there are weapons created which causes the wound fester and cause infection."

"What do you think is going to happen?"

"I haven't any idea." He sighed. "I suspect Lilith would have gotten hold of these types of weapons. It would make killing us much easier."

"How do you kill a demon?" Reika asked.

"It's fairly simple." Samael explained. "All that must be done is to stab the demon in the temple." He pointed to the side of his head. "The knife must be driven into the brain."

"So, a helmet is probably essential to any suit of armor?"

Samael nodded. "The helmet is the most crucial portion of your armor, never forget to wear it. Let's go inside and we will fit you with the armor."

Reika nodded and smiled. "Alright." She again took Samael's hand and they stepped inside the barn.

Chapter Fourteen

"Sebastian Luciano, age 18, was reported missing one week ago. The police say there are no signs of a struggle, or foul play. If anyone has any information about Sebastian's disappearance, please contact the Callisto police department." A blonde newscaster's voice echoed through the darkened living room at the Avel residence. Yuri sat, Lynde holding her while Meredith was locked in her room, as she had become accustomed to doing.

"I can't believe they're both gone." Yuri whispered. "What happened?"

"I don't know." Lynde sighed out. "He probably got brainwashed by her, and decided life wasn't worth living without her."

"I don't believe any of these stories." Yuri heaved out. "Reika was a little weird, but she wasn't insane like all these news reports make her sound. Mom hasn't talked to me about any of this since she brought me home. I just want answers."

"It's a little too late for that, Yuri." Lynde said. "They're gone now. You're just going to have to move on."

"That's not possible." Yuri sat up, her eyes wide with irritation. "Regardless of what people say she's my sister and I loved her. Things were getting weird near the end, but she wasn't that different from usual."

"Did she normally torment people like she did to Camille?"

"If you got on her bad side, yes." Yuri smirked. "I saw that girl take down six guys in a single fight. One had grabbed her ass, another grabbed her arm. She actually hit the one who grabbed her ass with the guy who grabbed her arm. She was fierce, not someone you wanted to mess with, but when she was your friend, you knew you were safe no matter what."

"I still think it's better you just let it go." Lynde said with a sigh. "Hanging onto her is only going to hurt you in the end."

Yuri stared at Lynde for a moment. "You know, death is never easy, nor does it ever stop hurting. You don't let go of those feelings of love no matter what, because it's all you have left." She smirked. "What's easy, is letting go of a piece of shit like you. You can leave, Lynde, and don't come back. I don't need your bullshit right now, I need a friend. Obviously you can't do that, so you serve no purpose anymore."

Lynde's jaw fell open in shock. "Seriously? You're going to be like that?"

Yuri stood up and went to the front door and opened it. "I sure am. Now get the fuck out." She pointed out the door.

"You're fucking insane, just like her." He said, shaking his head as he walked out the door.

"Thanks, I take that as a compliment." She grinned, winking at him. She slammed the door shut behind him and walked into her room. She closed the door, and leaned against it, sliding down to sit on the floor. Tears welled in her eyes, as she buried her face against her knees and began sobbing.

"Why did you have to leave?" She whispered through her sobs. Her question wasn't directed at a specific person, but to all who had left her. First, her father, then Reika, her mother wasn't stable enough to be supportive in this moment, now Sebastian and Lynde.

Isolation was taking it's toll on her, and she just wanted someone to be there for her.

Yuri took a deep breath, grabbed her boots and coat. She pulled them on quickly and left the house. She began walking down the street, and towards the town cemetery. The sun stained the sky in shades of reds, oranges, and pinks as she hurriedly made her way through the wrought iron gates. She began running, and found her father's grave. She stopped, and knelt down, her cries shaking through her small frame. "What do I do, Daddy?" She whispered. "I need you." She crumpled down, into a ball on the ground, scattered with colored leaves that matched the skies above her.

"Excuse me, Miss?" She heard a male's voice. "I'm sorry to bother you, but are you alright?"

She looked up, glaring at him. "Do I look alright to you?!"

Electric blue eyes peered out from underneath a hood darkened face. "No, you don't. That's why I wanted to check on you." He knelt down and pushed his hood back, revealing his face. "Can I help you at all?"

"I don't know if you can." She whispered. "Everyone's left me, and all I want is to see them again."

"Who is everyone?"

"My whole family." She sighed. "My mom is still alive, but she's no use. She goes to work, comes home and locks herself in her room." She looked up at the man. "Why am I telling you all this?" Yuri shook her head. "I don't even know you."

"Don't worry so much." He said softly, with a smile. "Sometimes you just need to talk to someone new."

She nodded softly. "You're right."

"What's your name?" He asked.

"I'm Yuri Avel."

"Your sister is Reika?" He asked. "I've heard of her."

"Yeah, she is." She paused for a moment. "Well, she was my sister."

"Yuri Avel, she still is your sister." He smiled. "Regardless of death, the bonds of family are still very much alive."

"You're right." She nodded.

He nodded some. "I've been through it before, I understand what it feels like. Can I ask what happened to your sister?"

"I don't know." She sighed. "They told me they found her body down by the creek at school. I don't know if she committed suicide, or if someone killed her. It could have been an accident too." She shrugged. "All I know is she's gone, and I wish I could see her again."

"Who identified the body?" He asked.

"Oh." She was caught off guard by the question. "Mom wouldn't let me leave to do it, so I don't know who did. They might have gotten the record store owner to do it, Rei was really good friends with him."

"You see, the reason I asked is because, I don't think she's dead." He smirked. "Sources say she is very much alive. If you wish to find her, look for this book." He handed her a slip of paper. "Find this book, and you may find your answer."

She opened the slip of paper. *'Occult Mysteries Solved: Practical Spells, Summons and Potions.'* Yuri bit her lower lip. "This sounds familiar." She looked up and the blue eyed man was gone.

She slipped the piece of paper in her pocket. She walked deeper into the cemetery, to a fresh grave. The only markings on it were a small sign with "R.L.A" on it. She knelt down and sighed. "Reika is that you in there?" She paused for a moment, but sighed once more.

"If it is, I'm sorry we weren't on the best of terms at the end." She said softly. "I missed having you around like it used to be, but you were scared of something. I knew you were cause you never acted like that. I hope these bones in this box beneath me aren't yours. I pray one day I'll see you again."

The wind picked up, the leaves began tumbling and dancing in the cold November breeze. She thought she heard a whisper on the wind, telling her *'I'm still here.'* Yuri felt a bone chilling shiver slam through her body. She stood, and made her trek back to her house. She entered quietly, and went into the computer room, where her mother had bookshelves lining the walls. She searched for the book the man had told her about.

Yuri searched and searched, to no avail. She was about to give up and return to her room when she noticed, on the top shelf, there was a spot where four books were sitting farther forward. She pulled a chair over so she could climb up and get a better view. She pulled the four books down, and behind it she saw an old book, the worn cover read *"Occult Mysteries Solved: Practical Spells, Summons and Potions."*

She grabbed the book down and replaced the books, keeping them forward so it still looked like the book was hidden. She slipped the book into her jacket and walked quickly into her room. Locking her door, she slipped the book out of her jacket off and threw it down on the floor. She pulled her boots off and sat on her bed, cracking the cover of the book open.

Yuri stared for a moment. "He never even told me what I was looking for." She whispered to herself. She ran her thumb over the side of the pages, and noticed one was folded over. She flipped to the page and read over the page.

'To summon a broker demon, you will need a piece of paper, a knife, matches and at least one candle. Make sure you know exactly what you wish to exchange for your soul before you summon a demon. Light the candle(s) with the match and turn the lights off. Cut yourself, so that you may have enough blood to write your name on the paper, then do so. Say these words three times over:

With this blood I give, I wish to make an offer.

I give you my soul, so that I may wander.

(Demon's name) Please come forth tonight

So that you may oblige my plight.

After you finish your words, blow your candle(s) out, and wait patiently.

Yuri looked over the page, and written before the parenthesis, was Samael. She sighed, pulled her phone out, and searched 'Samael.' She couldn't find much information on the man. She began flipping through the book, trying to find any demon summoning spells which didn't involve selling your soul. She couldn't find one, so she chose her own words. She lit her candle, and began chanting her own words.

"Samael, I summon you to me tonight. Please, come to me, I have questions, and it seems you're the only being who may have answers. Please grace me with your presence." She repeated herself three times, before blowing her candle out.

Yuri held her breath as she waited. She watched the extinguished flame's smoke dance in the darkened room. After a while, Yuri didn't think anything would happen. She stood, and turned her light on. She was about to turn, when she heard a voice call to her.

"Good evening, Yuri. You called for me?"

She turned to see a dark haired man sitting on her bed, dressed in all black. His leg was crossed over the other, and his hands in his pockets. He was perfectly sculpted, from his tall build, to his sharp cheekbones, and mysterious silver eyes peering out from heavy black lashes.

"Samael?" She whispered.

"It is what I am called." He pulled his hands out from his pockets, and leaned forward. "In your summons, you didn't say you wanted to make an offer, you just have questions. What are you seeking so desperately, that you must call upon the angel of death?"

"I went to my sister and father's grave today. This man with blue eyes came, and gave me a paper of a book title. I looked at the book, and in it, there was a page marked to summon a broker demon. Your name was written on the page. I don't want anything badly enough to give you my soul. I just wanted to know if she was still alive. The man said he believes she is still is. If she is, I want to be with her again. I'm alone, Mom isn't really living anymore."

"A man with blue eyes, you say?" Samael looked at her, intrigued. "Did he state his name?"

"No." She pulled the paper from her pocket. "He only gave me this."

"Adrian." He said to himself. Samael looked to Yuri. "You wish to join your sister once more?"

"If she's alive, yes." Yuri's eyes met Samael's. "This solitude is killing me."

Samael thought for a moment. "Gather what things you wish to keep from here, and you may come with me." He stated. "Only a few things, for you will be well taken care of."

Yuri nodded and gathered a few things. She grabbed a necklace her father gave her, her diary, and her computer. She put them in a bag, and turned to Samael. "I'm ready."

"I shall take you to the estate, you'll wait there, I'll get Reika for you."

"That's fine." She said with a nod.

Samael grinned, and held his hand out to her. "Come with me."

Yuri hesitated for a moment, then placed her hand is his. Her eyes closed the moment she felt her body being pulled into a void, and screamed out, her voice stifled by the void around her. Finally after what felt like an eternity, she opened her eyes, and was greeted by a magnificent living room.

"Welcome to the Blake House." He said with a grin.

Realization struck Yuri's face. "You're the Dean of Locke Academy."

"I am indeed." He smirked. "I placed myself in the position so I could get close to her. It seemed to work perfectly."

She nodded. "It makes sense. Where is she now?"

"Reika and Sebastian are both at the cabin. I will retrieve them shortly. I wanted to get you settled first."

She nodded, and took a seat. "I'm settled enough."

Samael smiled. "Strong willed. You learned well from the elder sister."

"I really did." She smiled in agreement.

"I shall return in a moment." Samael turned away from Yuri and let the darkness engulf him. He returned to the cabin and saw Sebastian, Reika and Darius sitting in the living room of the cabin, Darius telling them stories.

"Papa! You just missed a great story!" Reika exclaimed.

"I am certain I did." Samael smiled. "Though, I have a story for you, yet I cannot tell you here."

"Where are you able to tell me?" She asked.

"Back at home." He smiled warmly. "I have a surprise for you. We will summon your items home later on this evening, but it is very important we return home at once."

"Papa, when you talk like this you worry me." She gave him a stern look.

"Do not fret, my dear. All is well." He disappeared.

Reika looked to Sebastian. "Are you ready?" She stood up, and he followed.

"I am. Let's go see this surprise of yours." Sebastian said, hugging her. Reika smiled, held onto him tight, and they arrived at the house. Immediately upon arrival a set of hands covered her eyes.

"Papa, is that you?"

"Holy shit!" Sebastian exclaimed.

"It's not your father, silly!" Yuri's voice echoed through her skull.

"Yuri." She whispered, touching the hands on her face. They dropped and Reika turned. She was greeted with the smiling face of her little sister. "How did you get here?!"

"I called on Samael. I asked him if you were still alive, and he brought me to you." She grinned.

"You didn't make a deal, did you?" She asked, hugging her tightly.

"No, I didn't." She hugged her back. "Not yet at least."

"Why would you? You have everything." She whispered.

"I don't anymore. Mom's lost it completely. I broke up with Lynde today." She sighed. "Everything fell apart once you left." Yuri sniffed back tears.

"I never meant for it to happen. I was hoping it'd be a clean break, and everything would be normal once I left."

"Nothing has ever been normal, Rei. It wouldn't matter if you were here or at home, nothing will ever be normal, and I wouldn't want it to be."

Reika grinned. "I couldn't have said it better myself." She pulled back and looked Yuri in the face. "Listen, if you want to make a deal with us, I understand."

"I haven't made my choice. I don't even know what all is happening." Yuri explained. "I need answers."

Reika took Yuri's hand. "Let's go to my room and we'll talk."

Yuri nodded and they walked down the hallway and entered Reika's room. Yuri looked around in awe of the beautifully decorated room. "Holy shit! This is amazing!"

Reika laughed. "It is! I love it." She sat down on her bed, and grabbed a pillow, holding it to her chest. "What questions do you have for me?"

Yuri sat down on the bed, and looked down. "I have a lot of questions."

"Begin where ever you want to." She said softly.

"What are you? You're obviously not human."

"I'm a demon."

"How long have you known?"

"Since the night of my birthday."

"Is that why you were sick?"

"Yes."

"Who are you real parents?"

"Lilith and Samael Blake."

"His secretary?!"

"Yes." She laughed. "Don't trust her. She's a bitch."

Yuri nodded. "Noted." She looked down at her hands, and then up to Reika. "Why did mom leave you at school, and take me home?"

"She wished for two children because she was infertile. Lilith gave her me, and the ability to have one more child. You are the flesh and blood of William and Meredith Avel. I am not. We're not sisters by blood, but by bond. If you still consider me so."

"I do, Reika. You're the only family I have left." She wiped at her eyes. "When the coroner and police showed up to tell us you were dead. Mom just shuffled away, back into her room. They said after a few minutes of standing there at the door, I passed out. I woke up, in my bed. They made sure I was okay, and Mom too. She wouldn't go identify your body though, or let me."

Reika took a deep breath, her face was contorted in thought. "I'm not surprised. Is she okay now?"

"No, she's still locking herself in her room." She shook her head. "I'm surprised she didn't come out when I was talking to Samael."

"That's not like her." Reika sighed. "Do you think she'll be alright?"

Yuri looked up. "To be honest, I don't know and I want to say I don't care." She sighed out. "I still do."

"As crazy as everything got, I do too." She shrugged. "She raised us. William too, at least up until he passed. They were a pivotal part of our lives, it's okay to care."

Yuri nodded, as she fought back tears. "I wish someone had told me that sooner. Mom made me feel so guilty for still caring about you. I kept asking what happened in the car, she wouldn't tell me."

"What happened to me is this, Yuri." Reika scooted closer to her, and took her hand. "The night of my birthday I went to sleep. I was swept away, and tied to a bed. It was this bed, actually." She laughed a little. "Once I was here, I was given two options by Lilith. I was to either choose to live my life as what I was born to be, this creature of darkness, or die. Yuri, I didn't want to die, but I didn't want to leave you either.

"That's why I started acting weird, distancing myself. I figured it would be easier to leave that way. It wasn't. I'm just glad we didn't have to say goodbye for long." Reika looked down at Yuri's hand in hers. "My eyes changed, because they are a sign of what I am. I became stronger physically. I didn't have to eat as much anymore, but I still enjoyed it. I won't have to sleep hardly anymore, once I get older. Mom saw my eyes, and that is what she remembered of my real parents. That's why she left me behind. I became what she feared the most."

"Why does she fear them, when she got her wish?"

"Because in death, she will become nothing." Reika sighed. "It's the hard reality of making a deal with one of us."

"What do you mean?"

"It's not for free, Yuri." She squeezed her hand. "You lose your soul. Just know nothing in this world is for free. If you ever choose to make a deal, one of us will collect your soul."

Yuri gulped. "How do you collect someone's soul?"

"There are many ways, but I prefer to do so by drinking their blood." She said softly, looking down once again. Admitting everything to Yuri was difficult, and it was even more so to look her in the eyes while she spoke.

"You mean like a vampire?!" She exclaimed. "That is so fucking hot!"

Reika looked up, surprised. "Yeah, like a vampire." She laughed. "Except, when vampires feed, they don't take the soul."

Yuri grinned. "That's so cool."

Reika smiled and nodded. "It's pretty cool."

Before either girl could speak again, the door flew open, revealing a flustered Sebastian.

"You guys need to come to the living room, now." He said and ran off.

Reika and Yuri exchanged looks and took off to the living room quickly.

Samael and Sebastian were staring at the television, Sebastian's jaw agape.

Flashing atop the screen were the words "MURDER IN CALLISTO."

"Oh my god." Yuri exclaimed.

"We have breaking news from Callisto, Ohio this evening. Neighbors of this home in the town reported to police that they heard a scream come from inside, and saw a figure leaving the home's back door. Police state the neighbor tried to enter the home, but all doors were locked. They called 911, but when help arrived, it was too late for Meredith Avel, age 47. She was found dead this evening, due to a stab wound. The neighbors tell us her 16 year old daughter, Yuri Avel, is now missing."

Yuri's face paled as the report continued.

"Police are seeking out Miss Avel, for she is a person of interest in this case. Police tell us there was a book of occult spells found next to the body." The blonde reporter stated. She looked down and placed her hand to her ear, as to listen to someone speak. She looked up at the camera, her face stern. "It seems it is a sad night in Callisto, as it has been reported that Brian Luciano, age 53, has been pronounced dead. Our sources state this as a homicide as well, and the suspect, Theresa Luciano, age 37, is in custody."

Reika looked from Yuri, to Sebastian, whose face shifted from shock to relief, and settled into melancholy.

"Both families have had their children go missing. Ms. Avel's daughter, Reika Avel, aged 18, was reported missing, and later was found dead in Stafford creek near Locke Academy. Police officials are still looking for Sebastian Luciano, 18 years old, and Yuri Avel, of 16 years. If any information of their whereabouts is known, please contact Callisto Police Department."

Samael shut the television off. "We need to make a plan quickly. First thing, I will make sure your mother has a top notch defense attorney. I will speak with Darius, he will be able to decipher if this was self defense." He turned to Reika and Yuri. "We need to fake Yuri's death, as well as yours, Sebastian." He gazed back to Sebastian. "The murder weapon she used, do you think it was the knife you used to summon me?"

Yuri took a deep breath, looked at Samael with dead eyes and nodded. "Yes, it was. It was one Reika had given me for my birthday. That damn thing was sharp."

Samael smirked. "I have an idea."

"What are you thinking, Papa?"

"I will create a scene, where Meredith murdered Yuri, and took her own life in Yuri's room." Samael nodded some. "As for Sebastian, I believe we should have your death be in the same creek as Reika's." He looked up and sighed. "Ah, two lovers meet their death in the same place, so they may meet once more in the afterlife." He looked at Sebastian. "Morbidly romantic, yes?" Samael snapped his fingers. "Everything should be in place, no need to worry. Though, I am truly sorry, my girls, Meredith was a lovely woman, with a big heart. It's saddening to see someone succumb to the madness which can occur when one loses their soul."

Reika turned to Yuri and gathered her sister in her arms and hugged her tight. "I'm so sorry, Yuri."

"Yeah, me too." She whispered, holding onto Reika tight. "Can I go to sleep now?" She asked softly.

"Of course. You can sleep in my room tonight." Reika replied.

"That sounds good." She said softly.

Reika lead her down the hallway and into her room. Yuri sat down on the bed once more. Reika went to her dresser and pulled out a shirt and pair of fleece pants. She laid them on the bed. "Here's something to wear to bed. If you need anything, I'll be across the hall, just knock before you come in. It's Sebastian's room."

Yuri nodded. "Thanks, Rei. I love you." She said.

"I love you too, Yuri." She smiled and left the room quietly. She returned to Sebastian and Samael.

"Is she alright?" Sebastian asked.

"As fine as she can be right now." She sighed. "Poor girl." She wrapped her arms around Sebastian's waist, and leaned against him. "Though I think her idea of going to bed is a great idea. I'm exhausted."

"Dear child, it might be time for another feeding." Samael said softly. "You as well, Sebastian. Rest tonight, we will take care of this in the morning. Good night my darlings." He smiled, and patted both on the shoulders as he passed through to his bedroom.

Reika yawned into Sebastian's arm. Before she could say anything, Sebastian had scooped her up in his arms, and began down the hallway to his room.

"Bas, you don't have to!" She said, yawning again.

"Apparently I do need to." He said with a smile. "You just look so precious, let me carry you in my arms for once."

She smiled and laid her head against his chest, savoring the moment. "You're the sweetest."

"Oh, you say that now." He smirked.

"What are you trying to say?"
"Not a thing, my love." He said softly. "Nothing at all."

He stopped in front of the door, Reika looked up and smiled. She reached down and turned the doorknob to open it for him.

Sebastian took her inside the door, and closed it with his foot. He laid her down on the bed, and joined her. Reika entwined herself in Sebastian's arms.

"I've missed moments like this." She said softly.

"Everything will fall back into place, and you'll never have to miss moments like these again." Sebastian replied. His fingers began combing through her hair.

Reika let out a soft moan. "We've been working hard, it should pay off in the end. Then we'll be free of it all. So will Papa." She sighed. "I can't believe he's dealt with her this long."

"Since the beginning, right?"

"Yes." She nodded. "It's terrible what she's done to him. Watching him speak of the old days, when he had all those children he adored, and how they were taken away because of what she did. It's sickening. Honestly, I'm surprised I've made it this far in my life with what she did to those poor children."

Sebastian nodded, and held Reika tight, cradling her head to his chest. "She won't get you. I won't let her."

"She won't take any of us down." Reika sighed out. "I'll destroy her before that happens."

"I know you will." Sebastian smiled gently. "You're a fierce protector. When I saw you on the streets, as mesmerized as I was by you, I was also terrified."

"Why were you scared?" She asked, pulling back and looking at his face.

He laughed some. "You've never seen yourself angry, or fighting. You're ferocious and it's just as seductive as it is scary. To know you're capable of such things is one of the most sexiest things about you, but it's scary. You're like a wild animal. You're unrestrained, and majestic. It's part of what makes you so beautiful." Reika nipped at the tip of his nose. "Is it your job to tame me?" She smirked.

"In some ways, yes. In other ways, I'm here to preserve your wild beauty." He placed a hand against her cheek. "Which do you wish for tonight?"

She slowly rose, straddling his hips. She wrapped her arms around his neck and lowered herself to press her lips on top of his.

"For every night with you to be like this." She whispered on his parted lips.

Sebastian wound his arms around her waist, holding her close to him. "My love, every night together will be like this, until the end of time."

Chapter Fifteen

"They moved back to the mansion." Adrian explained. "They have the human girl as well." He dipped the sponge in his hand in the bath water, squeezed it, and washed Lilith's shoulders. "How shall we proceed?"

"I know a way inside the house. I want to steal away Sebastian, the girl, or both. It depends on how fast I can move." Lilith leaned her head back against the tub. "Reika will undoubtedly come to rescue them. Once she is in the vicinity, I will slaughter them all."

"To see you covered in the blood of your victims would be a dream come true for me." Adrian cooed in her ear.

"And for you to clean it off of me in whichever way I command is mine." Her silver eyes gazed into his blue orbs. "Now kiss me." She smirked.

Adrian obeyed her command and laid his lips on hers as she began to kiss him furiously. He submitted to her, letting her have her way.

Lilith pulled away. "I shall need my towel now." She said dismissively.

Adrian laid the sponge down on the edge of the bathtub and went to the long marble counter and retrieved the towel he had laid out for her. "Here you are, my dear."

She stood, and took the towel from him, and stepped out of the tub, onto the rug. She wrapped her body in the large towel and made her way onto the balcony.

"I will get my revenge." Lilith hissed. "That wretched whore thinks she can take him away from me and get away with it!" She yelled. "I'll make sure to take everything from her! I should have killed her that night Samael brought that rat into my home! She didn't deserve to live! She doesn't deserve to take my place! I am the queen of night, she can't take that from me!" She screamed out, her eyes lit in delirious anger.

Adrian came to her, taking her hands gently. "You still are queen." He said softly. "No matter who says otherwise, you are my queen."

She ripped her hands out of his, and knocked him to the ground. "It doesn't matter if I'm your queen! You have no power!" She hissed. "None of your subjects listen to you! You're a spineless leader!"

Adrian pulled himself up, rubbing the back of his head where it struck the hard floor of the balcony. "You're right." He said softly. "I haven't any control over my subjects." He turned and left her alone.

He walked into his room and locked the door and sat in silence. He thought to himself about what a mistake it was to take in Lilith. He knew her end was near, he just didn't know how soon.

# # #

"There's how many?!" Reika shouted, her eyes wide with shock.

"Twenty-five." Samael grinned. "Each want to die by the blade, and each soul is yours."

"I have to battle them all at once?!"

"No, it will be in groups of five." He put a hand on her shoulder. "I promise you will be alright."

Reika looked into Samael's eyes and nodded. "Alright. I'll do it."

"Sebastian and I will be there in case you need help."

"Sebastian will be watching?" She asked, a devious smile crept across her lips.

"Indeed he will be."

"Let's go to the cabin." She said, eagerly clapping her hands together.

Samael nodded. "Go fetch Sebastian and we will make our way there together."

She nodded and ran off to the library. When she entered, she saw Sebastian sitting in front of the stained glass window. Reika came over and took his hands. "We're going back to the cabin today!"

Sebastian smiled up at her. "What's happening there?"

"I have twenty-five souls I need to consume, and then twenty-five men I need to kill." She sat down next to him and wrapped her arms around his neck. "Papa said they wish to die in combat, and I am to give them their wish."

"Sounds brilliant." He smirked.

"Let's go meet with Papa and we'll head there!"

He kissed her cheek and set his book down. "Let's go." Together, they walked from the library to the living room where Samael waited. Yuri and Darius sat together watching a movie.

"Darius, take good care of our dear Yuri." Samael said. "We shall return by nightfall, I imagine."

"Have no worries, Samael. She is in good hands."

"We'll be fine!" Yuri smiled. "We're having a movie marathon!"

Reika laughed. "They'll be fine. Yuri will be distracted all day."

"We'll see you guys later." Sebastian said before they disappeared from the house.

They looked around the barn, where Reika's armor sat on a mannequin, waiting for her to put it on. She grinned, and looked to Sebastian. "Sometimes I need help with corsets, but today, I need help with armor."

Sebastian smiled. "I would be glad to help you."

Samael smiled as well. "I will prep our warriors whilst you prepare yourself." He turned and left the barn.

Reika looked to Sebastian. "I'm probably too excited for this moment."

"I think you're a perfect level of excitement." He kissed her forehead. "Don't feel guilty over this, because you're just doing your role in this world."

She nodded. "I'll do my best." She turned away from him and began to strip down, to put her padding on beneath her armor. First she wrapped clothe around her chest, slipped a loose shirt over top, and put on a pair of cotton pants. She slipped each piece of armor on, and Sebastian tied the cords to hold them in place. Sebastian wrapped her belt around her waist, and secured her sword. Finally, she took the helmet from the head of the mannequin and turned to Sebastian. "I'm ready."

Sebastian took the helmet from her hands and placed it on her head gently. "You look deadly gorgeous in this." His proud smile shone brightly in the dim light of the barn.

"Thank you, love." She said softly. Reika's stomach dropped with the weight of what she was about to do. Not only was she nervous of the battle before her, she felt something tragic would happen. She looked up, her concern saturated her irises. "If I get in trouble out there, will you come to my aid?" She asked.

"Of course." He said.

Reika wrapped her arms around him. "Thank you, my love." She said softly. "Sorry, I'm sure a hug in armor is not very comfortable."

"You're fine, dear." He smiled. "You'll be fine, I promise."

"Could you give me a moment alone?" She asked.

He squeezed her hand and nodded. "Of course. Come out when you're ready."

Reika nodded, and took a deep breath. She tried to calm her churning stomach. She pressed her hands together and breathing deeply, calming herself. She whispered words to herself, drawing her inner strength, and centering her mind. She opened her eyes, and felt much more relaxed about her situation. She took one final deep breath and stepped out of the barn. Sebastian and Samael stood, looking down at the bottom of the hill.

"It seems they are all ready." Samael stated. "We will start out having one versus one due to skill levels, and the lower skilled fighters will take you one in groups." Samael smirked.

"There's a group of six who haven't fought a day in their life." Sebastian commented

Reika looked up at them in confusion. "They wish to die by the blade?"

"Those who wish to die by the blade with no experience wielding a weapon seldom put up a fight. Usually they are the first ones to kneel down and offer up their necks." Samael smirked. "Their souls have been collected, and I have placed them in a bottle for after your battle. You will need the energy from them after this."

Reika nodded. "How do we begin?"

"There aren't really any rules. They just pick who goes first." Sebastian shrugged.

"Go to the bottom of the hill, and your first opponent shall present himself." Samael nodded. "Just as you have dueled before, draw your sword, wait for your moment and strike."

She nodded. "I got this."

Samael stepped forward, and took her helmet off. He kissed her forehead. "You will be extraordinary." He placed the helmet back in place and smiled down at her. "I would not have arranged this opportunity if I did not think you could handle such an event."

She smiled softly. "I can do it." Reika turned away from the two and made her way down the steep hill where twenty-five men awaited their death by her sword.

Samael set his gaze on Sebastian. "Let the blood bath begin."

"I think I'm more excited for this than Reika is." Sebastian grinned like a child.

"Your words do not surprise me." He laughed. "There have been many a time Lilith was given this very opportunity, and it was a glorious mess." He shook his head. "Ah, then there was the wonderful moment I met our dearly departed friend, Countess Bathory. She was intrigued by how young both Lilith and I seemed.

The poor girl was told by Lilith it was bathing in blood, as well as consuming it. I assume you know the rest of the story?"

Sebastian nodded. "I do know the story."

"She truly was beautiful, even whilst bathed in blood." Samael said. "Enjoy your view." He smirked.

Both Samael and Sebastian fell silent as the saw Reika stop in front of the group of men. "Who wishes to meet their end first?" She asked, her voice strong. "Step forward, so that we may cross blades." Despite the confidence she let flow through her body, she still held that slight unease in her stomach.

A young man came from the center of the group and stood before her. "I shall meet my end with honor and dignity." He said, his head held high.

"Why do you wish for this end?" She asked.

"I was diagnosed with an incurable cancer. I was to join the military, but I was denied. I won't live much longer. I have no family left, and want to meet my end in a way which is memorable."

Reika nodded. "Very well." She tried not to let her smile flicker on her face. "Draw your weapon."

The man, who was barely clothed drew a short sword. Reika drew her's and she watched. He took a deep breath, and ran towards her, his sword raised above his head. He yelled out as he charged forward. Reika stepped to the side, and plunged her sword into his stomach. She heard the shocked gasp escape the man's lips. She held firm to the sword with one hand, and placed another on his shoulder. "Rest now, warrior." She whispered in his ear, before ripping the sword out of his body.

She stepped back, and watched him fall to the ground, a soft smile was etched on his face. Reika's eyes rose to the group of men once more. "Who is next?"

One by one, the men came forward, and met their deaths, until only five men stood before her. Reika's body was covered in dripping red, and grin across her face. She looked to each of the last five and nodded.

They formed an arch and drew their weapons. Reika's eyes were wild with adrenaline. The man in the center came forward, and attacked. She dropped her body, raising her sword over her head, and struck underneath his arm. Each man attacked and fell, one after another, until only one was left standing. He smirked at Reika, opening his arms, beckoning her forward.

She raised her sword above her head, holding it straight towards the sky. She waited, watching his body.

A battle cry erupted, and Reika charged forward. Her eyes watched carefully for signs of her enemy's retreat, or feint. He brought his sword up, to pierce her, yet Reika stepped away just in time, and struck him in the side.

The man whipped around, to strike her in the head. She blocked, and kicked him back. The man fell backward, landing with a thud on the ground. His sword flew from his hand. He looked at it, wide eyed. She stepped forward, bringing her knee down on his chest, and drew her sword across his neck. She looked up to the sky as the spray of blood from his final heartbeats washed over her.

In the setting sun, Reika wiped the blood from her blade and sheathed it. She turned towards the hill, where Sebastian and Samael were struck with awe. She climbed the hill in record time. She knelt down in front of her father. "The deed has been done."

"It was quite the spectacle, my dear. I shall draw you a bath inside, and we will give you your prize." He winked, and tapped the end of her nose with his index finger. Samael stood, and licked the tip of his finger as he entered the cottage.

Reika stood and took a deep breath. Sebastian joined her, his eyes were bright with excitement. "Come, and we'll get you out of this armor." He smirked and took her hands, leading her into the barn. As soon as she entered the barn, she placed her helmet upon the mannequin. Sebastian turned her around and began unlacing her armor, He laid it out to clean later, and pulled Reika into his arms once she was free from her metallic casing.

"Sebastian!" She said in surprise. "What's gotten into you?"

"Seeing you like this, is indescribably arousing." He growled into her ear.

She looked at him with a smirk. "I wish I could oblige right this very moment, but I need to take care of something important."

Sebastian nodded. "I'll be waiting for you, my sweet."

She kisses him hard and left the barn once more, her eyes were struck with dark clouds rolling across the horizon. She quickly made her way to the bottom of the hill, where she took each man's weapon and stabbed the blade into the ground where they died. With the last sword in hand, she gazed around in confusion. "Only twenty-four?"

She felt the rain begin to trickle across her skin. She smiled, closing her eyes and tilted her head back, forgetting her thoughts. The cold rain against her body felt glorious. She could taste the blood, sweat and rain rolling down her face, onto her lips. Though something didn't feel right.

Reika's eyes flashed open as she felt another presence near her, one she didn't recognize. She turned, the last man's sword still in hand, though she couldn't find the source of the aura.

"You should never let your guard down!" She heard an unfamiliar voice call out. Before she had time to react, she felt his blade slice her right side open. She could feel her blood cascading down, from her waist, over her hip. She drew the sword back, and swung with fury. The man dodged her. She took a deep breath, regaining her composure. She raised her sword over her head, the blade in line with her body. She was much too reckless though, giving the man another opening.

He thrust his blade forward, it plunging deep into her side. At the same time she swung once more, with all her power. The sword sliced right through his neck. The man's head landed on the ground with a thud. She stumbled backwards, pulling the sword from her side, and threw it on the ground next to the man's body. She watched as his blood poured over the ground.

"I may have forgot, but you didn't take me with you." She said, holding her stomach. She dropped the blade, and tried to make her way up the hill to the cottage. Each step took more and more energy from her. She felt sluggish, her surroundings looked dim with each step. She cried out, the pain finally seeping into her bones. Dropping to her knees, she clung her stomach, screaming out.

"SEBASTIAN!" She cried out. "PAPA!" She began pulling herself farther up the hill, still crying out for them. She had almost made it to the top, before her vision went black.

# # #

Faint cries from outside were barely audible over the rushing water of the bath. Samael turned the faucet off, and listened closely. He heard her scream one last time, and frantically ran out the door to find her. He checked the barn first, but heard Sebastian call out to him.

"Down here!" He yelled out.

Samael ran out and looked down at Sebastian. He was cradling Reika's limp body in his arms, trying to keep pressure on her wounds. Samael slid down the hill and ran to his side. "What happened?!"

"I was cleaning her armor, and I heard her cry out. I came out when she screamed for me, but she was already unconscious." He said through panicked sobs. "I don't know what to do, she won't stop bleeding."

"We need to get her inside." Samael said. He placed his hand on Sebastian's shoulder and they transferred to the bathroom of the cottage. The worked quickly to remove her clothing, and clean her quickly. Samael swallowed hard at seeing the full extent of Reika's wounds. "I need Darius."

Darius appeared the moment his name was mentioned. "What happened?" He asked, trying to remain calm.

"I don't know." Samael said, his face was blanketed in anguish. "I came out, Sebastian was trying to apply pressure to her wounds. We brought her in, and cleaned her up, but the wounds are still bleeding profusely."

"Let me take a look." He said, retaining his calm demeanor. Darius knelt down and examined the wounds carefully. "I need clean bandages, disinfectant, a needle, suture thread, and lots of gauze." He said.

Samael nodded, and grabbed a medical bag he had in the cabin. "I think all should be there, if not, please let me know."

Darius nodded. "This will take me a while. Might one of you apply pressure to the puncture wound while I stitch the other?"

Sebastian nodded. "I'll do it." He came over to him. Darius gave him a pair of gloves to put on first. He put them on, and took the gauze and pressed down on the puncture wound just above Reika's hip. Samael grabbed a couple towels and covered her. He sat down on the stool at the vanity mirror and held his head in his hands.

For what seemed like hours, Sebastian sat, pressing on Reika's wound. Every so often, when he saw red peek through the top layer of gauze, he added more. "It hasn't stopped." He said, his voice hoarse.

Darius cut the end of his thread and covered the wound he had just stitched. "I'm hoping I'm wrong." He said softly. "Though, it's possible these wounds were created by a holy blade."

Samael's head shot up, his eyes wide. "A blade of Michael?"

"It's possible." Darius said softly. "If it were, any creature which holds darker disposition in this world is susceptible to horrifying wounds from the blade. I can only think of a few ways to cleanse such a wound, but I need further research. The stitched wound should fare decently. I may need to close the second one until research gives me some answers." He sighed softly. "Until I find what I need, it's all I can do to help."

"What shall we do until then to help her?" Sebastian asked.

"We need to keep the wounds cleaned, and bandaged. She will need to be fed. If she hasn't claimed her souls from the battle today, it could help greatly."

Samael nodded. "Close the second wound." He said, his voice muted. "I will make sure she consumes what she needs."

"Very well." Darius said. "I shall take care of it." He came over to Sebastian's side. "You and Samael may sit in the living room. Once finished, we shall take her to the bedroom."

Sebastian nodded and they both shuffled out of the room. Sebastian sat down and went to put his head in his hands, but was stopped by the blood stained gloves on his hands. He closed them in tight fists and tried to fight back the hot tears he felt brimming in his eyes.

"Sebastian, if you must, let it flow." Samael said, his voice still void of emotion. "It doesn't make you weak to show your true nature. You're among those who feel the same."

Sebastian ripped the gloves from his hands and dropped them on the floor. His hands balled into fists in his hair as he began sobbing. "I can't lose her." He whispered. "Not now."

"You won't." Darius said, entering the room. "We'll save her."

"Do you think Lilith is behind this?"

"It is almost certain at this point." Darius said. "She must have gotten wind of the execution, and had someone infiltrate the group."

"She must pay for this." Samael said through gritted teeth. His knuckles were white, as he clasped his hands together. "She must be in Michael's bed as well as Adrian's is she was able to come into possession of a holy blade." He shuddered. "It is difficult to know what will happen from this point on." He let out a tired sigh. "Darius, who is a Demon to pray to in need of guidance? A being lost from the light of the world certainly couldn't call upon God."

Darius was shocked by the words drifting from Samael's lips, but he thought for a moment. "One would assume he would pray to himself, implore his own powers, invoke his own name. He certainly holds enough power to handle the task before him, he needs to muster the strength within. If praying to himself would do so, then pray he must."

Sebastian's lips tugged at the corner gently.

"How correct you are." Samael said softly.

Darius smiled. "Everything will turn out for the best interest of everyone in this family. I must go and find my research material. If Reika needs anything, give her the bottle of collected souls first, if she still needs anything, I am certain either of you have no problems letting her feed from you."

They both nodded in response.

"I shall return shortly." Darius said softly, and disappeared before their eyes.

Samael looked to Sebastian. "Are you doing alright?" He said softly.

"Do you want me to answer honestly, or lie?" He asked.

"Speak the truth, my son." He offered as much of a smile to Sebastian as he could. "The truth is always welcomed in my presence."

"I'm scared. I feel like I can't do a damn thing to help her, when it's all I want to do." His body shook as he was on the verge of tears. "I don't want to lose her."

"Believe these words, Sariel." He whispered softly. "Reika will live forever. She is a force which is almost impossible to destroy. There is a strength within her body I have not seen in any living being." Samael's eyes were full of conviction. "She will live."

Sebastian nodded. "She will." He looked up. "Sariel?"

"It is your name." He looked at the wall, his eyes glazed. "As Reika's middle name is Lilin, your middle name is Sariel now. It signifies your parentage."

Sebastian nodded. "I understand."

"When you are summoned by anyone in the human world, you will be summoned by Sariel, unless someone knows your real name."

"I doubt anyone from school will realize what I am now."

Samael smirked. "One would be surprised at how quickly urban legends are built."

Sebastian jumped as he heard whimpering coming from the bedroom. "She's restless." He said softly. He got to his feet and walked towards the room. Samael stood and followed. When they entered, Reika's eyes fluttered open as she let out a cry of pain.

"Papa." She cried out through her tears. "Papa, please make it stop. It burns."

Sebastian and Samael went to either side of her bed and took her hand. Her grip was tight on their hands.

"Love, what would help?" Samael asked.

"I don't know." She whimpered.

"The bottle." Sebastian said. "The souls."

Samael held his hand out, and a bottle appeared in his hand. It fit in the palm of Samael's hand, and the dark liquid glowed with a deep red hue. "I hope this will help." Samael whispered. He looked down to Reika's face, and then back to Sebastian. "She will need help taking this."

"What do you mean?"

"She will not be able to sit up to drink from the bottle." Samael handed it to Sebastian. "You'll have to take it yourself, and give it to her."

Sebastian slipped his hand out from Reika's grip and sat down beside her on the bed. He unscrewed the cap from the bottle. "Rei, are you ready?"

"Yes." She said breathlessly, opening her eyes.

Sebastian took a small sip of the bottle, placed it on the night stand and leaned down, placing his elbow down next to Reika's head. He brought his lips to hers, and parted them. He let the liquid flow into her mouth and she swallowed it down. Sebastian pulled back, and looked down into her face. "Was that alright?" He asked her.

"Yes." She whispered, her eyes gazing into his. "More."

Sebastian repeated the process, until he only had one small drink left. He took the remnants of the bottle into his mouth and gave her the last bit. He went to pull back, but a weak hand touched his thigh, beckoning him to stay.

'I love you, Sebastian, my saving grace.'

'I love you as well, my warrior. Now please, get better. Is there anything else you need?'

'Stay with me.'

'Forever, I will be by your side.'

'And I by yours. Good night, my sweet.'

Sebastian sat back up, and brushed the hair from Reika's face. Her skin was hot, and damp with sweat. "She has a fever." He frowned.

"I'll get a clothe." He said, kissing the back of Reika's hand before leaving the room. Sebastian leaned down and kissed her forehead.

"Reika, my dear." He whispered. "You will make it through this. You are by far the most resilient person I've met. I believe you can survive anything. You're a fighter, and you need to keep fighting."

"You are my strength." Reika whispered drowsily. "Do not waiver."

"Never." He said, biting the inside of his cheek to hold back the tears threatening to spill over. "I will stay strong, for you."

"Do it for both of us." She tried to move, and yelped in pain.

"Don't try to move." He touched her cheek gently. "You'll hurt yourself more."

"I hate sleeping on my back." She grumbled.

"You can't really sleep on your sides." Sebastian said. "Do you remember what happened?"

"I cut that fucker's head off." She growled out. "He stabbed me, and slashed me. I'm still alive, barely." She laughed some, but moaned in pain. "I wish I could kill him a thousand times over."

"Rei, you really need to rest." He kissed her gently. "You're not going to heal if you don't rest."

"I'm not healing at all right now." She sighed. "I can feel them bleeding."

"Do you need more blood?" He asked her.

"I need it, and to sleep again." She looked up at Sebastian, her eyes wide. "It hurts so fucking much. I don't want to feel it anymore."

"Close your eyes." He said softly. Reika obliged, her dark lashes laying down against her ever pale skin. Sebastian brought his hand to his mouth and bit into his own flesh. He touched it to her lips, and she parted them, letting his blood flow into her mouth. Sebastian thought to himself, how he wanted his blood to calm her, and take her pain away, so she may rest. It didn't take long until she fell asleep. He leaned down, and kissed her lips once more. "Sleep well, my love."

Sebastian stepped out to the hallway to see where Samael was. He and Darius were standing in the living room. In Samael's hands was a metal bowl, and a clothe.

"I don't know where she is." Darius said softly. "She was in the living room, watching a movie when I left. When I returned, the room was a wreck and she was gone."

The bowl dropped from Samael's hand. "They stole her away."

"They got Yuri?" Sebastian asked.

Darius looked to Sebastian with saddened eyes. "She's gone."

Chapter Sixteen

"Welcome to my home." Adrian cooed. "It's so nice to see you again, Yuri Avel. I actually believed you to be dead. How wonderfully convincing Samael's cover story was."

"You know?" Yuri whispered, her eyes wide. "How do you know?" Her jaw dropped. "You were in the cemetery that night."

He brought a finger up, and closed her mouth. "You look much more intelligent with your mouth shut." Adrian smirked. "Though it's difficult to look smart when you're bound in ropes."

"Well, when some psycho fucking demon comes in your house and takes you hostage when you're only a human, you tend to not have a choice on whether you get bound in ropes or not." She hissed.

"Pathetic little girl, you mistake me for one of those disgusting creatures." He shook his head. "Satyrs are much more majestic."

Yuri laughed. "A majestic satyr? You mean those half goat men with harps and bows? How the fuck is that majestic? Where are your damned hooves?"

"We've learned how to conceal those." Adrian said, clearly not amused by Yuri.

"Evolution at it's finest." Yuri snorted. "I would kill myself if I had horns, and a fucking half goat body." She gagged. "I already can't stand my legs being hairy, but to be completely furry would be hell! Oh, maybe that's why you guys are evil, you're tired of hairy legs." Yuri couldn't help but laugh.

Adrian drew his hand back and cracked her across the face. "Enough with your senseless banter! You idiot, do you even realize what's going to happen to you in my custody?!"

She smirked. "I do."

"You'll meet your own death her." Adrian grinned.

"Not if you meet yours first." Yuri said calmly.

"What do you mean?"

"You've brought a hostage into this game you're playing." Yuri stared at him. "Are you seriously telling me you can't think of anything backfiring due to having a human hostage inside your walls who is protected by some of the craziest motherfuckers out there? Maybe you're the dumb ass here and maybe it's a good thing I'm in these fucking ropes otherwise I'd punch you in your fucking face."

"You and Reika are indeed sisters." Adrian laughed. He leaned forward and licked at the corner of her mouth, where a small trail of blood dripped down.

Yuri slowly leaned in, as if to kiss him, and bit down on his tongue. "Don't think it's alright to fucking touch me with your nasty goat tongue."

Adrian cursed under his breath as he stepped back, and put a hand to his mouth. His eyes were filled with fury as he struck her in the stomach. "Don't ever think you can try anything smart like that again!" He growled. "You will obey, or you will die! Do you understand?"

She groaned out. "Yes, master." She said, trying to hide her sarcasm.

Adrian grabbed her chin. "I asked if you understood!"

"I do indeed understand." She glared at him. "I'm not deaf."

Adrian dropped her chin and left the room, slamming the door behind him. Yuri sighed.

"This is the life." Yuri rolled her eyes. "Being tied to a chair in some cell, oh yeah, this is paradise." She leaned her head back and closed her eyes. "I better not die here, or I'm going to haunt the shit out of all of you."

# # #

A week had passed since Reika was attacked. Her wounds still appeared as fresh as the day they had been dealt. Darius and Samael sat at the table in the small kitchen, pouring over ancient books.

Darius groaned. "Couldn't these alchemists written these instructions in an easier language to understand?!"

"If they did, everyone would have become one." Samael sighed out. "I think our only option is the paste you had found in your first book."

"We shall try." He said softly. "I have a theory though."

"What are you thinking?"

"If the blade had been blessed by holy powers, do you think that something as unholy, so to speak, would be able to void it?"

"What do you mean?" Samael asked. "The only unholy items which could be used would be the tongue of a demon, or his blood."

Darius smirked. "Now you're thinking."

"Are you saying if we cleansed her wounds by the tongue of a demon, they might start to heal?"

"By the tongue of wickedness, all which is holy shall fail." Darius said. "Those possessed by the demon's tongue are bound by the chains of hell. They shall never see the light of the one, so long as the darkness flows through their body."

Samael nodded. "Darkness shall consume all light held inside, polluting it to a beautiful black."

"You remember." He smirked. "Are you willing to try?"

"I will attempt anything to save her life." Samael nodded.

"Let us test this theory." Darius said, standing. Samael followed.

Sebastian had fallen asleep in the chair next to Reika's bed. She had just woken up.

Samael knelt down next to the bed. "How are you doing, child?" He squeezed her hand.

"It still hurts a lot." She said, groggy. Her face was pale, with dark circles under her eyes. "I'm so tired." Her voice was weak. "I shouldn't be, I sleep all the time."

"It's the so called Blessing of Michael." Samael said. "We may have found a way to rid you of it."

"Will it hurt?" She asked, turning her head to look him in the eyes.

"It might." Samael touched her cheek. "If it does, it will only be for a moment. Once the pain of the blessing being removed has passed, you will be able to heal properly."

"What must you do?" She leaned her head against his hand, closing her eyes.

Samael made a funny face. "I must lick your wounds."

"Papa, we aren't dogs." She murmured.

"We aren't human either." He said softly.

Sebastian stirred, opening his eyes. "Everyone's here." He said with a yawn.

"We're going to need your help." Darius said.

"With what?"

"Hold Reika's hand. Samael is going to cleanse her wounds. It might prove to be painful. Moral support is always needed in times like these."

Sebastian nodded, and took Reika's hand. "I can absolutely do that much." He smiled softly.

Darius pulled the blankets back from Reika, and pulled her shirt up so he could remove the bandages. He winced as he saw the red edges of the wounds. He looked to Samael. "I really hope this works."

"One must draw on the strength within." Samael said. "There is enough power within me to do such a deed. I will succeed."

Darius smiled. "I am glad to see you've returned, my friend."

Samael smiled softly and looked down to Reika. "Shall we begin?"

Reika murmured. "Yeah, go for it." Sebastian nodded.

Samael knelt down and looked at the wounds. He swallowed hard, closed his eyes and ran his tongue over the first wound. He could feel his tongue begin to burn, but took a deep breath, and completed the process to the second wound. He could feel the smoldering sensation growing in his mouth and clenched his fist.

Reika blinked her eyes a few times. "I don't feel anything." She looked confused.

"Perhaps it didn't work." Darius said, his brow furrowed.

"No." Reika said, her voice strained. "It did work, it just took a moment to start." She whimpered, squeezing Sebastian's hand tight. Her muscles tightened, and she writhed in pain.

"The light which burns painlessly inside, shall be snuffed out by the blanketing darkness. The coals will smolder, blistering the skin from inside, until nothing but ash remains." Darius said softly.

"What the fuck does that even mean?!" Reika growled through gritted teeth.

"It means it will burn until the blessing is gone." Samael said softly.

She cried out, grasping Sebastian's hand and the bed sheets in an iron grip.

Samael took his clothe and wiped her brow. "Try to relax, child. The more you strain, the more it will pain you."

"It's hard not to when your entire body is on fire!"

"Reika, he's right though, all you can do is try." Sebastian whispered.

She took a deep breath and looked to Sebastian. "I'll try."

Sebastian leaned down, and kissed her lips gently. "It's all we ask."

A soft smile bloomed on her face. "All I ask is for another moment where your lips steal away my mind's focus on this awful burning hell inside of me."

Darius smiled, and looked to Samael. "And a kiss of love shall resurrect the damned."

"Breathing life into the ashes, lifting them so they may dance once more." Samael smiled in return. He nodded towards the door and left the pair alone.

"Bas." Reika whispered through her pained whimpers. "Kiss me again."

Sebastian leaned down, bringing his lips to hers. "Is that all you wish for right now?" He asked.

"No." Her breathless voice danced across his lips.

"What do you wish for." He asked, caressing her cheek.

"Let me drink." She whispered. "I want to taste you." She took a sharp breath in, tears streaming down her cheeks.

"Do you believe it will ease your pain?" Sebastian asked.

"I do." She whispered.

"I love hearing you say 'I do,' my dear." He smiled, laying his lips upon hers. He placed his hand against her cheek. "If you believe it will help you, you can have it." Pulling his hair back, he exposed his neck to her. "Take as much as you need."

Reika brought her arms up as far as she could, to hold him in place so she could bring her lips to his neck. She kissed and sucked at Sebastian's neck. She parted her lips and press her teeth into his flesh.

Sebastian let gasp escape his lips as she drank. He wanted more than anything to pull her into an embrace, but was afraid to hurt her more. He gently caressed her shoulders as she sucked at his neck. He moaned, the sensation driving him wild. Finally, she pulled away, he could feel the droplets of blood forming on his neck.

Reika pulled away, but first licked at the wound before she laid her head against the pillow once more. She looked up to Sebastian, and a soft smile rested upon her weary face. Sebastian ran his thumb against the corner of her mouth and wiped the tiny scarlet drip from her mouth.

"You are prone to making a terrible mess when you eat, my dear." Sebastian said with a smile. "If you could only have seen yourself at the birthday dinner."

"Mm, well, you see, there are two dinners you speak of. I probably made a mess of myself at both of them." She laughed softly. "It's no matter to be discussing now." She smiled, eyes closed.

"Are you feeling better?" He asked.

"I am." She said softly. "I'm so tired though." She whispered, her silver eyes peering up at him through hooded eyelids. "My sides don't ache nearly as much anymore, but I just want to rest."

"Then rest my love, you'll be watched carefully." Sebastian smiled, kissing her forehead. "You'll need your strength."

"You're right." She said, yawning. She was surprised the pain had almost complete subsided. Reika smiled softly. "Thank you." She slipped into a restful sleep.

Sebastian stepped out of the bedroom after laying another gentle kiss on Reika's forehead. He looked to Samael. "What are we going to tell her of Yuri? Is there any news of her yet?"

"She has called out to me, but I cannot seem to find her." Darius sighed. "I know she is in the confines of Adrian's fortress. My powers nor Samael's are able to penetrate the walls."

"I wish there was something I could do." Sebastian sighed out.

"We're working on a plan." Samael said. "We must stay as fluid as possible, because there is always a possibility of Adrian moving Yuri."

"He is also a blundering idiot, many things are possible. " Darius interjected.

# # #

"You guys are terrible hosts." Yuri groaned out. She was tired, her bones ached, and she had a hunger she had never felt in her life. "Starve your guests, leave them tied in a chair, and you use a hose to clean me up." She said to the door. "Maybe it's best you keep me tied to this fucking piece of shit chair." She slumped forward, exhaustion taking it's toll on her body. "I just want to go home."

"I just wish you would shut the fuck up." A harsh woman's voice snapped, as the door was flung open, crashing against the wall.

Yuri jumped, hissing at the sensation of the ropes digging into her skin. She looked up and saw a woman with bright red hair, dressed in all black. She sighed. "Great, the crazy bitch has finally showed her face. What are you coming to tell me? Your plans to kill me to get revenge on my sister, because she and her father have a normal, healthy relationship, and you just can't handle it? Or how you plan on torturing me more?"

Lilith laughed. "Quite a spirited young girl, especially for being in this room for a week now. However, I'm not here to tell you what I am going to do with you, I had a proposition."

"A proposition?" Yuri snorted. "'Join my side, and I'll spare your life,' is the first one to come to mind. Sorry, bitch isn't really my style. I'd much rather die than be a part of your fucked up agenda."

"I was afraid of that." She smirked. "There's another option, though it really isn't a choice for you."

"Oh, what's that?" Yuri stared at her, unimpressed.

"I'll release you, but you'll have to dine with me after we get you cleaned up."

Yuri cocked her head to the side. "You're going to release me?"

"You've proven to be the most annoying hostage I have ever had." Lilith said. "Honestly, I can't stand having you in my cells anymore. Every night, all I hear is your incessant whining."

Yuri laughed. "I knew I was going to be a terrible hostage. I never did well with time out."

"I'll have one of my servants retrieve you, and they will get you cleaned up. Once you're," Lilith curled her lip, "presentable they will bring you to eat dinner."

"You're *so* gracious." Yuri said.

Lilith turned and left. She snapped her fingers, and two women came into the room and cut Yuri's ropes.

"Thank goodness." She said softly, rubbing her wrists. "Now what are we doing?" She asked.

Both girls, with light blonde hair, stared at the floor. "Now we take you to the wash room." One of the girls said, neither looked up. They took Yuri by the hands and helped her stand up. Yuri was shocked at how unsteady she was on her feet.

"Damn, how far is the wash room?" She asked, feeling sweat bead all across her skin.

"Not very far." They said in unison. The girls began walking slowly, taking Yuri down the hallway to a large room with a bath the size of a small pool. They walked down the steps together and they sat Yuri down in the water, and pulled off the mangled remains of her clothing. She sat still as the two girls took soft clothes to her skin, washing away what filth the hoses hadn't in the past week. Exhaustion finally had caught up to her, as she yawned over and over.

"We're almost done." One girl said. "Then we shall dry you and dress you."

Yuri nodded, the whole scenario was strange and unsettling. She wanted to go back home, that she decided it was best to follow along.

The two girls helped her from the pool of water and up the steps once more. They wrapped her in a bathrobe and continued out the door, and down the hall once again. Everything Yuri was seeing was a complete blur. For late November, the grounds she saw were lavish with rose bushes in full bloom. The trees and shrubbery were still a lush green. The air smelled of salt, and the buildings surrounding her were made of marble. Before she could catch a glimpse of anything else, she was pulled inside a powder room.

She gazed around the bright room, seeing a single vanity, and beautiful seat in front of it. The two girls lead her to sit upon it.

One of the girls picked up a brush, applied a sweet scented oil to the bristles, and began brushing Yuri's tangled hair. The other girl went to a small armoire, pulled out a black dress and laid it on a lounge chair.

"What are your names?" Yuri asked.

The girls did not respond.

"Tough crowd." Yuri said through a yawn. "Are you allowed to talk at all?"

The girl brushing her hair laid the brush down, shaking her head. Yuri let out another sigh. She offered her hand to help Yuri up. She took it and they went over to put the black dress on.

"You look much better." One girl said.

"Um, thank you." Yuri responded. She still felt nervous about the entire situation, but only thought of the outcome, of being able to go home.

The two girls took hold of Yuri's arms and lead her out of the room once more. They made their way to a gazebo in the heart of the rose garden. A small square table was set in the center. Lilith sat alone facing the stairs. She waved the two girls away, and they quietly left.

"My, do you clean up well." Lilith smiled. "Please, have a seat." She gestured towards the seat in front of her. Yuri sat down, sitting on top of her hands. She looked down.

"Are you really sending me back to Reika and the rest, alive?" She asked.

"I am." Lilith said as she pouring wine for Yuri, and another liquid for herself. "I assume since you are still human, and would much rather not partake in the lifeblood of those you still share a common bond with, so wine it is for my guest!"

Yuri nodded some. "If you're sending me home, what's in it for you?"

"There is only my solitude and sanity." Lilith smirked. "To not have to hear your screaming and whining anymore is enough for me." She raised her glass. "May we toast, to our sanity!"

Yuri picked up her cup, and tapped it against Lilith's. "Yes, to our sanity." Yuri said before taking a sip. She screwed her face up as she swallowed the drink. It was bitter, and dry. "I was expecting sweet wine." She muttered.

"Worry not, child. You will get used to the taste. It isn't something many people enjoy their first sip of."

Yuri nodded. "It's understandable. It's alright, but at first it's off putting." She took another sip. "It begins to grow on you after a while."

Lilith smiled. "Indeed it does." She snapped her fingers, and two plates of food appeared on the table. "Now we shall eat."

Yuri looked in front of her and was salivating by the delectable looking plate of roasted vegetables, seafood and rice. She reached for the fork, but stopped for a moment. "How do I know you're not trying to poison me?"

"If I wanted you dead, you would not be sitting at this table with me." Lilith said in reassurance.

She nodded softly, and took a bite of her food.

Lilith smiled, and joined her. Yuri stayed silent through her meal, with each sip of wine, her eyes became a void of life, hazy and matte.

"Are you ready to return home, Yuri?"

"Yes." She said, her voice came out as a monotone whisper.

"Are you aware of what you must do?"

"Yes." She repeated in the same blank tone.

Lilith smiled. "Good, you are released." She snapped her fingers and Yuri disappeared from the table. She let out a heavy sigh. "Now the little brat is out of my hair." She picked her glass up and swallowed the contents and threw the glass to the ground. Lilith smiled as she saw the sparkling shards in the sunlight. "Adrian!" She called out.

"Yes, my love?" He asked, appearing immediately.

"We have many activities to attend to." Lilith said. "Our first stop is the dungeons. We need more blood."

"Yes, my dear." He said. Adrian swept her off her feet, carrying her away.

# # #

Yuri stood in front of a cabin, she blinked a few times and groaned. "Well, fuck." She looked around and decided her best option was to knock on the door in front of her. She stood waiting, hoping she hadn't made a mistake.

The door opened only but a crack. A pair of green eyes peered out, but then the door opened completely. "Yuri? What are you doing here?" Darius asked, shocked.

"Darius." Samael said cautiously.

The two men exchanged glances and Darius stepped outside. "How did you get here?"

"Honestly, I don't know. One minute I was sitting at a table with Lilith, drinking wine. The next minute I'm here, and have no idea how I arrived."

He thought for a moment. "You were drinking wine? Yuri, you're under age."

"Oh, gee, Mr. Gregory." She said, her tone dripping with sarcasm. "I'm a seventeen year old, walking dead girl. I think the cops would be more interested in the fact that I'm alive, than my blood alcohol content."

"I am more interested in why you would partake of anything she would set in front of you."

"She promised me it was safe."

"Her promises are ever made in vain, Yuri." Darius said. "One would be a fool to trust any word slithering out from those poison lips."

"I just wanted to come home." She whispered. "I don't know where home is anymore, I figured it was with Reika. I need to see her."

"The only person she's allowing to see her is Samael and Sebastian."

Yuri glared at Darius. "You haven't even told her I was here. Wouldn't she want to see me?"

"She's hardly awake." Darius said.

"You rushed out of the house, leaving me alone because she needed help, and I was taken away." Yuri said. "I want to know how my sister is!"

"Yuri, she is doing well. She is resting. I cannot go back on her wishes of only wanting Samael and Sebastian in her room. I am only allowed entrance when I am to dispense medicine to her. I am sorry I cannot be of more help."

"Let me speak to Samael." She demanded, crossing her arms. "I'll wait here, bring him to me."

Darius sighed and nodded. "As you wish." He made his way back into the cabin and looked to Samael.

"What troubles you, friend?" Samael asked. He waited for response, but Darius stayed silent.

'She is under a spell of sorts. I cannot tell what kind, but it cannot be a pleasant one. She only wishes to see Reika, which makes me believe she has a poison in her blood. She's here to kill her.'

'I wish I were surprised by Lilith's current attempt, though I am not. How do we handle this?'

'Yuri is very strong willed, but I don't fully trust her to break through this on her own. I may have something which can break her through this. Do you have contact with any shape shifters?'

'The only ones I know, I loathe.'

'You do not need to love them to put them up to this idea.'

'Darius, I do not wish for senseless death in this war we wage. Too many have died in the years passed.'

'We may only know her intents by using a decoy.'

'Her intent is simple, Darius. Lilith wishes for Yuri to kill her. To let Yuri kill someone who is or isn't her sister would be torturous. The human psyche can be delicate, and she would suffer greatly due to it. I cannot allow it.'

'Though that is the worst of all outcomes, I do not believe it would happen. I will respect your wishes though. I believe we will need to remove her from this property, to a safe location. Somewhere both her and Reika can be safe. Do you have any of your sleeping serum left?'

Samael smirked, and nodded. He walked into Reika's room, and returned with a small vial. "It is all I have left." He said, finally breaking their silence.

"I can make you more." Darius smiled. "I'll take her to my place."

"Sleeping serum, and taking a young woman to your home, Darius." Samael gave him a chiding stare. "We will speak on this matter later."

Darius glared at him. "You know this our best option."

"I do." Samael smiled. "Behave yourself, Darius and take excellent care of her."

Darius nodded, and embraced his friend. "I will inform you when I know more, and I promise you I will."

Samael nodded and went with him to the door. "Farewell for now, friend."

Darius nodded as well, slipping out the door and returned to Yuri.

"What's the verdict? Can I see my sister?" She asked immediately.

"Not yet." Darius said. "We need to go to my home and get more herbs for her."

Yuri nodded, her facial expression softened. "Okay, let's go."

Darius held out his hand for her. "Let us."

Yuri took his hand, and everything went black.

Chapter Seventeen

The setting sun splattered pastel pinks, oranges, and yellows across the blanketing clouds. Yuri looked out from the balcony of Darius' secluded home. Her eyes were greeted by a growth of sky high buildings shining, like mother of pearl in the setting sun. She hadn't any idea what city she was looking upon, but it was a beautiful contrast to the splendid trees surrounding her.

"Yuri, the tea is ready." Darius said, peeking his head out the sliding door.

She turned towards him and smiled. "I'll be there soon."

Darius slipped outside, and stood next to her, leaning against the railing on the balcony. "This is my favorite place to think, I believe you've found why."

"It's beautiful." A smile gently rested on her face.

"May I ask you something?"

"What is it?" She looked to him.

"What happened while you were held by Adrian and Lilith?"

"They tied me to a chair, and mostly left me alone." She sighed. "Occasionally they came in and threatened to kill me, but mostly I just sat and complained about being hungry and smelling bad. They came in with a hose and sprayed me down after that. Then finally, Lilith came in, saying she was going to send me home, after we had dinner together. These twin girls came in and took me to a wash room and then to a gazebo. I remember having a drink of wine, and then I appeared at the cabin."

"You have no recollection of what happened after that moment?"

"No." She sighed out. "I wish I did, but I have no idea. I think she did something to me, I just don't know what. The joke's on me for trusting her." She looked down. "I just wanted to come home."

"You are home, and we will figure out what she has done to you." Darius said softly. "May I ask one more question about this?"

"Yes." She nodded, her eyes still cast to the ground below the balcony.

"Why do you feel so desperate to see Reika?"

"I," She stammered, "I don't know. She's hurt, and I want to see if she's okay." She said, but sounded uncertain.

"She's doing well." Darius said, reassuringly. "Come, before the tea gets cold."

She nodded, and followed Darius back inside his beautiful home. It was decorated in light colors, and rich wood. Yuri sat down on the couch, and Darius brought two tea cups in, handing her one. Yuri took a sip, and smiled. "This is really good, thank you."

"You're welcome." Darius said softly. "We will figure out what Lilith has done to you, and reverse it."

Yuri nodded, and yawned. "I'm sure we will." Yuri took another sip of her tea. Another yawn shook her. She set her cup down and leaned back against the couch. "I'm so tired." She muttered, as she closed her eyes and fell asleep.

Darius waited a moment before taking her, and laying her down fully on the couch. He laid a blanket over her. "I am terribly sorry, Yuri. It is the only way I can reverse this." He knelt down next to her, placing a hand on either side of her forehead and closed his eyes. In a language not spoken by any mortal, he began chanting.

Moments passed, his words which hung heavy in the air faded into silence, and he drifted into slumber.

Reika woke in a cold sweat, panting. Her wide eyes searched out Sebastian. He was asleep in the chair next to her bed. She smiled gently and took deep breaths. "I'm okay." She whispered.

Sebastian yawned and opened his eyes. "What's the matter?"

"I had a really weird dream, that's all." She said softly, smiling at him. "Nothing to worry about." The dream had been one of the worst she had experienced since childhood, but what calmed her most were Darius' words at the end. *'This is only a dream. Speak to no one of it.'* She kept repeating his words, reassuring herself the dream wouldn't become reality.

Sebastian nodded and stood. He walked towards her bed and sat on the edge. "If you say there isn't anything to worry about, then there surely isn't." He leaned down and kissed her forehead. "How are you feeling today?"

Reika slowly pulled herself up, and leaned back against the wall. She grinned. "Really good. Maybe I can get out of this bed finally."

"I think you'll be able to." Sebastian smiled. "Could I check your wounds?"

Reika nodded, and pulled the blanket down. She lifted her shirt and leaned forward just enough so he could unravel the bandages.

"Holy shit!" Sebastian exclaimed.

Reika jumped a little. "What is it?"

"They're gone!" Sebastian grinned. "Let me go get Samael."

Reika watched as Sebastian ran off. She was excited, she felt no pain finally, and they were finally closed fully.

Samael came in with Sebastian. He came to the side of the bed and knelt down. He ran his finger over Reika's skin, tracing the scar. She laughed some, trying to pull away.

"Papa, stop that!" She tried to move away. "It tickles!"

Samael stood, his face beaming with the same excitement as Sebastian and Reika. "I think it is time to step out of bed!" He took her hands in his. "Do you think you are ready?"

Reika held tight to Samael's hands. "Yes, I am."

Samael instructed Reika, she moved slowly, bringing her legs over to the edge of the bed and pulled herself away from the wall. She held tight to his hands as she pushed herself up to her feet. She smiled up at Samael for a moment, before her legs gave out and she fell back on the bed with a groan.

"That was short lived." She grumbled.

Samael sighed. "It will be alright. After long bouts of bed rest, this is not uncommon. It will take some time to adjust. You are ahead naturally because of your genetics." He smiled. "It's the perks of being a demon. Give it time, child. You have come a long way already, the end of this is near."

She sighed once more. "You're right."

"Let's try again."

Reika sat up once more, slowly. Again, she took Samael's hands, and brought her to her feet once more. She smiled, it felt good to be on her feet once more, despite the instability of it all. She felt

her legs start to give way once more, she became light as air. Samael

had scooped her up in his arms and carried her into the living room,

and gently set her in a reclining chair.

She looked up at him. "Change of scenery?"

Samael laughed. "Yes, take a look out the window." Samael

stepped aside.

Reika looked out the window and grinned. "I don't think I've

been so happy to see snow in my entire life." She watched the fluffy

white flakes dance in the early morning light.

"The holiday season is upon us." Samael sighed out happily.

"I enjoy the festivities more than most in our world."

"You do?" Reika asked.

"My dear, I view my role in this world as merely my

employment. Death and despair do not excite me like they used to.

Battles like yours are still a wondrous spectacle, but murder and

senseless violence is nothing I rejoice. I love nothing more than to

see these humans embrace their short lives and celebrate every

moment they are given."

"Papa, you told me once humans are destined to be part of your domain once they perish, and they should just give up, relinquishing their souls to you. What has changed?"

"I believe my words were misinterpreted that night." Samael said. "The ones I spoke of, are those who have already given up. They are the people desperately seeking something to patch their soul. They consider themselves broken, they are mistaken. They aren't broken. There isn't a soul in this world which is broken. Only those who need polishing, because they let the worlds' filth accumulate around them, and encase their soul in an almost impenetrable crust. They are imprisoned by their own habits and their own inconsolable emotions.

"They continue to spiral down, deeper and deeper until there is no where else to go, but to take the demon's hand, and shake on an agreement most humans would never dream of doing. They destroy any hope of their situation getting better, for a demons' contract may be based upon the wishes of these beings, but are perverted by those who grant them. It is part of the price which must be paid. I pity these beings the most, for they will live out a reality much more horrifying than before they met fate, so to speak."

Reika nodded. "Though you said I shouldn't waste my time pitying them, why?"

"Because, my dear child, I spend enough time pitying these unfortunate beings enough for two people." He knelt down, and placed a hand on her knee. "You have said it before, people who cross you do not deserve your pity, only your wrath. Please keep this in mind, but do not let it consume you. Do not become a carpet in which these souls use to clean their feet upon. You are strong, continue to stay this way."

A smile rose on Reika's lips, she took her father's hand and squeezed gently. "You have no need to worry." She looked down at his hand in her's. "The only thing I'm worried about right now is getting a bath."

Samael laughed. "I am certain it would be deeply beneficial to you. I shall arrange it. There are some wonderful oils I shall put in the water as well." He smiled, kissed her cheek and went off to take care of it.

Reika sat alone for a moment, her eyes glazed over as she watched the snowflakes flutter through the air. Leaning her head back and closing her eyes, she smiled at the sensation of a strong pair of arms descending around her shoulders and embracing her.

Sebastian laid a gentle kiss on the top of Reika's head. "The bath should be ready in a moment. Samael asked me to help you."

She leaned her head against his arm. "Alright." She whispered out.

Sebastian slipped away from her for a moment and circled the chair. "Do you want to try to walk?" Sebastian asked, holding his hands out for her to take.

Reika laid her hands in his and looked up at him, biting on her lower lip. "I want to try, but I'm afraid."

Sebastian knelt down, still holding her hands. "Fear is normal, to move past it, you must face it." He offered an encouraging smile.

"You have been around Papa and Darius for much too long." Reika laughed. "You're right though." She squeezed his hands tight. "Let's try."

Reika and Sebastian worked in unison to get her to her feet. Sebastian held one hand as he wrapped an arm securely around her waist. Slowly, they began walking towards the bathroom. Each step Reika could feel her unsteadiness dissolve, though she relied heavily on Sebastian to guide her forward. Once in the bathroom, Reika sat down on the bench to a white and gold vanity stand.

Samael smiled at the two. "I'm almost finished here." He said, as he took a vial in his hand, uncorked it and wafted the scent to inhale it. He smiled, and poured it into the steaming water. Pleased with his work, he looked to Reika and Sebastian once more. "A mixture of essential oils which should help greatly for your body. I expect a full recovery within a few days. You're resilient, my dear. I shall leave you two." Samael nodded his head gently and walked out the door, closing it gently.

Sebastian knelt down before her. "Are you ready?" He smiled gently.

Reika nodded. "I am."

Sebastian helped her disrobe, and with ease, scooped her up in his arms to carry her to the bathtub. He lowered her slowly into the hot water. He smiled, hearing the relaxed sigh escape Reika's lips.

The scent rushed over Reika as she leaned her head back against the tub. The scent was rich with cinnamon, ginger and sandalwood. Turning her head, she looked to Sebastian. "Thank you." She said softly.

"For what?" He asked, a confused smile upon his face.

"For everything." She smiled. "You're so wonderful to me."

"We're supposed to take care of each other." He said, leaning closer and cupping her face. "It's just another way for me to show you how much I love you." He chuckled gently. "I'm sorry, it sounds so cliché."

"Don't apologize." She smiled up at him. "I enjoy it. If you didn't say cute cliché things, I'd be worried."

He laughed, a warm smile on his face. "I'm so glad you're finally better." He said, his expression slipping to a somber tone. "For a while there, I was afraid you weren't going to make it. It was terrible." He swallowed hard, looking down. "The wounds wouldn't stop bleeding. I don't know how to made it, but I'm so happy you did."

"I'm not ready to leave." She said softly. "There is so much more in this world for me to see, and do. I can't leave yet. I can't leave you."

Sebastian leaned forward and kissed her forehead. "No, you can't, neither of us can. We both just entered this life. We're not done yet, not for a long time."

"Not until dawn rises on this eternal night." She closed her eyes. "A dawn in which this world will never see. For the light may rise each morning, it still cannot chase the shadows away."

Sebastian smiled. "Even if that day were to come, we would face it together. I will always be at your side, Reika."

"We will be able to achieve anything." She smiled back at him, her eyes opening. "Let's not dwell on this too much. I still need to pay Lilith back." She sighed out. "The time will come soon."

"Reika, Sebastian, I must go back home to retrieve some items and make a few mixtures. It may take me some time to complete them. If I do not return, this is why." Samael called out from behind the door. "I will contact you soon. Take care, both of you."

"I love you, Papa. Be safe." Reika called out.

"Take care of yourself, Samael." Sebastian said after Reika.

"I love you both." He said, and left them in silence.

Sebastian looked down to Reika. "Let's get you cleaned up, and I'll cook for you."

Reika grinned and nodded. "That sounds perfect!"

Sebastian kissed her forehead once more before finding a sponge. He buffed her skin slowly, trying not to be too rough. He washed her hair, massaging her scalp. Finally, Sebastian rinsed her after letting the water out.

Reika smiled up at Sebastian. "Though we're already tied together, I cannot wait for the day we can truly say our bond has been sealed." She reached up, taking his hand. Her trembling fingers intertwined with his. It brought her warmth, and strength knowing he loved her enough to care for her this way. In her heart, she knew she would do the same.

"Once this is over, we will be able to." He smiled brightly. "It is only a symbol, Reika. A simple reminder which will adorn your hand." He leaned down, pressing his forehead against hers, and gave her a soft kiss. "Let's get you dry and dressed." The soft giggle which escaped Reika's lips tickled his. He grinned, scooping her up in his arms, and setting her on her feet on the mat just outside the tub.

Reika held tight to Sebastian, but she felt different. Her legs weren't trembling under the weight of her body, she could feel her strength once more. She looked up to Sebastian with a large smile. "I think Papa's bath worked." She whispered up to him.

Sebastian peered down into her ecstatic face, and smiled with the same happiness. "Are you sure?"

She nodded. "Let's try something." She ran her hands down his chest and took hold of his hands.

Sebastian stepped backwards once, giving her some distance. "Whenever you're ready."

She looked from his hands, to his face, and took a single step towards him. She still felt slightly unsteady, but a grin burned over her cheeks, knowing she could walk on her own once more. "It worked!"

Sebastian squeezed her hands gently. "Let's get you dressed. Maybe some food will help too."

She laughed. "Food makes almost everything better!"

Sebastian kissed her forehead. "It does."

# # #

Deafening silence struck Samael's ears as he woke in his bed. Slowly, he rolled to his side, and sat up. The scent of his brewing potions filled the air. He smiled softly, knowing the potions would greatly help Reika's recovery. "Only a few more days, and they shall be ready." His voice carried in the silence.

Samael pushed himself up off his bed, and dressed himself for the day. He left his chambers and headed towards the kitchen. Any moment he had alone, Samael made coffee before starting any project. He sat down at the table, the sounds of the coffee machine gurgling made him smile. Closing his eyes, he inhaled the rich scent of the coffee.

Though, his peaceful moment was broken by the sound of heeled footsteps echoed through the halls. His eyes shot open and he looked behind him once the cadence of steps halted.

"You're finally alone." Lilith cooed out. "It's so wonderful to have you back."

"Oh hell." He murmured, as she came closer.

"She's finally dead, and I can have my love back at last." Lilith whispered. "I saw it all, Samael. You must be heartbroken, but do not worry. I can take your pain away, and we can start anew. We can create a new family, a better one."

"You understand nothing, Lilith." Samael said, his face somber. "I would much rather spend my days in solitude, than see your face again, than hear your screeching tongue carry in the air. Losing Reika is a pain which will never subside. It will burn through me for all eternity. I can only thank your pathetic jealousy and rage for such agony." His eyes stared blankly at the floor, as tears welled over his lashes.

"My fierce love could soothe the burning agony within you." Lilith said, pressing herself against him. Her long fingers came up to caress his cheek, yet he turned away.

"Why must you insist upon this?" Samael said. "I am no longer your partner, once you left, and joined Adrian, I was relinquished. I am no one's other than myself." He said, moving out from under her, putting distance between them. "I shall never be your lover again, nor shall I ever love again."

"I cannot believe my ears." Lilith hissed under her breath. "You dare deny me?"

"I dare deny anyone who wishes ill will upon those whom I love, or have loved." Samael hissed back. "You are a vandal, Lilith. You annihilate everything you touch, everything you have ever loved, all which you've treasured, including yourself. I will not allow you to destroy me, not after I have spent centuries reconstructing every bit of damage you have done to me. You are the one who desperately needs to disappear from this world."

"I am not leaving!" She screeched, her words sharp. "You are mine, and I will see your end!"

Samael laughed, smiling cruelly. "You are mistaken. Have you forgotten such a day already? You were created to be equal to man, you did not want to be so. You were cast out, and I took you in, I took your soul. It is I who may lay claim to you, not the other way around." He shook his head. "Indeed it is true that those who are given immortality by those who consume souls are struck by madness."

"I am mad, but not in the way you think!" She glared at him. "I am furious over the fact you would choose that little brat over me!"

"You honestly believe after all you have put me through in the millennia we have spent together, I would choose you over an innocent child? Especially one who only wishes to learn and love me for who I am? You are sorely mistaken. Reika became my priority once she came into my life again. You should have expected it, though you are much too narcissistic to realize it."

"All I had expected was for you to teach the wench and send her on her way. You are not supposed to get attached to your servants."

"Servant?!" Samael roared. "She was our flesh and blood! You dare call her a servant?"

"She did your dirty work, didn't she?" Lilith asked, stepping back and leaning against the wall. "Those twenty-five men?" She shook her head. "It's too bad the twenty-fifth man didn't do his job properly. The poor little girl wouldn't be tormented by her conscious for killing her beloved older sister." Lilith made a clicking noise. "What ever will she do now? I am certain Papa Samael could never forgive the girl even if she begged at his feet."

"You are absolutely mistaken." Samael said, his voice coming out softly, somber, like a hymn. "The one who could never be forgiven is the one who continues to speak this very moment without any recollection of events caused by unwarranted rage and jealousy. I cannot blame an innocent for a crime committed by one who cannot control their emotions. The source is to blame, not the one who acts upon a spell without knowledge of doing so."

Lilith sauntered forward, and looked to Samael's face. "I did what I needed to do, and you did no such thing. I will continue to do what I need to, until this world is mine and if you choose to stand in my way, I will make sure to destroy you too." She hissed.

"Do your worst." Samael taunted. "I am certain I can best such attempts."

"You may have taught me well, but so have the satyrs." Lilith smiled.

"Though they may have taught you, neither party has taught you fully what you are capable of." Samael grinned. "Once again, you are mistaking yourself as someone with great value, whereas you're only a pawn. Birthing children for me, making contracts, dealing with Michael. The list goes on for miles." Samael's grin twisted into a devious smirk. "To say I loved you would be a complete and utter lie. I merely only tolerated your existence until it was time to relinquish you."

Lilith's smile faded, a concoction of sadness and anger whirled in her mystical silver eyes. "You are the next to be eliminated." She said, her calm voiced belied the wrath within. A slender hand came up, and engulfed Samael's throat. "It will be slow." Her eyes ran up and down his body. "You will beg for the end, to be erased from existence, but I won't give it to you, not until I'm ready. I want to watch you suffer as much as I have felt in these years together." One corner of her mouth curled upwards. "It could take months, or even years, but you will perish in the same fashion my heart did because of you."

"Did you only make the decision now?" He choked out. Samael wrapped his hand around her's and forced her away.

"No." She hissed out, backhanding him. She grabbed his arm and dragged him along, to the bedroom he had just been in and threw him onto the bed.

Samael was shocked at her strength. He laid back, carefully watching her every move. He took a deep breath and waited

Lilith turned, and grabbed his arm, tying it to the bed posts. She repeated it, until he was fully tied down, and placed a blindfold over his eyes. Looking down, pleased with her work, she pulled the knife from her thigh holster. The bright steel glimmered in the dim candlelight of Samael's room. "The beginning of the end has arrived, Samael. Are you ready?"

"I've been ready since the day Michael slaughtered my children." He growled out through gritted teeth. "This is far more welcomed than you could imagine."

# # #

Yuri looked up at the sky from the balcony at Darius' house. She sighed out, barely able to see the stars in the sky. The door behind her slid open, and Darius came out to join her.

"How long until we can go back to the mansion?" Yuri asked. "The spell's broken, what are we waiting for?"

"We are waiting for Samael's sign." Darius said softly, taking a seat next to her on the floor of the balcony. "Lilith believes Reika to be dead, as we had hoped for, now we are just waiting for reality to happen. We are waiting for Reika to kill Lilith."

"Why is it she has to kill her?" Yuri asked. "Shouldn't Samael be doing it?"

"As much as Samael wants to do the deed himself, he cannot."

"What do you mean?"

"He is also a victim of a curse from Lilith. He knows, yet there is only one way for it to be broken."

"For another to kill her?" Yuri asked. "What curse is he under?"

"He may never fatally harm her. I feel there is much more to the curse than I can sense. Samael's being is like a chasm. It is deep and knows no end." Darius sighed. "Not even I can seem to break the surface. I pray he will be able to come through this."

"If Reika inherited even a small fraction of his strength, he shall come through this stronger than when he entered." Yuri sighed out, leaning her head against Darius' shoulder. "It's too bad, I'm not as strong as them. Just a dream of killing someone has my mind spinning, I miss my parents, and I'm scared. Darius, I'm fucking terrified."

"What's scaring you the most right now?" He asked, wrapping a comforting arm around her.

"It's not just one thing, it's everything." She whispered. "I don't even know why I'm telling you all this. I miss Reika so much. I miss my mom, and I feel guilty over her killing herself." She felt hot tears sting her eyes. "Maybe I should have stayed, maybe if I didn't leave she'd still be alive."

"What happened with your mother is not your fault, not in the slightest." Darius said softly. "She wasn't in her right mind, nor would she ever return to a competent state. You shouldn't blame yourself for such things, Yuri, please trust me, I know the fate which lies before you if you continue to lay blame where it ought not rest."

"I trust you, but, can I ask how you know?" She said softly. "You don't have to tell me, I'm just curious."

"Samael and I share similar stories." Darius replied. "Before Reika, Samael had a bounty of children whom he and Lilith raised. Samael did his best to be a good father to his children, Lilith would undo his work in the most extravagant way I had ever seen." He sighed out. "Michael slayed his children, because he was commanded to do so. They were marked for death by the one.

"I had one child. Her name was Neela. I found her in the desert late at night. My duties in this world is to watch, and to listen. I was listening that night, and heard an inconsolable cry flooding an abandoned camp site on a trade route in Africa. The baby wouldn't stop crying, and I decided it was best to see what was happening. There she was, laying in the sand, wrapped in tattered clothe." His voice was strained, body trembling as he recalled the story.

"I hadn't any idea how to care for a child." Darius let a small laugh out through his misery. "I asked for Samael's help, and help me he did. This was after all of his children were slain. He brought me everything I would need to raise a human child. To this day, it still intrigues me so, that a man, whose purpose in this existence, is to lead those who have met death, into their afterlife knows so much about rearing children."

Yuri listened carefully. "Neela." The name rolled from her lips, and met Darius' ears like an incantation. "What a beautiful name."

"She was a beautiful soul." Darius said. "She captured my heart completely and I loved her deeply. She hadn't been my flesh and blood, but there was no denying she was my daughter. I spent every moment with her, and she adored me so." Darius sighed. "It all came to an end, however, on her sixteenth birthday."

"What happened?" She asked.

"Michael came to me." Darius said, his voice became deathly quiet. "He explained to me, having a child to care for was causing me to neglect my duties." He bit his lip, stopping the sob which threatened to escape. "He called her name out, and so cheerfully, as if he were singing her praises. Neela skipped into the room, with the most beautiful smile on her face. She looked to Michael, and was in awe. He stood, made his way to my precious Neela and wrapped his filthy arms around her from behind. He pulled a sacred dagger from his belt and slit her throat right in front of me."

Darius couldn't stop the tears from streaming down his face. "I cannot forget the scream which emitted her lips. The sound of her choking on her own blood." He pulled Yuri close. "The look of terror on her face as she took her last breath in my arms, and there was nothing I could do."

"Darius." Yuri whispered as she wrapped her arms around him. "I'm so sorry."

"Michael was gone before I could do anything irrational." He said, sniffing his tears back. "Some days I wish I would have been taken from this world that day as well."

"As much as it hurts you, I'm glad you are still here." Yuri said softly. "For what it's worth, what happened to Neela wasn't your fault either. You cared for her, and from what I've heard, Michael is an overpowered prick. You shouldn't blame yourself either. You gave her a life, you weren't the reason it was taken away."

Darius pulled away from her, a melancholy smile finely etched across his face. "Yuri, remember your words, because you must believe what you said for yourself."

She nodded. "I do, now especially that I've heard your story."

Darius nodded in return. "You are going to be just fine." He said softly. "I promise you this."

"I wonder what is taking Papa so long." Reika murmured, looking out the window at the cottage. Snow sparkled and danced in the frigid breeze in the midnight starlight.

Sebastian looked up from the fire he was tending in the small fireplace in the living room. He looked up and shrugged softly. "I dunno, Rei. I wish I knew."

She walked over and knelt down beside him. "I want to trust him, but I'm worried he's in trouble."

"You're allowed to feel both of those." Sebastian said softly. He turned to Reika, offering to take her hands. As she placed her hand in his and he lead her to the couch facing the fireplace. He sat down, pulling her into his arms. "You love your Father, you're allowed every bit of worry you feel, but also know, Samael is no fool and if he needs help he will call."

Reika wrapped her arms around his neck. "You're right, on both counts. I'm still going to worry until I hear something from him. I know the potions shouldn't take this long to brew. I've seen the recipes he uses frequently, and they only take three days at most."

"Just give it time, we'll hear from your Papa soon."

"When we do hear from him, I'm certain of one thing." Reika sighed out.

"What are you sure of?"

"It will be time a call for help." She turned and looked at Sebastian. "It will be time to kill her."

"How do you know?" Sebastian asked, a puzzled look on his face.

"I had a strange dream one night, and it wasn't just a dream." Reika began, but a knock at the door stopped her.

Sebastian kissed her cheek. "Just a moment." He said to her, and went to the door. He slid from the couch, and went to the front door. He turned, smiling to Reika, and opened the door, revealing Darius and Yuri.

Reika grinned. "I'm so glad to see you guys!"

Darius nodded with a smile. "I see you're doing well."

"Much better than the last time you were here." Reika nodded. "What brings you here?"

"There's something I think I should give you." Darius said with a smirk.

Yuri held up what looked like a wad of clothe. "You're going to love it!" She said, a grin on her face.

"If anyone knows me in this world, It's you." Reika laughed.

"Well, after seventeen years in hell with you, I'm bound to know you better than anyone else."

"I didn't think it was so bad." Reika chided.

"Well, you weren't the one getting tormented." Yuri shook her head.

With a laugh, Reika nodded in agreement. "You do have a point. So, what brought you here?"

"Darius had something he thought would help you with this battle against Lilith." Yuri handed Reika the clothe bundle. "Be very careful though, it's dangerous."

Reika sat down on the couch, and laid the clothe on her lap. She carefully began peeling back the layers of the beige cotton, to reveal a golden sheathed dagger. The sheath was decorative, with filigree, and deep blue inlays. "This is beautiful." Reika whispered out. She pulled the blade from the sheath to admire it.

Darius sat down on Reika's other side, and placed a hand over her's and closed the blade. "Do not touch the blade, Reika. This is the same style blade which almost ended your life." He explained. "It will be of great value when the time comes for you to slay Lilith."

"You need one only one blow, and it will all be over." Yuri said softly. "You know which one I speak of."

Reika shuddered. "I do." She rubbed the side of her head. "I wish I didn't, but I do."

"I'm sorry." Yuri said softly.

"What am I missing?" Sebastian asked.

"Oh!" Reika exclaimed. "I was about to tell you before they got here."

"As much as I wish you could explain the happenings since you woke from all this, Reika, it is best if you did not speak of it. To speak the truth into existence will ruin what we have created."

Reika looked to sad eyes. "I think I'll have to wait until after everything is done to explain it all to you."

Sebastian's mouth twitched, but he smiled. "It's alright, I understand."

Darius looked to Sebastian. *'Child, listen carefully.'*

'Darius?' Sebastian looked to him, confused.

'What has happened, is Yuri was under a spell by Lilith, to kill Reika. We used the spell in the best way we could. In a controlled dream, we had Yuri kill Reika. The images were projected into the world, and Lilith believes them to be true.'

Sebastian nodded in understanding.

"I'm glad we got here before you spoke it." Yuri said softly. "I know honesty is needed, but sometimes things are better left unsaid."

"They can still be shared, however." Darius added.

Reika nodded as well. She looked to the dagger in her lap and to Darius. "The end of this nightmare is closing in."

"Occasional nightmares are the cost of walking the night." Darius whispered. "Sometimes we are the nightmare, stalking our prey. Sometimes we are the ones who are haunted by dreams which seem to never end."

"It's time for me to end this nightmare." Reika said, holding the dagger close to her chest. "I'll become the creature she and all others should fear most. The creature I was born to become. I am Lilin, a child of night, a child of death."

# # #

"Do you submit to me yet?" Lilith whispered, staring down at Samael. She perched herself atop his body.

"No." Samael whispered through cracked lips. "I never will submit." He smirked, his face bruised, and stained with blood though his spirit wasn't broken.

"I'm sad to hear such words." Lilith said softly. "Though, I am pleased it means my play will continue for a while longer."

"It's too bad my pain fuels your addiction." Samael laughed softly. "I'd much rather it kill your spirit, bore you to death to the point to end this all."

"Why do you wish for this to end, yet you will not submit?" She asked, leaning down, her face inches from his. "If you wish for your end so badly, why do you continue you to say you're not ready for the engulfing bliss of eternal numbness?"

"It is because I am not done tormenting you."

She slapped him across the face. "Will you ever be done tormenting me so?"

"No." He said, his voice breathless. His eyes sparkled with a life Lilith hadn't known. He could see the fear in her eyes. Lilith hadn't broken his spirit, he would never allow for such an act to happen again. She had done her damage, and he had felt the pain emotionally, now he was feeling it physically. The resolution of emotion pain brought peace to his being.

"I don't understand!" She shouted. "I can't do anything to bother you!"

"When seated in the proper mindset, it is nearly impossible to knock someone from their throne." Samael whispered.

"You're impossible!" She shrieked, her hand striking his cheek once more. "What would it take to destroy you?"

Samael laughed, his stomach shaking beneath her. "You honestly think I'd tell you what it would take?" His stomach shook harder beneath her center. "After four thousand years and you haven't a clue? The only thing I am able say, is I was such a fool."

"I was the fool!" She howled. "You were?!"

"I was the fool, a jester in which I thought the queen loved me unconditionally. Unbeknownst to me, I was a king in peasant's clothing. I am the god of death, you are merely a subjugate of my reign." His teeth stained with blood glistened in the dim candlelight. "You are nothing but a whisper among the morning breeze whispering in my ear. It's a soft call within hurricane winds. Now I know it's nothing worth wasting my thought on. My thoughts are best spent on thoughts of myself."

"I cannot understand what you even mean!" She whispered, her face cemented in frustration. "It's like we speak another language."

"We have spoken different languages since the moment we met." Samael whispered out. "I spoke the tongue of angels, you spoke that of man. We've been on parallel paths since the moment we met. Different languages have reverberated these vocal chords in different tones since the moment we were brought into this existence. Love may have brought us together, but in the end, I hold your soul, and the love. This relationship has been doomed since the words to bring you into my life were spoken."

"Those words were only born because I left the garden."

"You were removed because you would not submit to Adam." He chuckled. "This sickness must have your memories distorted as well. You were meant to be a subjugate of man, and I turned you into a tyrant. I can only blame myself for what has happened. End this life when it pleases you, for it does not matter to me anymore."

"Ever classy, Samael." Lilith laughed. "Even when he is looking in the mirror, he greets death with dignity and honor. How pathetic!" She spat.

"When you have made peace within yourself, looking in the mirror isn't a painful experience. I have noticed any room you dwell in does not have a mirror, Lilith. Why is this? Are you afraid of your own reflection? When I gaze upon the face of the woman who calls herself Lilith I am greeted by limitless beauty, yet it is just a facade." He smirked once again. "Beneath a porcelain thin veneer is a chasm of grotesque hatred. It knows no source, for she was born with it inside her. Every being makes mistakes, and to have created you was an understated one. To let you live is unforgivable."

"There isn't a thing you can do to end my life." Lilith leaned closer, whispering in his ear. "I have control over you, Samael, in ways you cannot even fathom. You may have my soul, but it doesn't hold any significance. The moment it left my body, I was free. You took on my burden, my pain, my suffering, and for what?" She laughed. "The faint memories of joy with your fleeting children? Are they really as joyous as you wish them to be, or do they cause you anguish every time they play in your head?"

"Anguish is the last emotion to cross my mind." Samael whispered. "The memories I harbor deep so deeply are the only happiness I have left." He chuckled. "It is the only thing you cannot take from me."

"If I take your life, I take everything." Lilith whispered, her lips brushing his ear with each word she spoke. "Every last bit of misery and ecstasy I will remove from your body and you will be nothing."

"Bring the knife to my throat, Lilith." He whispered back. "Drag it across my flesh, and let the blood flow. Make sure to listen carefully to the babbling of my last breath leaving my body through the river of my blood rushing to join the universe once more. It will be the most haunting melody to greet your ears, and it will do just that. It will haunt you until you are mad, so lost in it's sound, you will beg to meet the same fate."

"I will never wish to join you again, even in death." She hissed. "I only wish to rid myself of such a burden as you."

Samael laughed. "Ah, I believe you have mistaken yourself once more. I am your burden? I am afraid not. You may have thought you were dominant in your role, but it was only a semblance of control. You have always been my burden, Lilith. From the day I took your soul I fell to the ground, laden with the mistake of consuming such tainted goods."

"How could I be considered tainted?!" She roared. "I was the first woman!"

"Now you see, you were the first of the succubi, not woman." He smirked. "There was another mistake made, and you needed to be disposed of. I happened to be the one to create the circumstances in which the garbage may be rid of."

"What are you saying?" Lilith said. She sat up, looking down, sneering, though terror coursed through her eyes.

"Soon you shall know." He said simply.

"I wish to take you somewhere." Lilith said, sitting up. "I must end this where it all began."

"To the garden we go." He sighed out.

# # #

Reika ran through the snow chasing Sebastian, throwing snowballs at him.

Sebastian fell to the ground after being hit by one of Reika's many snowballs. "Dear woman!" He shouted. "You have slain me!"

She fell on top of him, laughing. "I didn't know snow could kill you!" She took his hands, and got to her knees, helping him up.

"It was only for the sake of the game." He smiled. "I'm alright, but how about we head inside."

Reika nodded. "Yuri probably has a fire going."

Sebastian took her arm, and they walked together to the cabin. Sebastian opened the door for Reika and stepping inside behind her. Reika stripped away her snowy clothes, , and ran off to change. Sebastian took a blanket from the couch and wrapped it around his shoulders. He went to the kitchen and began making a batch of hot chocolate.

Reika ran back into the kitchen. Sebastian looked over at her, her face frantic as she was tightening the strap to her thigh harness for her dagger. "He finally gave me the sign!" She said, her eyes wild. "I gotta go!"

"Reika, calm down, we'll go with you." Sebastian said.

She grabbed hold of Sebastian's arm and they disappeared from the cabin.

Darius looked to Yuri, who was shocked. "What just happened?" She asked him.

"Samael made the call for assistance, finally." Darius said. "This could get quite ugly, and I do believe it is best we stay behind. Reika is more than capable of handling this situation."

A warm breeze carried the scents of cedar and salt through the air. Reika looked around in the dim twilight glow peering through the trees. She slowly crept her way towards a flame in the distance, towards the voices talking in hushed tones. She turned to looked back, and Sebastian followed quietly behind. Reika held her hand up to signal Sebastian to stop, as she finally was able to see what was happening. She took her hand and placed it over her mouth to stifle her breathing.

In the flickering light brought on by torches, Reika saw Samael tied to a sycomore tree. His face was drenched in blood. Lilith stood with her back turned towards them. A blade in one hand,

Lilith held it over the torch in the other. Lilith turned towards Samael, her blade enclosing on his chest. Reika ran as fast as possible, her arm drawing back and struck Lilith in the jaw with all the strength she could muster.

Lilith fell to the ground with a thud, the blade flying from her hand. Reika came down, and grabbed Lilith by the front of her dress, and pulled her to her feet. "You treacherous wench!" Reika growled, hitting her again. Lilith grabbed hold of Reika's arm and twisted it. Her grip broke off, Reika tumbled backwards and sprung to her feet. She drew the blade from her thigh holster and waited patiently.

Lilith's eyes glinted with fear for only a moment, but she grabbed another dagger from her side and readied herself. Reika waited still, collecting herself. Patience was a warrior's friend in battle. She had almost forgotten it in the rage that took over when seeing Samael tied to the tree. Lilith charged forward, bringing her arm up with her dagger. She brought it down, trying to strike Reika in the head. She side stepped, cutting Lilith in the side. Lilith staggered, coming around Reika, and cut her forearm. Reika ignored the injury despite the searing pain and closed the distance between them.

She came close, striking Lilith in the leg, causing her to fall to her knees, panting. Reika kept her composure. Though she was injured, Reika knew victory wasn't hers yet. She kicked the dagger from Lilith's hand and pushed her onto her back. Bringing her knees down on Lilith's shoulders, and brought her dagger to her neck. Lilith's eyes caught a glimpse of the jewels in the hilt. Reika could see the panic flash in Lilith's eyes, and smiled wickedly.

Reika ran the blade across Lilith's throat, light enough to leave a small gash. "As the sun sets beyond me, everything before me is washed in red. Now, as your past comes back to haunt you, like this setting sun, all you shall see is red. The life will be drained from you, just like the sun from the day and all you shall see is black, forevermore." She threw the knife up, and caught the handle as the blade pointed down towards Lilith, driving it through her temple.

The scream emitted from Lilith's rouged lips echoed throughout the valley. The animals of the valley fled away from the ghastly screech which lingered through the branches like a heavy rain. Even Reika wished she could have run from the sight she had created before her. As Lilith's blood poured from her wound, her skin began to shrivel around her frame until there was nothing left but dust.

Reika stood, and tossed the dagger into the pile of dirt. She looked over at Sebastian and Samael. Sebastian had just freed Samael from his bindings.

"Child, come here" Samael said softly. He held out one hand, as he held Sebastian's in the other. "I cannot thank you enough, both of you."

Reika hugged Samael, trying to be gentle. "I'm so glad you're alright." She whispered.

"Me too." Sebastian said.

"Let us go home." Samael smiled. "It is Christmas after all, and there shall be a wondrous meal and gifts awaiting us."
"Since when do demons celebrate Christmas?" Sebastian asked.

"Ever since a demon named Samael was brought onto this earth and discovered the beauty of cooking." He said with a smirk. "If it is a holiday which involves food, expect me to celebrate it."

"Noted!" Sebastian and Reika said in unison.

"Next stop, the Blake House." Samael said, the smile on his face was far more bright than any Reika had seen. It warmed her heart to see her father free, finally.

Epilogue

"Luna, you outdid yourself again!" Reika shouted in happiness as she gazed at herself in the full length mirror in her bedroom. "This is gorgeous!" She surveyed herself in a beautiful red gown. "I can't wait to see the look on Sebastian's face when I walk down the steps to the party." She said, trying to keep herself from tearing up. "Thank you, Luna." She turned and hugged her.

"My dear, you're so welcome!" Luna hugged her back. "I'm really excited for you."

Reika smiled. "I'm really excited too." She let go of Luna to take one last look at herself in the mirror. "I'm ready."

"This is going to be so beautiful." Luna sniffed. "Let me get Yuri and your father." Luna went out the door for a moment, and returned with the two.

Samael walked slowly towards Reika, his hands extended and took hers gently. Months had passed since Lilith was slain, and their wounds had healed, but everyone still felt on edge. Samael hoped the warm May weather would melt away the memories of a blood soaked winter.

"You look stunning." Samael whispered. A sweet, prideful smile graced his lips. "No fairer woman has ever graced this earth. Sebastian is quite the lucky man." He winked.

Reika felt blush rise in her cheeks. "Papa, you're so sweet." She hugged him. "It's not even the wedding day!"

"I know, child." He chuckled. "An engagement party is a very beautiful choice. I am pleased you realized rushing to the altar wasn't in the best interest. You have all of eternity to do so."

Reika nodded. "The night will continue to be ever dark, and there is plenty of time for dancing in the dim light of the heavens."

Yuri smiled at Reika. "I'm glad to hear you've finally found your voice." She came up and hugged her sister. "You and Sebastian are perfect together. I'm so happy for you."

"Thank you, Yuri." Reika said, hugging her tight.

Yuri pulled back and looked up at Reika. "Don't get all mushy and disgusting at this party, I don't want to be embarrassed!"

"I'll do what I want!" Reika glared at Yuri.

"It seems sisters will never change, no matter the time, or powers each hold." Samael said to Luna.

"It's true." Luna laughed. "My sister and I are the same way, even after seven hundred years."

"I'm not surprised." Samael shook his head. "Alright, I believe it is time for the festivities to begin! Luna, go with our dear Yuri, and join the party. Reika and I shall join in a moment."

Luna nodded, and took Yuri's arm, leaving Samael and Reika alone.

"There was something I wanted to give you on your wedding day, but I cannot wait any longer." Samael took Reika over to her bed, and they sat down on the edge. He produced a small silver box from his pocket. He held it in his open palm, a small note on the top read *'To my little Lily'*. The box had been cleaned, but there was evidence of blood stains upon it.

"How did you get this?" Reika asked, staring at the box, as if a ghost had appeared in the room.

"The day William Avel passed away from the car crash, I went to his side immediately." Samael said softly. He hadn't the strength to look Reika in the eyes as he spoke. "I felt I owed him greatly, and to just let his soul pass through like any other did not settle well with me. I personally escorted his soul to the afterlife. Before I left the scene of the crash, I found this in the passenger seat. I knew it would be of great importance to you one day. I believe today is the best day to present this to you."

"Papa." Reika said, her voice straining to hold her tears back. "I cannot thank you enough for doing this."

"And I cannot thank William Avel enough for raising a tremendous woman. Both of your human parents did right by you child, I cannot deny that. I'm terribly sorry still over how your relationship ended with Meredith."

"It's alright." Reika said slowly.

Samael placed the small box in Reika's hands. "It's still sealed."

Reika looked down, and turned the box over, slicing through the tape with her fingernail. She slid the top from the bottom, and a beautiful cameo necklace was revealed. She tried her best not to cry, but a laugh emerged. "He knew me well, a skeleton cameo necklace."

Samael chuckled. "It is fitting for you, Reika. Shall we put it on?"

Reika nodded. "Yes, I would love to."

Samael took the necklace in his hands and unhooked the clasp. He laid it upon Reika's bare neck and fastened it. "Now both your doting fathers can share this spectacular moment with you." He smiled sincerely. "Shall we begin the party?"

Reika grinned. "Yes! Let's do it!"

Samael escorted Reika through their home, and to the back yard. The stepped through a set of french doors, to a brick patio lit by the setting sun. Samael had gathered a few good friends to share the moment with. Darius and Sebastian waited at the bottom of the stairs to the patio. Reika looked to Sebastian, and the expression on his face lit her heart. He was overjoyed, almost to the point of tears. She took Sebastian's hand and they turned to the small crowd.

Samael stood behind the couple, and began to speak. "Today we wish to announce Miss Reika Lilin Blake is to marry Sebastian

Sariel Luciano. In the many months I have had to get to know these two as a couple, I can say with absolute confidence they were made for each other. The dynamic between them is ever present. They wish to be wed on All Hallows Eve, under the stars. I hope you all may join us on the day, for now, we celebrate Reika and Sebastian!"

The small party applauded, and the festivities began. Darius was the first to approach them.

"Samael, I am afraid I must leave momentarily." He whispered to Samael.

"Return when you are able, my friend." Samael smiled. "I assure you, we will be here all night."

Darius nodded. "I will return shortly." He disappeared, cloaking his presence and brought himself a few feet from a dark dressed figure peering over the garden's wall. Darius listened carefully.

"The Demon's daughter is to be wed on Halloween." A man's voice carried out from under the cloak. "It will be a perfect time to strike." Before Darius could hear anything else, the man ran off. Darius disappeared once more, leaving the party to continue

without any knowledge of intrusion.

Made in the USA
Monee, IL
24 February 2022